Everyone
Knows
How Much
I Love You

Everyone Knows How Much I Love You

A NOVEL

Kyle McCarthy

BALLANTINE BOOKS

NEW YORK

Published in the United States by Ballantine Books, an imprint of Random House, a division of Penguin Random House LLC, New York.

BALLANTINE and the HOUSE colophon are registered trademarks of Penguin Random House LLC.

Grateful acknowledgment is made to Forrest Gander for permission to reprint an excerpt from *As a Friend* (New York: New Directions, 2008) by Forrest Gander, copyright © 2008 by Forrest Gander. Reprinted by permission of the author.

Hardback ISBN 978-1-9848-1975-8
Ebook ISBN 978-1-9848-1976-5

Printed in Canada on acid-free paper

randomhousebooks.com

1 2 3 4 5 6 7 8 9

First Edition

Book design by Caroline Cunningham

To my mother and father

Everyone knows how much I love you.
All your gestures
Have become my gestures.

—Variation by Forrest Gander on a translation by
Kenneth Rexroth of an anonymous Japanese poem

Is love the word for these strange deep ancient
affections, which begin in youth and have got
mixed up with so many important things?

—Virginia Woolf, *A Writer's Diary*

PART ONE

The Joining

As many times as I've tried I can't go back. As many times as I've sat writing at my desk—so many different desks, in so many different cities—that exact moment on the road remains blank. What was in my mind? I've tried to find it. I've conjured. Fibbed. Faked it, and let it remain the lie in the middle of my novel, the improvisation, the patch. The caulk over the crack in my memory.

At the time everyone wanted to know what I'd been thinking, and maybe lying so often lost me access to the truth. Not the truth, but the *feeling*. "You just . . . overshot the curve?" my mom said. "Was there a deer?" a cop asked. "Another car?" his buddy guessed. They were so desperate to understand. To diminish what I'd done. Decipher it. "So you swerved . . ."

I did swerve. But it wasn't a flinch. It wasn't a mistake. There was a column of rage in me, a crackle of blue flame, clarifying. The whole problem—as I recall—was that Leo kept talking. Leo wouldn't shut up. It was past one in the morning and he wouldn't stop talking about Lacie and so I turned the wheel.

Did I simply want to scare him? That might be too generous. But even now, all these years later, trying once again to summon the moment, all I find is static.

The moment afterward I remember. The moment afterward, indelible. Before the sirens, before the ambulance, before all the flashlights and noise and shouting, there was just a quivering hush, the trickling creek, and my beautiful boy, my best friend's boyfriend, his warm blood all over my lap.

August, and a gray sweaty shimmer lay over Bryant Park. Cops stood around looking bored. A homeless man keened. Women in pencil skirts unwrapped greasy sandwiches with quick, surgical fingers, or forked up massive bites of salad. They ate quickly, alone; they had come to enjoy being outside, in this "urban oasis," yet their shoulders were hunched and their eyes lowered.

But who was I to judge? I, too, sat at a little green table with my shoulders hunched; I, too, tapped my cell phone and darted my eyes. Wishing I had chosen a coffee shop—someplace normal—though at the time Bryant Park had made sense. Lacie lived in Brooklyn; I was staying with my cousin in Queens. There was the meeting with Portia Kahn, my so-called agent, which would bring me to Midtown anyway. And I was broke. Even four dollars for tea—especially four dollars for tea—seemed unbearable to me. So I had suggested this glade of green where we could sit for free.

While I waited I watched a woman at a sandwich kiosk feebly disguised as an antique gazebo. She wore a loose black jumpsuit and espadrilles. She had a tote bag. Her brown curls were carelessly pulled into a messy topknot. She was not like the office drones; in fact, I could almost imagine myself, once I had settled into my New York life, dressing something like her. Up at the green-black trees she gazed. Then she turned.

Everything slowed. My lizard brain knew her. Even from across the park I knew. That tilt of the head, the squint as she scanned the tables. I had a sudden instinct to hide. Too late—she had spotted me, was even now rushing across the park, calling "Rose!"

Then she stopped short. We met each other's eyes. We stared deep. We looked the way you look in a mirror when you are alone: blatant, utterly unself-conscious. "Wow," she murmured. "It's been so long. It's been forever."

Time had sharpened her face, and it was strange to see her with a few strands of silver hair. Yet in her gray eyes, and the vexed, pointed chin, there was still Lacie.

The spell broke—she broke it with a tentative smile—and we embraced. Inside my arms she smelled of sweat and summer. Everything came back to me. Lacie, Lucinda Salt. Here. I shuddered.

She pulled back. "Want to sit? Do you still have some time?"

"So much time," I said, and then regretted my honesty. I couldn't stop looking at her. Her eyes, I thought. What drives men crazy are her eyes.

She had come back into my life in that most quintessential of contemporary ways, the email. A shy, tentative email. Twelve years it had been. Not a word since high school, and then suddenly her name on my screen. *I've been seeing someone you know . . .* Ian, apparently, had brought up my name; he had been the one to share my email address.

"I can't believe you know Ian," I said once we had settled ourselves at my table. I tried to keep my voice offhand.

"I can't believe *you* know him." She twisted the cap off her iced green tea and took a tiny, nervous sip. "When he was like, 'My friend Rose is moving to town,' I thought, I used to have a friend named Rose . . ."

Used to, so casual on her lips, startled me. I tried to match her bright tone. "So you guys are dating?"

"Apparently." An ironic twist to her lips. "I hope you don't mind me reaching out. It was his idea."

In the hollow of her throat, a tendon was jumping. I felt it in my own neck. The rigid angle of her arm: my arm, too, was oddly bent. Always between us there had been this symmetry, this sympathetic pain, born of thousands of hours of sleepovers and creek walks, born, I think, of being children together. A kinship between our cells. I realized what I should have known right away: she didn't want to be here. She had come for him.

We locked eyes again, and in that moment I knew—but the kind of knowledge that is like a dream, so that you doubt it afterward, if you even remember it—that I had haunted her twenties the way she had haunted mine. I had lived inside her brain. I knew it.

"How did you guys even *meet*?" I found myself saying. "How long have you been dating?"

"At a gallery. I don't know, like, six months?" She pursed her lips, as if to say, *Who even keeps track?* and then continued unwrapping her sandwich, a steaming mass of avocado and slippery roasted red pepper. "Do you want some?"

"No, no, I'm fine. I'm not going to take your *lunch*." I rolled my eyes to underline the largesse of such a gift. "So where do you work? Somewhere near here?"

"Yeah, it's a magazine. I do graphic design."

"Oh, nice. What magazine?"

"*Tablet*? It's Jewish. It's small." She nibbled the edge of her grilled bread, then looked at it quizzically, as if it didn't taste quite how she had expected. I squelched a smile, and when she met my eye, something unlocked between us.

"A panini's really just a grown-up grilled cheese, isn't it?" she asked, and I giggled and agreed.

After that, we talked more easily. I described my horror of the subway platforms, hellish in the August heat, and she commiserated, saying that summer in New York made everyone "completely hysterical" and "basically insane," and then telling a long elaborate story about the night she bought an air conditioner, all the cabs and tips and smiles it had taken to get it home, the drama of installation, the fear that it might tumble from her fourth-floor window. When she told me about waking up in the middle of the night to pat it, as if it were a fussy baby, I laughed and laughed, more from relief that she was being nice to me than anything else.

We chatted a bit, too, about the past decade. Not high school, not college, but our twenties: her stint in art school, the series of graphic design jobs she had held, my peripatetic wandering across the country, the time in Iowa and Oakland, the stints in Montauk and Nebraska.

"Iowa?" Her gaze sharpened. "Iowa City? The Workshop?"

This was a revelation: in certain New York circles, the entire state of Iowa was reducible to a single graduate program. I nodded, thinking she would be pleased, even impressed, but instead she pouted. "You're not writing plays?"

In high school I had written a one-act in which the biblical Eve fights with the biblical Adam, then stabs him in the heart. Senior year, it had won all sorts of prizes, local and eventually national, but before that, when it was just an extra-credit project for English class, I had cast Lacie as Eve, and her boyfriend, Leo, as Adam. For six glorious weeks I had rehearsed them in the English teacher's classroom.

"Oh, that," I said now. "That was just kind of a high school thing. In college I got more into fiction writing."

"But you were so good!" she protested.

I caught my breath. She did not sound upset, did not sound like she was even *thinking* of the accident.

"I just got into fiction," I said again, more firmly this time, and she dropped it, asking instead what I was up to in New York.

"Oh, just—writing. I'm working on a novel." I flinched. "I'm going to try to tutor rich kids too. I think it's the easiest way for me to make money. I mean, without taking off my clothes."

This was my line, and I felt a surge of triumph and relief as I delivered it, thinking I sounded debonair, as if I *would* strip, if SAT prep weren't so damn easy.

But Lacie wasn't that easily distracted. "What's your novel about? Can I ask?"

"Ah, you know." I coughed a little. "I'm actually not telling anyone."

"Oh, okay." Lacie's face scurried in understanding. "Yeah, totally. That's what writers do. I get it." She crumpled up her napkin and waxed paper. "Well. This is a tease, I know. But I should get back."

We said goodbye ambiguously. Or maybe not. If I had lived in New York longer, I might have understood that Lacie's "Let's hang out sometime" essentially meant "Let's never see each other again," but as it was—especially because she gave me her number—I believed her.

Her last words to me were "Well, give me a shout if you're ever in Ditmas Park."

My expression must have been blank, because she added, as if I had caught her out, "Okay, technically it's *Prospect Park South,* but nobody knows where that is." She raised her eyebrows at some unspoken irony.

I gulped, nodded, and watched as she walked away. Her loose tendrils, the boxy glasses, the jumpsuit at once unfussy and hip, were all so artlessly graceful, so casually perfect, that from within me came jealousy's old familiar throb.

After another hour baking in Bryant Park, I was sweaty and damp, yet Portia Kahn was nothing if not gracious when I was ushered into her office, cooing "Such a pleasure!" while ignoring the darkened half-circles beneath my pits. "After all our conversations on the phone." She pressed my hand. "How long has it been? *So* nice to see you again. What you've written, it's just incredible. Your voice is so *raw*."

If you have been writing in the dark for the greater part of your twenties, if you have scraped by on glorified secretary jobs while your college classmates pulled down six figures at Google or launched themselves into *exciting* and *rewarding* careers as immigration-reform lawyers, if on the cusp of your Saturn's return you moved to a small Midwestern town simply to find relief from all the mind-numbing office work, if you then labored in the cornfields for two years, rising in blue-black January mornings to icicles dangling daggerlike from the attic windows of your garret apartment to write your little thermal-wearing heart out, working and working and working on the almost prerequisite and certainly predictable thinly veiled autobiographical novel, then these words will be balm. Grace. All you've ever wanted to hear.

My final year, Portia had come to Iowa as a visiting literary agent. A tiny elegant bird with silver earrings and pearly pink nails, she had stood before us and assured us that she *loved* the short story, *loved* a good collection, which we all knew meant: *I hate story collections, story collections don't sell.* Like every other agent, she wanted novels.

When she left two days later with a stack of manuscripts I had been confident, though I made a great performance, as did everyone else, of exclaiming over how terrible my novel excerpt was. But I knew: what I had done as a teenager was so shocking that there was no question it would hook her.

When she called a month later, I had again pretended great humility. Alone in my attic apartment, I hummed polite demurrals while she exclaimed, "Rose! You're so talented. And this novel! It's just extraordinary."

There were, though, just a few things. Some minor points. Questions, really. For the next two hours she talked, and I typed, and when we were done I had a five-page, single-spaced Word document with structural changes, character questions, plot notes, suggestions for added scenes and deleted scenes, narrative arcs that might be "strengthened," and interiority that might be "more fully revealed."

But who was I to complain? She had called my novel extraordinary.

So for the next three years I wrote and Portia advised. Always success seemed right around the corner. As I traveled from Iowa to Oakland to Montauk to Nebraska, she followed, a voice on the phone, cajoling and promising, sweet-talking and demurring. Urging me forward, but cautioning "not yet." Not quite yet.

And now here she was. Draped in black, with the same pearly pink nails and silver earrings, she was still almost unbearably elegant, but when she said, "Your prose has this . . ." and then avoided my eye to stare into space to find the exact phrase, "*granular* specificity," I saw—as I hadn't before—that behind this smooth woman there was a nerdy girl who had once taken refuge in books. It made me trust her all over again, this dweeby, eager bookworm poking out behind the classy façade of *Portia Kahn*.

Not surprisingly, she thought the book needed "one last" push, that the stakes of the book needed clarifying. "This depiction of female friendship, it troubles me," she explained. "There's so much jealousy in the book. And the best friend. I still don't have a sense of Lacie."

All my sweaty parts went clammy. Even knowing it was coming, it was strange to hear Lacie's name on Portia's lips. I told myself firmly that the Lacie in my manuscript had nothing to do with the stylish thirty-year-old graphic designer I had just met, that they were separate, one fictional, one real.

Yet listening to Portia talk about character, the need for more *details,* I flashed back to Lacie's espadrilles, trying to decide whether they would make sense in a story set in 1999. Or was there something in her head tilt, or the way she touched her hair? The important thing was to convey her charisma. Her allure.

After I had thanked Portia profusely for these thoughts, she clicked off on her tiny heels to a back room and returned with three bound galleys, saying, offhandedly, "People are pretty hyped about these. I'll get a letter off to you next week. I just wanted to share these initial thoughts, but really, Rose. I couldn't be more excited."

Ten minutes after the appointment for which I had waited two hours had begun, it was done.

No matter. I burst out onto the street, buzzing. The city glinted with promise. All I had to do was throw in some telling details, get Lacie *down,* and I'd be launched.

But first, the tutoring interview. By slinging around the name *Harvard* I had quickly landed interviews at four companies, but from the beginning I had had my eye on Ivy Prep Consulting, the most expensive and exclusive "academic and test preparation firm" on the Upper East Side. Wild rumors flew about them: their top tutors made a thousand dollars an hour, they regularly flew on private jets with the families, the College Board itself sought their consultation. Half their tutors, it seemed, had *graduated summa cum laude;* all of them, the website bragged, ranked *in the 99th percentile for every test they tutored.*

Reading this, I decided to doctor my SAT scores, carefully inserting into my cover letter, "While I don't precisely recall my SATs from more than a decade ago, I believe I scored somewhere in the high 700s for both math and reading," knowing full well that I did not break

700 on the math, knowing, too, that I could say whatever I wanted, that my lie would not only be believed, but that it would confirm the whole set of assumptions already operating around me, that I came so fully outfitted in the trappings of success—*Harvard, Iowa*—that embellishment to cover any gaps was practically obligatory.

Then, interview scheduled, address received, I nearly blew it: 9:07 the morning after meeting Lacie found me racing from my cousin's living room to bathroom, from bathroom to front hall to couch, not quite *late,* but becoming increasingly dependent, with each passing minute, on the good karma of the F train, and then 9:57 found me run-walking, and then flat-out sprinting, down Eighty-Fifth Street toward Third Avenue, having spent the previous train ride staring straight ahead, my gut churning, too full of self-recriminations to read or even think about what I might say to Griffin Chin, founder and director of Ivy Prep, Harvard-trained lawyer, and "educational consultant" who regularly appeared on Bloomberg TV.

Griffin's office, in a residential building, had probably formerly housed a family of four. The living room had the black leather and glass-topped table of an executive suite. SAT prep books filled the kitchenette. When I arrived he ushered me to what must have once been the dining-room table and offered me a Poland Spring from the full-size refrigerator.

I was three minutes late—a negligible amount, especially in New York, where everyone is at the mercy of trains and traffic—but I could see he had noticed. "Rose." He squared his legal pad perpendicular to the table's edge. "Thank you so much for coming in. Now, as I said on the phone," though he had not said this on the phone, "you're very qualified. People in the office are very into you. So let's think of this not so much as an interview as a chance to get to know each other better."

I nodded and subtly wiggled my shoulders, trying to make my cheap Pashmina slide down my back. What do I look like? I am a girl, a girl who can look many different ways. When I want I can put on a nice professional, demure dress, and brush my hair so it is soft and luxuriant and smooth, and wear my grandmother's pearl earrings and a tiny gold watch; I can look utterly familiar, utterly unremarkable, except, perhaps, for my stained teeth. I am slender, with a long pale face that blushes easily, and strawberry-blond hair from which I pluck the occasional strand of gray. When I was young I looked much more unusual because I didn't give a fuck. I thought that's what you did if you didn't want to get trapped. Now I had convinced myself that freedom lay on the other side.

Reverentially Griffin spoke of the top "independent" schools, ticking them off on his fingers—Brearley, Dalton, Horace Mann—and then mentioned, for the second time, that his daughter was off to Yale next week ("How wonderful!" I exclaimed, though with less enthusiasm than before).

There was something funny going on with his teeth too. They diminished in a diagonal that culminated in pale pink gum. The back of his hair flipped out in a ducktail that couldn't have been intentional. His suit was expensive, his grooming impeccable, yet still his body's strangeness asserted itself.

He became serious. "Rose," he said, "there is no cynicism in what we do, absolutely none, because then everything would fall apart. And I believe the student is absolutely at the center of what I do. I don't care who's paying the bill. The student is my sacred trust."

I tried to imagine him coming home to his wife, unbuttoning his shirt, making a crass remark about money. That part of him was so utterly hidden that I suspected it must be large. Nonetheless, I was careful when he asked why I wanted to tutor. Not for the money; certainly, no!

"Well, kids are great." I shook my head, still stunned by their greatness. "I mean, kids are kids, right? It doesn't matter if their parents are on financial aid or are really, really rich, kids are always just—sweet." Even I was unconvinced by myself. I added hesitantly, "Of course, you know, if they're entitled, that's a little hard."

"Entitled." He shook his head, genuinely grieved. "Now, that's a word I just hate to hear. It's so sad when you see it in the kids."

"Yeah, absolutely."

"It's one thing when you've been alive for forty, fifty years, when you've made enough money to support your family for ten generations, okay, fine. Be entitled. But when you haven't done anything, and you expect things?" He shook his head again.

But did he mean—he *did,* didn't he?—that the adult residents of the Upper East Side, the bankers, the entertainment lawyers, the venture capitalists and heads of PR firms—deserved their ludicrous, indeed historically anomalous, wealth? I was just absorbing this when he added, "Well, as I said, the people in the office are *very high* on you, and I think we might just have a few kids for you.

"Now," he added, after I had burbled my gratitude, "what we like to do at Ivy Prep, we like to figure out what each person is *extremely* good at. Take Claire Pryor, for instance. Now, Claire is a graduate of Georgetown, which is a *very* good school"—the way he said "very" meant *not at all*—"and when she came here, I gradually realized, it's the strangest thing, but she's exceptionally good at grammar. And so now, she's the one who trains our Harvard PhD tutors how to teach grammar!" He beamed happily at me.

"Wow, that's great." I shook his hand. "That's such a good way to do it."

His beam widened. It wobbled. Griffin was not a stupid man: he sensed my disdain. The gracious mask he wore as easily as his silk shirts slipped, revealing a man confused, a face in the act of seeing its mistake. At that moment I almost liked him.

I started to text Lacie the good news but hesitated. Why should she care? We hardly knew each other anymore. But she had said to stay in touch. Following up was only polite.

To my surprise she wrote back right away, with exclamation marks and charmingly inexplicable emojis, including a rather festive dolphin. I considered sending her back a whale or a dragon, but both seemed too literal, somehow. In the end, I didn't reply, but that didn't mean I wasn't pleased. Her response was so much warmer than I had expected.

On the subway a few days later I watched a pair of high-schoolers engage in that particular social ritual known as "I Want to Fuck You but I Can't So I Will Laugh Hysterically at Everything You Say." Their bags were scattered everywhere, as if this Q train were their living room, and they sprawled along the benches with their feet up and their heads close. City kids. I envied their ease.

The boy, despite acne, was cute. In three years he'd be a heart-breaker, with his brown curls, puppy-dog eyes, and insouciant red socks. The girl, in a gauzy long skirt and black hoodie, reminded me of Lacie, Lacie with Leo: a little hippie, but nervy, too, under the skin.

Those kids! Leaning into each other and laughing, the girl exclaiming *Oh my God, I'm, like, obsessed with it!* while the rest of us sat, sullenly polite, knees together, bags on laps. They didn't know how desire stamped their bodies, how we all saw it. When the boy stretched out his arm, and the girl, giggling, nudged the crook of his elbow, they were totally unself-conscious, as if they had, just this minute, invented the language of longing themselves.

Meanwhile, someone's little sister sat across the car, nose buried in a book, a pale ghost in a pink T-shirt. Will you think it self-pity if I say she reminded me of myself?

Then a young man was ushering me into an elevator reeking of piss. Apartment viewing number three, and though the crumbling brick studio and the overpriced railroad apartment had not discouraged me, this one-bedroom—which turned out to be filled not only with a partially disemboweled sofa but a silent middle-aged woman in curlers who glowered at the broker's cheery greeting, slammed her coffee mug down, and lit a cigarette—left me a mite dismayed.

It was a child's game, this making of a New York life—my friends had mostly done it when they were twenty-two, and either had left the city by now or zipped along to higher incomes, better apartments, decent jobs. They'd outgrown their starter set, and I, embarrassed at how I needed everything—job, apartment, *life*—had not called them. Instead I was staying with my cousin in Queens, who, though she was deep in her surgical residency and hardly ever slept, had answered her phone right away and invited me to crash with her.

Now, standing in this shoddy apartment, I felt as though I were making my life from the cardboard boxes I had played with as a kid: they were printed to look like solid brick, but light enough for a child to knock over.

Patiently I listened as the broker detailed the "prewar" features and opened closet doors for me. The fake wooden siding on the cabinets was curling off. The countertop was chipped, and the shag carpeting smelled of mildew. "I love the . . . the . . . *space,*" I said, thinking that whatever price he quoted me, however reasonable it might seem, would undoubtedly be hundreds higher than what the people around me were paying. I would become a harbinger of gentrification, treated with derision and distrust, and I would deserve it.

As we walked out, I said I loved the neighborhood, and old buildings, and old *charming* buildings, and buildings with good bones. I was by then so sure that I would never take the apartment that I became desperate to convince the broker that I might.

This often happens to me. As soon as it becomes clear not merely that things are not working out but that a grotesque misalignment has occurred, that there is *no way* that I will ever take this apartment, accept this job, date this man, I become obsessed, *obsessed,* with hiding my hesitation. "I'll call you," I said, shaking the broker's hand. "I'm so excited!"

———————

Walking toward the subway, I felt loose and empty, reluctant to go back to my cousin's, but unsure what to do with myself. A clutch of teenagers glowered as I walked past. One said something, and they all collapsed into laughter. I felt fourteen again. I didn't belong here, but I couldn't stomach the long ride back so soon after leaving.

I got out my phone and hit Maps, though in truth I already knew. When I had called the broker, I had known. Now, looking at the blue dot pulsing near the soft gray letters of DITMAS PARK, I thought: Well, I could just walk over. I could just go see.

Church Avenue was broad but traffic-choked, delivery trucks double-parked, a beat-up Lincoln making a three-point turn while horns roared. Racks of cheap printed dresses fluttered in the breeze of a passing B35 bus. A broken man with red, runny eyes sat cross-legged on the sidewalk, rhythmically rocking. Following my phone, I walked past John's Liquors and GEMS GEMS GEMS, past the Golden Krust Bakery and the Island Waves Caribbean Market, past a fishmonger hawking pale, icy flesh, and a Chinese restaurant with starry, bullet-burst glass, dodging as I went pooling piss, and a spongy pizza slice, and melted ice cream, its dye curling out from the cream in a long pink trail.

Then I turned off Church to a quiet, leafy street. Everywhere, mansions and lawns. I stopped, amazed. There was a Tudor, an English cottage, a Southern colonial. A Victorian in orange and green, done up like a pagoda. A medieval castle, all turret and balustrade. Over the green swells of land bloomed English tea roses and tall, triumphant lilies, late-season honeysuckle and purple allium balls. Another world.

Down the block a film crew had set up, its silver trailers hugging the curb. Half a dozen klieg lights brilliantly flooded the cherry-red door of a colonial. A No Parking sign taped to a lamppost announced the filming of a popular TV show, one that took place in a studiously "normal" American town, and that was when it hit me: Swarthmore. This neighborhood reminded me of home.

After two blocks the street hit another commercial strip, less hectic than Church, with sun-faded awnings and an upscale ramen joint. I passed a "wine shoppe," an upholstery store, and three hair salons. There was check cashing and craft beer. A Mexican restaurant, a school. A bar that doubled as a flower shop.

By the library, I came upon a bevy of white four-cornered tents, like a caravan set down for the night. A woman called to me; did I want to fight fracking in New York State? Hastily I shook my head and waded in. It was slow-going. Fathers with strollers and older women clogged the sidewalk, leisurely leaning over the eggplants and pulling plastic bags from overhead hooks. There were homemade pies, a freezer of turkey meat, veiny gray shrimp. Potted herbs. Zucchinis and berries and endless, endless tomatoes, heirloom and cherry, plum and Roma, yellow and green and scarlet and that wonderful flat pink-red.

By the Bread Alone tent I saw her. In a pale peach sundress, with her hair atop her head, she floated in the eddy of shoppers. When she leaned over the lettuce heads, her shoulder blades tensed like twin hearts.

For a long moment I stood, half-hidden, watching. Lacie moved as if there were no one around her, as if each brimming basket of tiny wild strawberries had been picked especially for her.

The cheesemonger's face softened like a peach when she approached. Laughing, he offered her a wedge of something gooey. She took it, smiling, nodding in agreement: delicious. And then she moved on. Yes, that was how she was—that was how she had always been with boys. But there was something new in her, too, something I couldn't quite name.

Then she turned, and looked directly at me. Something live flew into my throat. I studied the sidewalk, and when I looked up again, she had turned away. I pressed through the crowd.

"Rose!" Awkwardly we hugged, her tote bags hitting my body.

"What are you doing out here?" she cried, with a sour note of aggression she didn't bother to hide.

Maybe that was the new thing: a little knife sewn into her childish voice, a butterfly skewer so light you hardly noticed it until the slice.

"I was just looking at an apartment nearby." I hoped I sounded breezy.

"And you came over for the farmers' market?" She sounded skeptical. "It's so small."

"No, I was just walking around. Exploring."

Pedestrians swiveled around us, some sending reproving glances behind them. Lacie began to drift along the stalls, and I followed, twisting my hips to avoid the strollers.

"So how was it?" she called over her shoulder.

"The apartment? Not great."

"Where was it?" She stopped to examine a cucumber.

I dodged a bobbing yoga mat. "Um, near the Parkside Avenue stop, on this big road—"

"Ocean?" She wrinkled her nose. "Yeah. Some of those places are in pretty bad shape."

We reached the herb tent, where she bought a bouquet of mint, and something called sorrel, counting out her dollar bills and carefully flattening each one.

"I can't believe how beautiful it is here, though." A sack of squash thunked my ribs. "The houses are just gorgeous."

She looked at me sharply, as if I were suggesting renting one of them. "A lot of them are still single-family homes."

We reached the end of the stalls. "Well, bye," she said with a tight little smile, her hand curling into a wave. I panicked. Apparently this was going to be it—she wasn't even going to remark on how strange it was that we had run into each other. I found myself saying, "Wait."

She turned back, surprised.

"You want to get coffee?"

"Ohh." She grimaced. "You know, I totally would, but I've got to get this meat into the fridge." She hoisted a bag, and I registered fully for the first time how many bags she was carrying, the way the straps cut into the pale skin of her shoulder.

"Oh, yeah, okay. Well, can I walk with you?" Her eyes narrowed. "I just want to see the neighborhood," I explained. "I don't know if I'll ever be back out here again." And then, because I could see she still wasn't sure—because I could tell she was puzzled by my zooming back into her life, and who could blame her?—I added, "I like it here. It reminds me of Swarthmore. It reminds me of home."

Her face opened. Swarthmore whizzed up before us, a snow globe of tiny houses and yellow streetlamps. "Yeah," she sighed. "I love living here," and when I fell into step beside her, she didn't object.

We headed up a graceful side street lined with more stately mansions, each one brightly painted, with wraparound porches and wild gardens and mature trees. Beech leaves crunched underfoot, a dry, summery sound. "It's funny," I said as we walked. "I thought Swarthmore sucked when I was growing up, but now I kind of miss it."

A shy, private smile played on her lips. "Yeah. We were actually really lucky to grow up there."

This admission filled me with squirmy, hot joy, as if she had said she was lucky to have grown up with *me*. "And now you get to live in an exact replica of your childhood town!" I gestured grandly at the streets. "I mean, almost literally, right? I saw them shooting something when I was walking over."

"They're always filming. It actually gets to be a little annoying." But she didn't sound annoyed. There was a lightness in her voice I hadn't heard before.

"It's so meta, don't you think? They're replicating your childhood all around you."

She laughed, a sound like cool water. "Yeah, totally."

When we reached her building, she paused, and the same desperate drowning feeling overcame me. We'd been profoundly out of touch—I wasn't on social media, and we'd cut ties long before email and cell phones—but now the ocean of fate had dumped her onto my shore, and I couldn't bear for the waves to swallow her again. "So this is your place," I said, craning my neck. A proper apartment building, six stories and made from brick, it was elaborately cut to maximize windows and balconies.

"Yep." She looked, too, as if seeing it for the first time. "Umm," she said, perhaps perplexed that I showed no sign of leaving. "Do you want to come up?"

"Sure." I smiled. "I'd love to."

Her foyer was dark and smelled of dried sweat. Following her lead, I kicked off my sandals and walked into a giant room of arrested chaos: a dining table cluttered with magazines and books, a drying rack of blouses and bras, and a small gray cat sleeping in an Amazon box.

I handed her the bags I had been carrying for her, and sank into the daybed, a veritable ship done up in red velvet with embroidered pillows of turquoise and tangerine. "Do you want coffee? Tea?" she called from the kitchen. The crisper door rattled on its track, and something clunked.

"No, I'm okay. Thanks." I didn't want to push my luck.

The furniture was motley but plentiful: overstuffed bergères, an epic dining-room table, a stray armchair done up in pink roses. Paperback novels and old *New Yorker*s littered the table, along with a sewing machine, a woodworking clamp, and a glass jar of colored pencils. On the mantel, a stack of old *Paris Review*s, a tiny lamp with beaded fringe, and a faded photograph of a Merce Cunningham dancer mid-plié.

"It's a mess," she said when she returned, handing me a glass of water.

"No, I love it." I meant it. "It's so warm."

She curled like a cat on the couch beside me. I wanted to say more about the jars of sequins and buttons, the careless heaps of books, the opened Moleskines marked with coffee rings, but I was distracted. She looked at me so expectantly that I knew I had to speak.

"Hi."

She laughed. "I can't believe you hunted me down at the farmers' market." I startled, but she was smiling, kidding. "Twice in one week, after so many years," she added softly.

"Yeah." I coughed. "Where's Ian?"

"What do you mean, where's Ian?"

"I don't know. I thought maybe you guys lived together."

She laughed and blushed at the same time. She was pretty when she blushed. "Oh, no, we really just started dating. It's all new." She looked at me shyly. "You guys were together . . . on this island?"

"Well, Long Island. But yeah. It was like this residency thing."

"Ian said you worked really hard. He said you were the best one there."

Now I laughed and flushed. "That's not true," I declared. "I didn't work *that* hard." But I was pleased. Ian was like a sore tooth I kept pressing with my tongue.

Another silence. "Well. Do you want the tour?"

When we stood, the little gray cat rose and trotted with us down the hall, like a dog. Briefly I glimpsed her bedroom: a swell of calico comforter, more books and journals, half a dozen glasses shimmering in the morning light.

At the end of the very short hall, there was a closed door like a door in a dream. "Here," she said, and flung it wide to reveal a room narrow and white, with a desk of heavy wood pushed beneath the window.

The room was immaculate. Pristine, studious, radiant. With it, the rest of the apartment suddenly made sense, chaos and creation anchored by clean simplicity. I loved it. Except: "What's that?" I pointed at a giant wooden contraption.

"It's a loom." She laughed. "I know. It's definitely the most ridiculous thing I own. It's like the beast in the corner." She scooped up her gray cat and kissed the top of its head. "My poor little beast. Totally neglected."

"What do you mean? You don't use it?"

She dropped the cat. "Not really. Not enough."

"It's so cool." I stepped toward it tentatively, as if it might snap to life.

"Yeah, I'm lucky to have it. And I have all these great ideas for projects, but when I get home at night"—she flung her hand out and expelled an exasperated puff—"I'm so tired I just sit on the couch."

"Oh. Well, you should work on your projects."

I realized as I said it how harsh I sounded. But these were familiar roles for us: I had always been the one to ringlead our school projects, to say we should just do it, that it was easy, no big deal.

She laughed.

"No, I'm serious. You should feed the beast. No, you know what you should do? You should move this whole thing into the living room"—a bark of incredulous laughter—"so you *have* to look at it, and then it'll annoy you so much you'll start using it. Really."

"And then what would I do with this room?"

"Let me live in it."

As soon as I said it I knew it was a step too far. We both blinked.

Quickly I added, "I'll help you move the loom." Theatrically I rolled up my sleeves. "Really. Let's do it right now. There's space in the living room."

"Ha-ha. It's a disaster out there right now."

"Oh, come on. There's space."

We were both grinning. I was ready for action; I wanted to skate over how sad it made me to think she had some big expensive piece of equipment she didn't even use. When we had been friends, she was always doing arts and crafts.

As we strolled back, I saw the living room differently. Maybe it wasn't humming with life. Maybe all the jars of sequins and woodworking clamps were only the detritus of stalled projects. Was there dust on the sewing machine? I had a sudden instinct to check.

As if reading my mind, Lacie said, "Yeah. Lots of good intentions, but I've got no follow-through these days."

"Hmm."

"But look. I'm happy for you. You're making art. You wrote a novel."

"Well, I'm *writing* a novel. Don't get too excited."

"I've always admired your dedication."

That was so unexpected that I really had to examine the carpet. When she was a teenager she never would have said something so heartfelt.

"No, really. In high school? You wrote that play on your own. How many kids would do something like that?"

"You made those amazing costumes." Embarrassed for both of us, I blushed.

"Oh," she waved me off, but I could tell she was pleased. "They were all right."

"No, they made the play! They completely made it."

And there we were, on the lip of the past. I almost asked. I almost said the name *Leo Kupersky.* But there was the cutting board with a golden boule, the cat sleeping on the chair, the mint growing in a clay pot. In me, a small motor of need. Rather than starting out in some anonymous, cramped box, I could have this. I could have Lacie. I wanted it; I wanted this neighborhood, and this house, and *her.*

Was it possible? I snuck a glance at her. She was taking a sip of water and avoiding my eye. The trick, I thought, would be to help her forget what I had done. And so I changed the subject. I stopped us from diving deep. I decided: not today.

M s. Keener, who wore her breasts around her waist like an incomplete inner tube, had decided it was too cold for outdoor sports, so she cued up the tape deck and divided us into groups of eight.

We were spindly ten-year-olds, fidgety squirrels. Jesse Grogan made farting noises while Leo Kupersky pretended to barf. Lacie, the new girl, was in my square. Solemn, tiny, all dark eye and bony shoulder, she rarely spoke, yet wore to school every day a pair of shorts, an audacity for which she was mercilessly teased.

In gym that day we learned the promenade and the do-si-do. Leo slapped a stray basketball her way and called her stupid: "You think it's summertime?" he cried. A pass and a turn to our corners later, I felt her hand quivering in mine. "You should wear pants," I told her. "Then he'll leave you alone." It was the first time we had spoken, but the drama of her refusal to wear warm clothes, coupled with her odd silence, had captivated me. I felt we had been talking for weeks.

"Why?" she spat back, her little white face flushing red. "This isn't cold. *Boston*'s cold."

At recess she paced the tennis courts alone. That day I joined her. She seemed neither grateful nor surprised. Immediately we fell into somber conversation. It made sense, walking beside her. I was lonely, too, though young enough that I didn't know it.

At last Ms. Keener decided: we must perform for our parents. A professional caller was hired, and we endured extra rehearsals, the reluctant boys threatened with revoked recess. On the chosen night my mother brushed my hair and talked me into a skirt.

The gym from afar was lit like a birthday cake. Inside, the square of raised wood gleamed. Parents, jackets crumpled on their laps, watched from the bleachers as we circled and swiveled, bowed and curtsied, even the most rebellious of us momentarily thrilled to step into this courtly vision.

In my chest that night there beat a melancholic sense of my own importance. I was Lacie's only friend in her new home. For weeks we had been drifting together, and now, under the motionless basketball nets, she looked so vulnerable, with her bright paisley shorts and thin calves, that I knew I must protect her. But she must not know that I was protecting her; she must not remember that she was the new girl. I trembled with feeling; the other kids twirled, and the caller called, but all I knew was the trust in her hand, the delicacy required to lead her through the dance.

Into that easy rhythm of my house–your house–my house we fell, tromping between homes with sleeping bags beneath our arms. Her family had two kids, mine had three; her house had one floor, mine had two, but these were just facts, the way the dates of the Civil War were facts, necessary but unremarkable. For me, at least, it was so; looking back, I'm less sure about Lacie. Once she said, "Your house is bigger than mine," and I said, "You guys get more pizza."

Her mom waitressed at the Inglenook until it burnt down one gloriously cold winter night. We all heard the sirens and ran, and our parents let us; our parents came too. Yellow flames jumped from the turret, and the firemen, burdened with tanks, forged through pale brown smoke. With a pop the windows burst and glass rained down, shards tinkling as they fell. Lacie and I stood, side by side, not moving, not talking, memorizing. I thought, This is happening to me, and right there is the church where I was a flower girl, and next to the church is Borough Hall, where the mayor gave me a ribbon one Fourth of July.

Afterward, when I walked down that street, I would think of the fire and the ribbon and the day I was the flower girl; I would hear little ghost whispers from my past childish life. Then Lacie would call, or jump the curb with her bike; then Lacie would suggest we make some prank calls, or spy on the neighbor. Though she was silent at school, at home she was reckless. She wanted to do everything.

Pain interested us. We were constantly perfecting our swagger. Once I dared Lacie to let a bee sting her. In a field of clover we watched a honeybee sink in its pointy stinger. Lacie gasped but did not cry. The next day she was not in school. I ran home after the last bell and called her: her arm and then her face had swelled up like a balloon, and she had spent the night in the hospital. "Awesome," I said; "awesome," she agreed.

For revenge we captured dozens of bees in glass jars and froze them to death. Then we zapped them back to life in the microwave. Mostly they exploded but one, left forgotten on the countertop, stirred after an hour. Gently, he flapped his cellophane wings.

Excited, we turned to proper science. We classified rocks and collected coins. We investigated whether her dog preferred Cheetos or Cheez-Its and experimented on earthworms. Lacie shrieked, "Keep chopping!" when she saw how they still wriggled.

One afternoon we microwaved CDs, looking for the blue sparks Lacie swore would fly. A thin burnt smell filled the air, and the smoke alarm shrilled. Her mother threw us from the house. "Do you think we could get lost in Swarthmore?" Lacie asked. We rode bikes to Baltimore Pike and the college woods and the condos, to Chester and Media and back behind the community pool, but no luck: everywhere we went, we knew where we were.

Boys, we were obsessed with boys. We wanted to smash them, destroy them, drive them mad; we wanted to bottle them and freeze them like the bees, but we settled for the soccer field. I loved them all: Leo Kupersky, who ran fast and light like a baby deer; Jesse Grogan, with his dirty blond mop; Mike Sibley, one of the Sibley boys, that legendary band of brothers who were all thick-necked, ram-headed, and put on earth to play ball. By sixth grade they were following us home, smacking Lacie and sneaking kisses. I smacked them back with my trombone case. I was nobody to them, just her protector, just an obstacle, just the girl who talked too much in class.

"I hate boys," I said. "Me too," Lacie agreed, and when my mom said, "Lacie's going to break hearts," I ignored it. I didn't know we had hearts to break.

The time came for us to write a novel; I told her, gravely, that we must know our characters *better* than we knew ourselves, and so we sat in her parents' parked Volkswagen and made lists of all we knew, not writing but preparing to write, filling entire notebooks with our heroine's likes and dislikes, the names of her aunts and uncles, the ages of her cousins, the grades on her spelling tests. We drew a map of her hometown. We decided that she had a sister, and so we wrote down the name of the sister and what she smelled like and what she sounded like, and we stipulated who got to ride in the front seat when and where the family went on vacation. All afternoon in the hot car we worked, passing the notebook back and forth, saying, "No, no, what if she . . ." and "I think we should say that . . ." and "We don't know enough yet, we're not ready." We wrote until we had created a model of the world as complete as the world we were in, but it was so beautiful, this world, all that we had mapped and all that we knew, that we could not bring ourselves to begin. Leaving the lines under "Chapter One" blank, we climbed from the car and rode bikes down to the creek, where there were baby salamanders under the rocks.

A s befitting an entity called Ivy Prep, our training was both self-important and useless, presented as exhaustive even as it degenerated into an empty exercise of form. None of us— there were seven new tutors circled around that gray kidney-shaped conference table—wanted to complete the twenty officially released SATs, as instructed by the agenda, and after a few days, when we had only reviewed the first section of the first test, it was clear we didn't need to, though our instructor, a beefy, middle-aged man who had once written screenplays, continued to make frequent reference to *all the officially released tests as listed in Appendix A of your agenda*. Appendix A, like all the pages of the agenda, was embossed with the crimson-and-gold insignia of Ivy Prep. That first morning, as the screenwriter talked, I rubbed the stamp until its ersatz gold stuck to my sweaty finger.

Along with refreshers in algebra and geometry, the training offered a tour of the ways tutoring could torpedo your artistic ambitions. There was the opera singer who taught graphing calculators, the in-evitable actor glossing reading passages, and the writer who explained prepositions. They were all "no longer young": their hair was thin-ning, their faces etched, and their waists thick. They were, Griffin had told us, the very best that Ivy Prep had found—no one knew graphing calculators better than this woman who had once sung at Lincoln Center. At breaks I asked, and learned: No, they did not compose music anymore, they hadn't had time for auditions, they had a kid, would I like to see a picture?

On the last day of training, Griffin himself came into the conference room. His sleeves were rolled up; he spoke to us kindly, as a father might. The rules were simple and, as we would agree, the epitome of fair. Compensation was determined as followed: The difference between our students' beginning SAT scores and ending ones was divided by the number of hours we had spent tutoring them; this provided a numeric representation of our effectiveness as a tutor. When we reached a certain number—confidential, of course—our rate would be raised. We would start at a hundred dollars an hour, but *if we were good* there was practically no limit to the money we could earn.

The guy beside me raised his hand. "What if we just happen to be working with a kid who's really bad at standardized tests? It seems a little unfair to get judged for a test we don't actually take."

Griffin gave a beneficent smile. "The only thing that overcomes hard luck is hard work."

Then came the checks—a thousand bucks—and a final speech. Griffin spoke to us directly, simply, making ample eye contact. We were to be the very best. We were not to try too hard. We should be confident, and never forget a million others would be thrilled to occupy our place.

Later that same week, I received my first assignment. Lupe Quiroz, of Eighty-Sixth and York, had a 1500 on her SAT, but her parents believed she could do better. Would I be available for a month of Sundays, an emphasis on math?

I began to calculate. Five hours, five hundred dollars. Four Sundays, ninety minutes each: six hundred dollars. And this was just the start. Sure, there were taxes, but April was a million years away. I said yes. When I slept on my cousin's couch now, I dreamt of calendar squares, each marked with tidy sums ending in double zeros, a wave of cash carrying me to a completed novel.

When I arrived at 450 East Eighty-Sixth, having hoofed it like hell from Lex to York, the doorman patiently waited for me to butcher "Quiroz" before sending me soaring in a silver box.

A woman in an embroidered blouse answered the door. "Hi! I'm Rose! So nice to meet you!" I exclaimed, hand outstretched. She looked at me sadly and muttered over her shoulder.

From the depths (but not the deep depths; this apartment did not have deep depths; even on the threshold I could tell) emerged a second middle-aged woman, wearing loose sweats. "Hi, I'm Araceli," she said. So *this* was the mother who sent emails from her DE Shaw account; *this* was to whom I should be directing my obsequious high-pitched flattery. It was the first time I had confused the housekeeper for the mother, but not the last.

I was ushered inside. Lupe, too, was in running shorts and a giant white T-shirt; everyone except the housekeeper was dressed as if for a slumber party.

We settled into the glass-encased breakfast nook, with its view of East Harlem's gray-and-brown geometry. The apartment, in addition to being spotless and small, was muggy beyond belief. In a far corner, an ancient air conditioner ineffectively wheezed. No wonder the family favored shorts.

Lupe was petite, with dark, serious eyes and delicate cheekbones. Beautiful, and angry: "So, are you guys connected to the Ivy League?"

"Um, it's sort of umm, a lot of the tutors went to Ivy League schools." I made a big show of getting out my new pad of paper and sharpened pencils, the folder neatly printed with her name.

"But it's not, like, official?"

"No."

"So you can just *call* yourself that? Isn't that illegal?"

"Well, it's not *illegal*," and I couldn't help myself, I smiled a little, and *that* got Lupe. "That's weird," she muttered, but she was done arguing. Adult condescension her Kryptonite, I noted. This was a girl who wanted to be taken seriously.

She was right, though. *Ivy Prep*. It was a disgusting name, coyly false. We were both trapped, her family so desperate for some *Ivy Prep* that they'd hire an *Ivy grad* to do the prepping; and me, the Ivy grad wandering further and further off the path of economic stability, capitalizing again and again on the brand-name school that was supposed to have served as a launching pad eight years ago.

"It is weird," I agreed. "But let's get out the diagnostic. How did it go?" The diagnostic was another Griffin tactic: before a family could even begin tutoring, the child had to take a mock SAT. Cost? $225.

Silently Lupe slid the test across the table. The thirty-one questions of MATH TEST 4—CALCULATOR had been completed in very faint, almost unintelligible pencil. "Oh, okay, this looks great. Um. This is good. Okay. Why don't we go over the answers real quick?"

A D C C B . . . a chain of letters like genetic code. She read, and I verified: she had answered every one correctly, save the second to last, which was an exponent-and-root question with enough checkmarks and cheeky superscripted numbers to resemble a three-story house. Number 29. What a coincidence. The coincidence was: I didn't know how to do number 29 either.

Lupe was looking at me with mild interest. "What's the trick?"

Behind Lupe's head there was a shelf of square glass jars with round wooden lids, the kind of jars where quaint coffee shops kept biscotti. These jars, however, were filled not with baked goods but with matchbooks. Hundreds of them, each stamped with a restaurant's logo.

"I thought I had it," she continued. "But the two and the three don't cancel out at the end."

What did the matchbooks mean? Was the father secretly a red-sauce Italian fanatic, did he go to escape the housekeeper's cooking and bring back, in apology, a little souvenir? Did Lupe, up late plowing through mountains of homework, ever lift a lid, plunge in her hand, and take out a book? Did she ever strike a light?

I forced my gaze down. "Well, yeah. This problem. This guy. Yeah. He's a bit of a sly one. I think the thing is . . ."

Here I wasted a good two minutes carefully recopying the question onto my yellow legal pad. Triumphantly I turned it to Lupe. "So what do you think the first step should be?"

"I showed you. I did this." With her mechanical pencil she made a series of pale gray lines.

"Good," I said skeptically, staring bewildered at the faint lines. She'd simplified it? Maybe? Is that how square roots worked? Could you do that? Damp pools of sweat formed in my pits. "And then what do you think you do?"

Lupe reclaimed the yellow pad, squinted, and made more pale marks. My gaze wandered to the next room. Sunk into the paisley cushions of the couch, a *man*. How long had he been there? Hunched over a manila folder, he seemed part of the furniture. The father. Spying on his daughter's tutor, hearing the bafflement in my voice. Thinking he had paid—what did Ivy Prep charge?—$300 an hour?—so $450 for this failed writer to fail at high school math.

Above his head, an antique clock was stuck at four minutes to three.

Lupe was scowling at the page. *Solve it,* I prayed. *Please, oh Lord, solve it.* I felt trapped in some Nietzschean dream of eternal recurrence, doomed to spend eternity here, several hundred feet in the air, shamefaced and sweaty beside a tiny teenage girl.

"I don't know," Lupe sighed. "I would think that you could do *this,*" she indicated a series of 7's and 9's with perky square-root signs, like overly exuberant checkmarks, "but the 3 still doesn't cancel out."

"Yeah, it definitely looks that way," I commiserated. On the couch the father coughed and the plastic crinkled.

"You've got to," I stalled. "Yeah, you've got to . . . this is weird." Lupe regarded me patiently. "This is a weird one. Actually, I think they may have—sometimes, these packets, they've got, like, mistakes in them."

"Oh."

The father coughed again.

"Yeah, I keep, like, asking my boss to fix them but the thing is, it's really hard to write a perfect SAT math question. They're really hard to replicate because they've been crowd-tested. So, this one, for instance, it's way harder than anything you'd ever see on the test. Plus, I think it even has a calculator error in it. It doesn't simplify. The answer is really messy."

My pits: drenched. God, it was hot. All that glass like a greenhouse in the summer heat. I pinched my biceps to my side and felt the damp patches cool my ribs.

"Ohhhh," Lupe hummed, and then, "I think . . ." The mechanical pencil hovered, darted, struck. A predator drone, that Bic. "Yeah, you do it like this."

She swiveled the pad around. The question was, in fact, solved. Square root of 2 and square root of 2, forever and ever, amen. "Amazing," I said. "Fantastic." I craned to see the green digit of the microwave. Seven minutes gone. Eighty-three to go.

Out, at last, on the gray cool street, I checked my phone and found I already had an email from Griffin. *How'd it go?* he asked. *Think you're going to rock SAT tutoring?*

Hurriedly, before I could feel too embarrassed for him, I wrote back: *Yeah! It was great. Lupe's great. I think I'm going to like tutoring.*

Then I was walking west with hope in my heart. About the next apartment, I had a feeling. It was very small and over-priced. It was on a beautiful block, in a beautiful neighbor-hood. It was foolish and maybe exactly right.

In the week since visiting Lacie, I'd spent every morning refreshing Craigslist and every afternoon and evening trekking along strange side streets, meeting real-estate agents on corners and following them to new or ancient or crumbling studios, listening grimly as they rattled off all the reasons I didn't know how lucky I was. But I never could get out my checkbook. With fees and first and last and security the total simply to sign my name often hovered near the $8,000 mark, but it wasn't only the money. I couldn't stop thinking about Ditmas. I couldn't stop thinking about how easy it would be.

But Lacie had been flat-out panicked when I had appeared at the farmers' market, though she had soon tactfully disguised it, and when, a few days later, I had asked her to the movies, she said she had plans. I suggested another night, and then another, but she kept dodging. Finally, awkwardly, I dropped it. She was too busy for me. She certainly wasn't interested in living with me. And the sooner I gave up that dream, and resolved the pesky question of where to live, the sooner I could return to writing.

There were other reasons to hurry. My cousin was getting progres-sively less good at hiding her dismay at finding me, every night, still parked on her couch. Next week Griffin had promised me even more tutoring students: "You're going to be busy!" he had chirped. It was time to find a place. It was time to make it work.

And indeed, this studio, two hundred square feet, with a shower jerry-rigged into the broom closet and the kitchen sink the only sink for ablutions, could work. More than work: it was bright and sun-filled and private, in a gorgeous historic brownstone of chocolaty purple. There was no broker's fee, no last month's rent. Right away I told Tony, a stocky Italian sculptor, that I wanted it.

To celebrate, we sat on the steps and shared a beer. He waved off my list of references. "Hey, hey," he said. "Listen. I don't do that. I don't need a guarantor. I don't need to hear about the size of your bank account or the fancy job you've got. Just look me in the eye and tell me that you're a good person. Tell me you'll pay the rent on time."

"I am obsessive about the rent," I assured him, unable to say, with a straight face, that I was *a good person*. "I've never missed rent in all the years I've been renting." I chuckled. "I'm *crazy* about rent. Just the thought of missing it makes me nervous." I scrunched up my shoulders to show how nervous it made me, playing neurotic writer to his primitive, sensualist sculptor; he may have been all brawn and intuition, but I was all brain, all twitchy, live-wire brain. Not a friend, and definitely not a potential lover, some hot young thing he could seduce into bed, no, no, just a type A, beige-dull neurotic.

Another woman appeared: young, pretty, tidy in a pleated skirt. "Excuse me? I'm here to see an apartment?"

"It's been taken." Tony winked at me.

Furiously she took me in: my unbrushed hair, my empty beer, my scuffed shoes. "You can't possibly have had time to check the references of *anybody*," she hissed.

Tony sighed and waggled his fingers at her. "Here, here, I'll take your, your whatchamacallit."

"My application." She brandished a silver folder. He flipped it open. Katrina Vosges had gone to RISD and worked in industrial design, where she made a healthy five figures—far healthier than my

five figures, which were, anyway, purely speculative, even if I had un-
dergone Ivy Prep's "comprehensive, rigorous, groundbreaking" training.

When she had gone he turned back to me. "I like to rent to artists.
We understand each other." He tore her application in half. Then he
giggled wildly. I joined him. I told him I would bring the check tomorrow. He suggested seven o'clock, and we shook on it.

hy hadn't I said to Tony that I was a "good person"? Why had I settled on "obsessive about the rent"? For I thought of myself as a good person, a *basically* good person. I donated to charitable organizations, I recycled, I held the elevator. I was a good listener, I was relatively close to my parents, every so often I made people laugh. I didn't lie. I hardly ever lied. But right in the middle of all this self-congratulation was a soft spot of rot.

Often I thought about what had happened at the pool. I knew I wasn't to blame, and yet when I tugged at the car crash, trying to unravel its threads, I always ended up thinking about that day at the Swarthmore Swim Club: they were yoked together in my mind.

It had happened the year we were ten. By then, we were old enough to ride our bikes to the pool, to sign in without parents, to buy greasy dogs at the snack bar with bills damply mashed in our hands. That summer we spent nearly every day there; we came to know all the pool's colors, its faded cornflower in the morning, the sparkling afternoon turquoise, its flickering white diamonds and the deepening sapphire of twilight.

I had passed the test for the deep end easily—I had done it the summer before, and the summer before that—but I stayed in the shallows with Lacie, who couldn't swim, and who doggedly pretended she had no interest in the shimmering depths, where the blues were more layered, where the boys played.

If we could have gone beneath the red-and-white buoys, we would have played a few paces from the boys, pretending we were oblivious to their presence. Instead we had to pretend we were oblivious from the shallows, which was much less effective. For hours we held cannonball contests and underwater tea parties, and not even when Leo Kupersky yelled that we were totally gay did we look over. It would have been beneath our dignity.

After swimming we would lie on the side of the pool like two shivering seals, our arms tucked under our torsos, the gritty sidewalk abrading our skin, and it was nice, somehow, after the blue water's give, to have tiny sharp rocks dig into our flesh. We rocked and baked in the heat. We soaked up all the sun stored in the pavement, and slowly the dark hairs on Lacie's arm would soften, slowly her goosebumps would disappear. Watching her was like watching myself in the mirror; what I saw in her body was happening to mine. Yes, I thought. If the color this summer is blue, the sensation is heat.

I could lie in the sun forever, rays prickling and crinkling my skin, heedless of burns. I could even fall asleep like that, right on the pavement, with the shriek of the high divers in my ears, which must have been what happened that August afternoon, for I didn't hear Leo come over, didn't see his long brown foot nudge Lacie. Maybe distantly their voices braided through the gauze of my dream, but then I fell more deeply asleep. When I woke, I was alone.

The air at once felt colder, the sun dimmer. I scrambled upright. The skin of my thighs was mottled and red from loose stones.

They were playing by the deep-end's edge, pushing and shoving, Leo grabbing Lacie and shaking her, her twisting free and raining slaps on his chest.

"Lacie can't swim!" Leo yelled when I came over. "Everyone knows how to swim!" and he punched her on the shoulder. She was giggling, a high-pitched hysterical giggle I had never heard from her before.

"Yeah!" I yelled, seizing Lacie's other shoulder. "Everyone knows how to swim!"

Lacie tried to wriggle free, but she was not very strong, and now there were two of us. She kept laughing, an exaggerated laugh that sounded like a sob, and screaming in a breathy voice, "Help! Help! They've got me!" while Leo and I chanted, "Everyone knows how to swim! Everyone knows how to swim!" shaking her, tugging her, as though she were our prisoner of war, and even now I can remember the feel of her sun-warmed skin beneath my palm, how I clutched it, how it felt good to grab and claw, to dig my nails in and screech near her ear, "Everyone! Everyone!" something mean and nasty in my hands, and while I was grabbing and shouting, Leo hooked his thigh around her leg and tipped her smoothly into the pool.

I don't think we actually believed she couldn't swim. When she dropped like a stone we were astonished. A moment later, she emerged, legs and arms flailing wildly in a spray of white surf. Then she disappeared again.

Neither of us moved. I almost thought she was pretending. It was like her weird laughter. Those fake screams.

Somewhere kids were shouting *Marco! Polo!* The diving boards creaked. There was a splash, and then the lifeguard's whistle. I looked at Leo, his tiny delicate face, like a lemur, pursed in concentration. The two of us, together. The two of us with a problem to solve.

It must have been less than five seconds, those moments of hesitation, though in my mind they go on forever. They last and last. Lacie in the water, and me looking at him.

Then Leo took off yelling. He bolted to the lifeguard's stand and grabbed the guard's ankle. Shouted. Pointed.

Lacie bobbed up. Her dark eyes were alive with animal fear. I stretched out my hand, and she lunged, though the distance was impossible. Again she disappeared beneath the water.

When I looked up all eyes were on me. The pool had gone silent.

Then the lifeguard blew her whistle: *eeeet! eeeet!* She dove: fingers together, toes together. I looked again into the rippled turquoise swirl, the flash of pink flailing *down there,* and then the guard emerged, elbows hooked through Lacie's scrawny arms.

I don't dream of water often but when I do it haunts me. Subway tracks brimming with black liquid. Creek beds meandering silver and brown. Diving deep into a swimming pool—something cinematic about this one, slowed down and hushed, always girl bodies, white bubbles, blown out in a stream.

To all the questions of *What were you thinking?* Leo and I hung our heads. When the manager at the pool, a middle-aged woman pleasantly weathered by sun and cigarettes, exclaimed, "She could have drowned!" Lacie, wrapped in a towel, piped up, "But I didn't. I'm fine," and faced with such nonchalance, the manager had no choice but to let us go.

Leo spun off to find the other boys. In a careful silence Lacie and I walked to the picnic grove. I had three quarters in my hand; I was going to buy her whatever she wanted from the vending machine. I squeezed the coins so hard they became slick and warm.

"You were going to save me," she said finally.

"I couldn't reach."

"You tried to save me," Lacie said again, this time with more conviction. I was embarrassed for her; it had been awful to see her hopeless in the water, but she didn't seem ashamed, or even that shaken up. "You're a hero," she added, and though she was kidding, she was also serious. I said nothing. The ridged edges of the quarters burred my finger pads.

Like most twenty-first-century American writers, I have a slightly tortured, carefully hidden, somewhat abashed but ultimately bedrock belief in destiny. Probably all writers, in all historical moments, do. To tell a story, you need to believe things happen for a reason.

So when Lacie texted me to ask me out just as I was bustling around my cousin's apartment getting ready to meet Tony for the lease-signing, it seemed like a sign, something destined, meant to be. She wanted to know: Was I by any chance free tonight? Like, in an hour? She had two comps to see a theatrical production of *Mrs. Dalloway*, and Ian had canceled. This she followed with another string of inscrutable emojis: eggplant, praying hands, lightning bolt.

This wasn't a real invite. I knew that. I was merely the person in her phone least likely to have Tuesday-night plans one hour before Tuesday night began. Still, it made my heart jig.

A round of Google mapping revealed what I had suspected: minus the ability to teleport, there simply wasn't enough time to drop off the check and still meet Lacie. Could I call Tony? No—we hadn't exchanged numbers. Either I showed up with the certified check in forty minutes, or that sunny studio would go to the next Katrina Vosges who came along.

I started to type back a polite refusal. Then backspaced. Tried again, this time capitalizing "love"—"I would LOVE to, but . . ." It sounded fake. Insincere. I tried a few different versions (thinking, all the while, of Lacie staring at her phone, watching those mysterious bubbles), before realizing that anything less than immediate, enthusiastic acceptance would read as snapping her olive branch over my knee.

All the way down the block I pretended to myself I was headed toward Park Slope. Even texting Lacie to suggest a quick pre-show drink, I was congratulating myself on my maturity. Then, at the last stop in Manhattan, I got off.

The cocktail lounge beside the theater was silky and hushed, with a red velvet curtain to shut away the vulgarity of the street. I spent a lot of time arranging myself on the stool, trying to find a hook under the bar, stuffing and restuffing my cardigan around my purse so it wouldn't hang onto the floor.

When she rushed in I thought: *Lacie.* In smart black booties and a wild floral wrap dress, she was her own weather system, kissing me on the cheek, slipping her purse easily onto a hook, cooing, "Thank you for coming! I know, it was so last-minute, I could *kill* Ian for canceling, I mean"—she lowered her voice while sliding onto a barstool—"I hear the show is *terrible,* but whatever. How are you, how's the hunt?"

My stomach clenched. Was I being an idiot right now? But sitting together with Lacie in public pleased me so much that I couldn't believe it was a mistake. Quickly I told her about the places I had seen, the elevator that smelled of piss, the studios that smelled of mold, the crumbly brick and half-renovated disasters renting for north of $2,000. Carefully I omitted any mention of Tony.

"It's just—moving here is hard. Apartment hunting is insane, but you can't talk about how insane it is without sounding like every other person who has ever moved to New York. But it turns out that knowing it was going to be impossible has not stopped me from being utterly amazed at how impossible it is."

She laughed. "No, totally. There are some things you just have to experience. Like, getting choked up at the ultrasound of your baby is totally clichéd, but everyone does it."

"Yeah. This is exactly like that, except bone-crushingly awful."

Our cocktails arrived, mine in a ladylike punch glass, fragile and ridiculous; hers in a highball glass, sturdy and serious. Instantly I regretted my choice.

Lightly she touched my arm. "By the way. You were totally right. I moved the loom into the living room, and I've been working every night." A glitter in her eyes as she spoke.

"Oh, really? That's great. That's wonderful, Lace." Carefully I hoisted my brimming punch glass. "To feeding the beast in the corner."

"To feeding the beast."

We clinked. When I met her eye, there was something live and febrile there. A dark warm river flowed between us.

Still, sometimes I think that if we hadn't seen a truncated, experimental *Mrs. Dalloway* that night, it might have gone differently. But when they got to the part about Sally Seton—*dark, large-eyed, untidy* Sally Seton, *with the power to shock*—sentimental feeling swelled in me.

Her way with flowers! The actors twirled about the stage. They all wore funny hats with flowers and stiff brims. *Cut their heads off, and made them swim on the top of water in bowls. Extraordinary!* they exclaimed in their horrible British accents, swinging around the beams of a framed-out house. They really got going with the flower bit. *Cut off their heads! Made them swim in water! Hollyhocks and dahlias, flowers never seen together! Extraordinary!*

It was honestly ridiculous, more like a spoof of experimental theater than experimental theater itself, and yet I found myself thinking how we, too, had once been mere children, loving one another in the deep, dumb way of the young. Memories began speaking brightly to me, a smear of warm light: our high, childish voices, our childish pleasure in having bodies, in using them. Riding bikes, walking on curbs, skipping rocks. Prank phone calls, epic sleepovers, endless summer days at the pool. It had all vanished. *But I didn't. I'm fine.*

Then, from the corner of my eye, I saw Lacie raise her hand. Delicately she dabbed her eye. My spine lit. Careful not to turn my head, I watched as she rubbed out the wetness on her cheek.

When the lights rose we gathered our bags in that special bubble of silence that comes after shows. She didn't turn to me and ask my thoughts, or make some wry dismissive comment. Carefully we edged our way up the aisle.

Out in the lobby, Lacie hooked her purse carefully over her shoulder. "Well." She looked bedraggled, as if she had just walked a mile in strong wind.

"That was incredible." I shook my head. "Just—incredible."

She nodded gravely. "There's such a sense of—worlds dissolving. It's just like—Peter and Clarissa, they love each other, you feel their love is more perfect than what's between Clarissa and Richard, but it's untested."

Ushers were locking the doors to the house and beginning to sweep, but she made no motion to go. I looked at her. Did she mean that we were untested? But the problem was that we *were* tested. Tested, and broken.

In my lungs there was still this kind of shattered feeling, as if a rib had gone somewhere it shouldn't, as if the air wasn't going in and out right. Before I could think too much about it, I found myself saying, "Actually, I was thinking about us, for a while, in there."

She smiled shyly. "Yeah, me too."

"Really?" I looked at her. Something real ticked between us.

"Yeah. All that crazy stuff we used to do." She laughed awkwardly. "I don't know. I hope I haven't been acting too weird or anything. It's actually really nice to see you again. It was surprising. But it's actually really nice."

Out on the street, in that soft gray, fuzzy New York night, we began walking north. At a crosswalk I stopped. "Lace?" The light changed, but she stayed still, watching me. "I'm sorry." I pushed the hair from my face. "I'm sorry for what happened. I want you to know that."

She whitened. She didn't accept the apology. But she didn't reject it either. We crossed the street and passed a man sleeping on cardboard. At the subway entrance she said, "Well, thanks for coming out."

"Thanks for asking me."

She paused a moment more, so that the moment stretched like taffy, almost as if we were on a date, that awkward, sweet moment of wondering whether you will kiss or just walk away, and then she was saying, "This is strange, I can't even believe I'm saying this, but would you ever want to move in?"

"Really?" I stiffened, thinking of that bare room, the dark trim and simple wooden desk, the solemn oak spreading its branches.

"I mean, I thought about it after you left that day. You're right, I'm not really doing anything with that room. It's sort of a waste."

"Oh my God, really? That's so nice. That's so nice of you." A strange giddiness rimmed my shattered lungs.

"Yeah, well." Suddenly she looked uncertain. "It could be fun."

So I moved in. I didn't have much: two suitcases, a duffel, and a cardboard box of old notebooks, all of which I schlepped over on a soggy overcast day in early September.

That first night was strange. I remember thanking her profusely for taking me in, and apologizing for leaving my suitcase in the hall. We were tentative around each other, overly polite about who should use the bathroom before bed first, quick to wash even our water glasses after use. When I finally shut the door to my room, I was relieved. We were like a couple on our first weekend trip together, plunged into unnerving proximity. I wondered if this had been a mistake.

The room, though, was perfect, dark and serious, ideal for finishing a book. When I had first seen it, there had been no bed, but apparently Lacie knew someone who knew someone, and by the first night, one had arrived: narrow and thin, with a saggy mattress, but all mine, and for free. When I thanked her, she waved me off.

As it turned out, Lacie knew lots of people, and they were all shedding furniture or mounting plays or opening tiny group shows in sub-galleries by the Gowanus Canal. She introduced me around, and soon things I needed—not just the bed, but a dresser, and a desk lamp, and a membership card to MoMA—came my way. Supervising this flow of things delighted Lacie: it was like a game to her. Standing in the doorway to my room, she'd say, "God, the overhead light in here is ghastly. Let me ask Sophie if they're still trying to get rid of that lamp," and before I could protest, her phone would be out.

When I timidly suggested that I take the middle shelf for groceries, she gave me her famous head tilt. "For what?"

"Well, just so our food doesn't get mixed up."

In her eyes, distrust. Clearly this was not part of the plan. "I mean, we could also just, like, keep track?" My voice climbed an octave, hesitant, and yet I was also flaring with injustice: *this*—sharing a refrigerator—was what made her decide I was not the person she thought I was? She had no idea. Sure, we had known each other as kids, but the quotidian details of my adult self—such as whether I preferred to share food with a housemate—were as yet mysteries to her. I couldn't already be disappointing her.

We were standing in the kitchen when this came up, and after my suggestion she slowly turned, as if seeing for the first time the ancient gas stove, the fridge plastered with snapshots, the glass canisters of rice and lentils and beans. Slowly she said, "I thought we could kind of— share food. I mean, I'm always buying too much anyway. And I don't want to feel like the apartment is divided in half." Her voice rose, even as she smiled self-consciously at her own sincerity. "I want it to feel like a home."

Home. I wanted so badly to believe in the myth of us, in the myth of all female friendships, the deep ones, the lasting ones: that they were more true than romance, more fun than children. That they were a place to live: *home.*

"Yeah, me too," I said. "A home. Let's do that."

Turned out, Lacie was that rarity, a single woman who had figured out food. She rarely threw out groceries, and yet there was always plenty to eat. When she came home from the farmers' market on Sunday mornings, she set about chopping, roasting, broiling, and steaming. Then she stored the cooked vegetables in Tupperware, ready to be tossed into stir-frys or stews. As the days cooled, she became serious about soup: parsnip soup, lentil soup, minestrone. Bread too—dough was often rising above the stove, ready for her to punch it down a few times and then bake at night. Meanwhile, carrots and cucumbers pickled in vast glass jars, labneh strained through cheesecloth, and chickpeas soaked beneath a tea towel.

Years of solo living had had the opposite effect on me: I was used to subsisting on cheese and crackers, on cutting open an avocado and spooning out the meat while standing over the sink, on cereal at ten P.M. and cans of soup and frozen burritos. Hunger to me had always been a problem to solve with minimal fuss.

Still, I tried. Using a recipe from one of her cookbooks, I made lamb meatballs, but they came out both charred and raw. I attempted a salad with a dozen ingredients, but after laboring for two hours, hacking at impossible gourds and slicing the tips off green beans, I devoured the whole thing and still felt famished. Every recipe I tried was incredibly complicated, full of strange, expensive spices and herbs, of which annoyingly awkward amounts always remained.

Soon I gave up. I still bought groceries, and urged Lacie to eat them, but I couldn't nourish her the way she nourished me. Every time I ate I felt both guilty and ravenous. Everything she made was so good.

Without making a big fuss about it, she often happened to be cooking when I got home, and always spooned me an extra bowl. While we ate she listened to me complain about work: the assignment to probe the "semiotic significance" of Huck Finn; the apartment with a yellow neon sign that read MY ASS IS HAUNTED; the sex therapist who dyed his eyebrows black but left his comb-over snowy white.

I confessed, too, that sometimes when a kid gave the wrong answer, and I didn't really know how to do the question, I lied and said it was right. "I just, like, have this moment of impatience and exhaustion. I'm just like, Yeah, that's fine. That's great."

"No, you don't!" She laughed wildly.

Then she would complain about *her* job, explaining the politics of the morning newsletter, the drama of lunch breaks, and what the new ownership meant for the editorial page. In those days we complained competitively, like athletes, spurring ourselves to greater and greater specificity.

On the best nights she would sit at the loom, clacking the harnesses, and I would sprawl out reading on the daybed, Cat nestled beside me. We could stay like that for hours, lost in our own projects, and yet sometimes I would say a name—Grogan, I'd call out, or that younger Sibley kid, the one with the freckles—and she'd say, he's a real-estate agent, he married Morgan, actually, yeah, they're still together, they live in Swarthmore. Oh, that makes sense, he was always kind of a homebody, I'd say, or, She likes to take care of people, and Lacie'd nod and agree.

"How's Ian?" I asked one night, and she nodded eagerly, as if she'd been waiting for me to ask.

"He's great, he's good. He's working on his show a ton."

"Yeah? Have you guys been . . . hanging out?"

"Yeah, sure. It's good." She looked pensive, and I thought she might divulge something, but she only asked, "Have you guys been talking? He likes you so much, by the way. He thinks you're great."

"Oh, that's nice." Through a supreme act of willpower I avoided asking what exactly he had said. "Yeah, we were close at the Barn. We've been texting a little, but we haven't really hung out. He seems busy."

"He is," she assured me.

In truth I was hurt that Ian wasn't making time for me. When I had thought about moving to New York, I had counted him among the handful of people who would stop me from imploding of loneliness. But he had farmed the whole job out to his girlfriend. It surprised me, though it shouldn't have. He could be careless with people.

I didn't have a current boyfriend to dissect, so instead I told her about my past, the mild schoolteacher, the Dutch Deleuzean, the contracts lawyer who loved to talk metaphysical defiance and jack off into my tits. I told her, too, about the guy who had been freaked out by my pubes. "He was like, Oh my God, you've got hair. As if I were a *freak*," and though I was trying to joke, raw hurt snuck into my voice.

"What an asshole."

"I know." I bugged up my face. "I can't believe I was with him." What I really meant was *Don't judge me for being with him.* I wasn't like Lacie, fat with male attention, assured of it, careless with it. I had been grateful this asshole wanted to go to bed with me. But I never could have said that aloud. It would be too pathetic, too nakedly begging for reassurances.

Now she sighed. "The whole shaved-pussy thing is gross anyway."

"Yeah. It's so transparently about porn. I'm like, Aren't you guys ashamed that you want to fuck prepubescent *children*? Don't you get that this is what this is about?"

"Yeah, it's disgusting," she agreed, and then, "Porn," she mused, in such a speculative, leisurely tone, that I giggled. "No, I mean really. It's a thing. It's a"—and she put on her best newscaster voice—"*it's a force shaping our world today.*" We both chuckled, loose from the red wine, and the air too was dilating, making space in our tipsiness for something to grow.

"This one time," she said in a wondering voice, "actually, it was the first time I was with Ian," and it was as though someone had lifted me up by the scruff of my neck, "I started to cry."

"Wait, why?"

"He was just being so gentle, so tender. And it had been so long, you know? So long since someone had done something more than just put me through a series of porn positions."

"Wow."

"You know what I mean?"

"Yeah, no. It's like a checklist. I had never thought about it that way before, but you're totally right. It's so mechanical."

Always, my most showy displays of submission—me on my knees, me whimpering, me helpless, or with my shoulders pinned—got the biggest grunts of satisfaction from men.

"I mean, I'm sex-positive, I believe that for some people, kink is a way toward intimacy. Absolutely. But a lot of it just feels like misogyny dressed up in new clothing. You know? It's like this massive collective fantasy of humiliating and overpowering women. And I'm like, actually? Being choked doesn't turn me on."

"No, it's true. It's depressing when I think about it."

It was depressing, and I also felt—what? Proud of Lacie for noticing it? Proud of her for naming it? As a teenager she had been so adored by men that now I loved hearing her trash them.

"Pornification is real," she declared.

It was real, but the tricky thing was that sometimes it turned me on. Sometimes I hated that it turned me on. My pride in Lacie withered to envy: yes, I envied Lacie, who hadn't gotten all scrambled by culture, who could definitively say she didn't want to be slapped or choked.

Tentatively I said, "This one time, I was having sex with this guy, and he kept spanking me. Just like, *Wham! Wham!* I mean, it hurt. And afterward I was like, Why do you like hitting me? And he said, it feels nice. And I thought, Really? It *feels* nice? We just met, we've never had sex before, and already it feels so boring you have to add spanking to the mix?"

Lacie was nodding. "Yeah, exactly. Good for you for asking."

I flushed under the compliment. I didn't deserve it: I had been stupid enough to be flattered by his answer. *It feels nice.* The truth was that I liked turning men on. I liked feeling them flush with pleasure. I liked feeling feminine and small and weak; I liked their gasps of disbelief. I couldn't be cavalier like Lacie; I couldn't afford her anger. The affection of men was too precious to me. But when I thought too much about *that,* I felt ill.

I wanted to ask—oh, how I wanted to ask—if Ian was still tender in bed. Wouldn't it be normal to say? Why were we still talking on this abstract level? But I couldn't find the guts. I didn't want to smash the warm circuit between us.

Lacie yawned and reached for her phone. "I'm afraid to look at the time, but let me just see."

Predictably, it was shockingly late. We groaned and chorused, "We have to go to bed," setting our wineglasses in the sink. Outside Lacie's bedroom we paused awkwardly. "Good night," she said, giving me a tentative half-hug. "This is so amazing. We get to have a sleepover every night."

I grinned at her. She looked so *pleased*. "Yeah. It's the best."

L acie left every morning around eight for work. Once the door slammed I would settle at my desk and open my laptop. I never started writing until she left. I needed to be alone.

Once she was gone, though—oh, how I wrote, with a faith that now breaks my heart. It was this simple: I believed I was writing a novel. For years I had believed this, but now I had an agent, and a solid draft, and all I had to do was fix it, fix it with all the vision and force within me, and glory would be mine. Though I am not that much older now, I look back on that girl with pity and frustration. She had such faith that her effort would be rewarded, that if she just dug in and *worked,* she would be lifted out of her life, the ordinary humdrum of tutoring teenagers, to a lifetime of mornings.

For my mornings—daydreaming at my desk, polishing a few lapidary sentences, scrawling out my dreams, sipping coffee—were the best part of my days. On the other side of publication there would surely be a lifetime of it. On scraps I tried out alternate exchanges of dialogue; breathlessly I whispered sentences, then swooped with my pen to correct errant syllables.

The novel focused on the friendship between two girls, one beautiful, the other plain; one popular and kind, the other closed like a fist. There comes between them a beautiful boy. Betrayal. Then violence—strange, ambiguous violence.

The problem, as you may have deduced, is that there are approximately one million other novels with this plot. The glamorous, beautiful one; the plain, smart one. A rueful adult narrator still puzzling over the past. Oh, it was all familiar territory—I was counting on my language, my beautiful crystalline *language,* to launch my career—but there was another problem too. Portia could no longer see it.

She kept sighing. "I just don't understand the *stakes* of this story. I don't get the *why* of it. *Why* does this book need to be written?"

The book needed to be written so that I could get on with my life. The book needed to be written so I could get a polite, middle-class sum of money, quit tutoring, which even after a month I already despised, and move into the adult part of my life.

But that was just me being glib. Glib was not a good strategy. I tried earnest: "The stakes are, she's a girl who never goes after what she wants, and you sort of *want* her to go after what she wants, but when she finally does, it's a disaster." Phone cradled to my ear, I paced.

"So what's the consequence of that? Why does this story matter?"

"Well, it's about guilt. And shame."

Silence. I looked at Lacie's bookshelves. Barbara Comyns, Barbara Pym, Elizabeth Bowen, Elizabeth Taylor. All the subtle British ladies who believed in subtle emotional devastation.

"I think, in this next draft," Portia spoke slowly, and I pictured her in her glassy gray office, eyes distant as she reached into my project, into *me,* "you should try—maybe even as an exercise—writing from Lacie's point of view."

"What, really?" The idea viscerally offended me. "Why?"

"I just think we need to understand her more." Portia's voice darkened like a purple-black bruise. A warning, almost.

After the phone call I wandered through the house, touching Lacie's things. That's what I did sometimes during these long lonely daylit hours when I was supposedly writing my book: touch Lacie's things and wonder about her. Why had she let her subscription to *Harper's* lapse? Why was she invited to Fabienne Hook's solo show about bioluminescence? Did she *ever* eat her dark chocolate?

Living with Lacie while writing about her had gone from deeply bizarre to completely normal in a remarkably short amount of time.

After all, I wasn't writing about the real Lacie, but the cipher in my mind. It seemed simple enough to hold them apart, though every so often I plucked a detail from her life. No harm in that. But now Portia wanted me to get into her head.

That day, I found myself standing in the doorway to her room, looking at the unmade bed, the accordion drying rack, the stacks of paperback books. Right, I thought. This is what I haven't let myself do.

I didn't snoop. I will say that for myself. Okay, maybe I opened her underwear drawer, but the sight of the Victoria's Secret bra—we're talking red lace, push-up, wires—discombobulated me. I thought Lacie was better than that.

Then I went through her closet, but only because I wanted to find the dress she had been wearing that morning at the farmers' market. It was a cheap dress, pale peach, with a sweetheart neckline. I saw her again, picking through those fresh herbs. The way the cheese man had held out his knife. Her fear when she had first seen me.

Soon I was kicking off my jeans. Pulling my shirt over my head. The dress swished as it settled around me, clung to my hips as it clung to hers, scooped a soft line above my breasts. I studied the mirror.

In the pale dress I looked like Lacie. Sexy. I smoothed my hand over my stomach, sighing. Was this what Ian liked? Had he seen her in this dress, did it make him want to fuck her? What was their fucking like? Did he still make her cry?

I hurried to my desk and began to type.

Once we were pirates.

Standing in the hot black wings, my face stiff with makeup, eyelashes gummy, lips tacky, I buzzed: with Leo, with Lacie, with *us*. Leo flicking dust off my costume, Lacie straightening his crinkled stockings, the two of them laughing and mouthing the words to every song. Best of all, the long fight, cheering on Captain Hook, our knees sore against the auditorium stage, Leo's thigh against mine. Scalding.

Why, even? He was just a boy. A pretty boy, long and lanky, with a loping walk and dark, smeary eyes. Skin so pale you could see blue blood beneath. He played the guitar. He was, in seventh grade, still nice to girls. Once he borrowed my eraser in math class; once he said he would write a song for me, though he never did. Leo, Leo Kupersky: every class has a boy like him, delicate, fawnlike, more beautiful than handsome, upon which adolescent girls can safely pin their fantasies. They should stagger under the weight of our dreams, these pretty boys, but no, Leo enjoyed our love, he loved it.

We roamed the halls of the school during the first act, pressing our faces against the dark windows of the locked classroom doors, our dull jail cells suddenly exotic on a Saturday night. In our striped tights and felt vests, we clowned around, slaying the dead hours cottoning our brief moments onstage. We squinted and said, "You've got lipstick on your teeth," and "Can you give me a back rub? My shoulders are tense." Leo always gave the back rubs, his long hands, muscled from guitar, working first Lacie's shoulders and then mine.

We were cast as Starkey, Bill Jukes, and Noodler, and our big moment came when we brought the theatrically squirming Tiger Lily to Captain Hook. Pure heaven: the three of us in a music classroom with Lydia Firkins and Walt Stevens, learning how to drag Lydia to Walt, how to coordinate our limbs.

"*Arrgh, Captain, look what we found,*" Leo was supposed to say, though he always mumbled it, and then I would burst out with, "*She was fixing to board the ship!*"

At the end of the final show, while the Darling children were singing in their nursery, Jesse and Leo tried to light themselves on fire. From the back corner of the cooking classroom I watched. Wedged together, they fiddled with a stove until blue flames shot up. Grinning madly, Grogan brought the sleeve of his Lost Boys costume close. Its fringe began to smoke, and slowly the room filled with a flat chemical stink.

All of us, pirates and Lost Boys and Indians, were penned in, ready for our curtain call. This was always the moment it seemed we might collectively go insane: the hours of waiting, the adrenaline of performing, the drama of who had missed their cues and smudged their makeup, ramped up all night, and would Joe get kicked out? Where was the cast party? What should we do with all this crazy energy, us sixth, seventh, eighth graders? Hyped up on hormones, teasing and pushing and whispering, we had so much electricity in our bodies that the parent volunteers could only stand by the entrance with their arms crossed and try to make sure we didn't set anything on fire, though they were obviously failing even at that.

It was up to Lacie, deftly maneuvering between the two boys, to twist her wrist and vanquish the flames. With an imperious nod she dismissed Grogan. He shook his head, balled his fists, and, with a twist of his mouth, drifted off to harass Tinker Bell.

From my post by the window I watched. The day before, I had explained to Lacie how Leo's thigh always lingered against mine during the fight scene, how I thought he was just a little too eager to give me a back rub. "I think he might like me," I had confided, raising my eyebrows. "Do you like him?" she had asked immediately, and though that was the obvious response, I was still somehow unprepared. "A little," I finally answered, and she nodded and agreed to investigate. Together we had worked out the exact wording, which struck us as precise, almost legalistic: "Leo," she would say. "Do you like Rose? Like, *like her* like her?"

Now Lacie leaned close. Seeing them together, I went cold. Lacie's lips brushed his ear. His eyes widened. She pulled back, and he shook his head. No.

A week after the play ended, I came swinging into the locker room after gym and heard from behind a wall of lockers a flutter of girl giggles, and then: *She was fixing to board the ship!* The voice exaggerated, humiliating in its theatrical growl. A round of glassy, high laughter. I stood in the shock of it, pressed against the hand-dryers, realizing I had become a joke, that there was something faintly ridiculous about me. I was aghast. But not, somehow, surprised. It was all there in how I said that stupid line: my dorkiness, my puppy-dog desire to please, the way I was simultaneously tainted by sex and helplessly a child. How could Leo love me? How could I ever have imagined he might? These girls despised me. They smelled what was eager on me. They scorned it.

These were the kinds of memories I wrote down. Wrote down, and embellished, trying to decipher their significance. Trying, also, to write from Lacie's point of view, though it wasn't easy. To enter her mind I had to go into a kind of trance, as if listening for a quiet song playing far away. I'd hear a lilt, and rush to write it down; sometimes the caught detail would lead to others, and I'd find myself scribbling a page or two, riffing about coming home every day to a depressed, withdrawn mother and an absent father; or having a gawky best friend lost in love; or discovering a strange power over boys but not knowing what to make of it.

I could never plan or force these scribblings; they just fell over me. I had the sneaking suspicion they were very good, maybe some of the finest writing I had done; on the best days, the book opened up. But work was slow and inconstant.

One day, pretending to myself that I was curious about Joy Williams, that I wanted to read the collection Lacie had carted off to bed last night, I found myself rifling through Lacie's underwear drawer again.

This had been happening to me more. Having broken the seal on her bedroom, I kept going back. I liked looking at her things. I liked touching them. They helped me feel her. They helped me get her on the page. In those minutes in her room I somehow felt closer to her than all the nights we spent talking.

Now I fished out the red Victoria's Secret push-up and pulled at the tag. We wore the same size. It was nice to see it declared there in a plain gray font.

Careful not to think too much about it, I pulled off my flannel top.

Unhooked my Macy's bra, and then threaded my arms through her straps, latched and straightened. Looked in the mirror.

The contraption pushed and hoisted, creating from my bony rib cage a valley of flesh. Was this what men liked? I touched the cups, twisting my body like an odalisque. It was all so cheesy. But maybe—I reached into the closet, back to where Lacie kept the peach dress, and slipped it on. Studied myself. Yes. In her bra, with—I scanned her dresser, snagged a tube of color, put her lipstick on my lips—I looked even more like her. I felt even more like her. Shifting my weight, cocking my head, raising first one shoulder and then the other, I tried to imagine how it would feel to wear these clothes in public, to snag second glances wherever I went.

Behind me in the mirror I could see her bed, all crumpled sheets and creased paperbacks, capped pens and shrugged-off sweaters and socks. The pillow crumpled up against the wall.

In a flounce I threw myself down. Inhaling deeply through my nose, I took in the sour smell of her sleep, the tang of sweat and something deeper, almost vaginal. On the pillow was a single dark hair. Beside it, a notebook. Opened.

I started flipping pages. I knew it was bad. As a writer I particularly knew it was bad. But I couldn't help myself. The book was already opened.

This was what I found:

A recipe for za'atar

A note to pick up cheesecloth

The phone number of someone named Sandy

A note detailing the dimensions of something called the EZ-5460

The date and time of the next JFREJ meeting

A diagram for what looked like a chrysalis

A second diagram of the chrysalis, this one more detailed, cross-hatched, with precise measurements (6'7¾", 4'3") in faint indigo handwriting

A sketch of a woman asleep on a couch. The woman was me.

For a long time I stared. My mouth was a slack hole, unrecognizable. But it was definitely me: she had even filled in the blond hair with a colored pencil. At the bottom, there was the date (9/13) and time (10:37 P.M.).

I remembered that night. She had stayed up late working on her loom, and I, lulled by the rhythmic clacking, had let my book slip from my hands and a deep sleep suck me down. As I had been sinking, some bright thread of conscious thought flashed: this is real friendship. To fall asleep in the same room, to let my guard down so completely. I was home. I slept.

And then she had taken a pen and recorded everything ugly about my face.

The doorbell rang. I swore. Lacie wasn't likely to waltz home in the middle of the day, but what if she had? What if she had forgotten her keys? I went to the door with my arms crossed against my chest, braced.

It was the UPS guy. "Lucinda Salt?" he asked, holding out a big brown box. More yarn, no doubt.

"Yep." With the stylus I signed, a big *L* and *S*. "Thank you so much," I purred.

"You're welcome," he gushed, taking in my short dress, my cleavage, my glossy red lips. Then he winked.

I was grinning as I shut the door. Her clothes were a kind of magic. With them, ordinary words, an ordinary moment, flushed pink.

Later, though, I felt disgusted and ashamed, bloated, as if I had gorged myself on candy. Lolling on the couch, back in my boring blue jeans, I vowed to stop.

When I was seven years old I had found my mom's journal, a lavender lily-covered thing. She had hardly bothered to hide it, just tossed it in the wicker basket beside her bed beneath a few magazines. It was easy enough to find. For a few days after my discovery, I didn't crack the cover. I would just go and touch it. I liked knowing it was there.

But eventually, I opened. I read. I was a good reader for my age; I could read her bubbly handwriting quickly, in the moments when she was downstairs flipping the laundry or fixing me a snack. In this way, I learned that when my father had forgotten my permission slip they had fought violently, in whispers, after I had gone to bed; that she felt he had never, never done his share of the household chores; that they hadn't had sex in eight months; that she hated her thighs.

Hardly earth-shattering revelations, and yet they scalded me. The idea that the cheerful, supportive, steady presence in my life hated her thighs, and occasionally her husband, broke over me like a thunder-clap. It was the beginning of learning that other people had private lives. It was the beginning of learning to write.

I'm still not sure how she caught me. I was always careful to put the journal back exactly where I found it. But one day I came home from school and found both my parents waiting. They sat me down in our white swivel chair and grimly explained that privacy and respect were more meaningful when freely given. They didn't want to live in a home where some things needed to be hidden, and they were wonder-ing: did I agree?

On and on they went, and the longer they talked, refusing to say the word "journal," the more my shame became rage. Why couldn't they be direct? Everything was soft with them. Everything was cloaked in cloth, and yet they were so self-righteous and sure. Mumbling my apology, I shook their hands, and that was that—no punishment, no consequence. As usual, just a "talk."

In an act of naïveté—or defiance, I could never decide which—my mom continued keeping her journal in her wicker basket, and I con-tinued reading it. We never discussed it again. Gradually I lost interest in her self-pitying complaints. Gradually I began to skim only for my name, which showed up with surprising infrequency. Reading her journal became less about cracking her psyche and more about sepa-rating myself from my parents. If they were going to be so smug in their self-control, then I would be the kind of person who had none. Who did what she wanted, and never apologized.

Not that I ever had the courage to execute that kind of stance in a public way. I just snuck. Snooped. All these years later I was still snooping, and as it fueled the novel I snooped more. Day after day, morning after morning, I went into Lacie's room. I lay on her bed. I tried on her earrings and turned the pages of her notebooks.

Then, after a morning of "writing"—that is to say, drinking Lacie's coffee and trying on her clothes—I would rise like an automaton and run the odd polygon that was Prospect Park, my legs mechanically pumping up the same hill, sailing past the boarded-up bandshell. Then I would frantically shower and stuff some more of Lacie's food in my mouth before heading out—backpack swinging, hair still wet—to tutor.

Standing on the Manhattan-bound Q platform at Church Avenue, bag loaded with College Board SAT guides, purse packed with power bars and water and gum, I would think over and over, *I hate this, I hate this,* and then, almost immediately: *Shut up, shut up. It's not that bad. It's just a job. It's really not that bad.*

To soothe myself I would think again of the hours already worked that week, of Lulu and Esme, Finn and Rome. If nobody canceled this month, if nobody got sick or had a baseball tournament or a long weekend in Hawaii or London or St. John's, this total, multiplied by four, would bring me . . . well, minus rent, minus health insurance, minus groceries, minus . . . I multiplied and subtracted, estimated and rounded. Moving to New York had turned me into a calculating machine.

When people asked, I always said that tutoring was "fine," that it was an "easy" way to make a living, that the kids were sometimes "fun." But that was a lie. Sitting in a cramped or dark or fussy apartment, craning my neck as a high-schooler penciled in her algebra, I felt berserk.

I especially felt berserk when the parents wanted to "check in." Although ostensibly *checking in* was a chance for me to tell them about their child's progress, the real purpose of *checking in* was for the parents to brag. After a few weeks of working with Lila, for instance, her father, a semi-famous sexologist with a series of YouTube videos ("Is Monogamy Necessary?" and "Sexuality: We're Learning More All the Time!") asked me to step into his office.

Jazzy red polygons squiggled across the gray industrial rug. He offered me a cone of water from the cooler. Then, leaning back in his executive chair behind his massive desk, he said, "My daughter, she's a wonderful human being. She's a delight. I couldn't be prouder of her."

"She's great," I murmured, though privately I thought she was dumb as a rock.

"And Lila, *the thing about Lila is,* she's never going to be a top scorer. That's not where she is. And my wife and I, we don't want to make her into something she's not. We don't want her to go to a school where she shouldn't be. But I'll tell you, *Barnard* could be an excellent opportunity for her. She does very well in an all-girl environment. And it's funny, I said to her, we only get a few days in our lives to change our lives. We only get a few opportunities. And this could be this for her, that day that she takes the test.

"And so, I just don't want this test to shut down any opportunity for her. I don't want it to be the reason she doesn't get into some school. Because once she's there, she'll be fine. She's such a kind, giving, generous young woman. But I just think . . . you know, once, I took her up to the roof of our summer home, in East Hampton, I did, and I taught her the times tables. I said, we're not going down until you've got the twelves. Because me, I happen to like numbers, I like math. You know, when I was a kid, I memorized my times tables, up to the fifteens, *just for fun.*" He laughed fondly. "And when we came down, it had started to rain, we were all wet, and her poor mother was like, Where did she go? What did you do to her?"

"You were really helping her," I murmured.

"Numbers," he said. "I liked *numbers.*"

When at last I spilled out to the sidewalk, I took great greedy gulps of air. Nighttime, and a borzoi was pissing on some chrysanthemums while the doorman wearily watched.

———————

Then came test day, too soon, a flurry of last-minute texts, *Good luck!* and *You're going to kill it!* and *You got this!* to which my charges mostly did not reply. Then the eager *How'd it go?*, also ignored, and then the waiting, and then the scores.

It wasn't precisely that the scores hadn't gone up, though from a strictly mathematical perspective, that was true. It was that the scores had gone up *and* down, up in some places, down in others, up for some kids, down for others. Eagerly I celebrated the gains to the parents. I reminded them that progress was never linear.

"What do you think is the average gain made by an Ivy Prep tutor?" Griffin Chin asked. It was the Tuesday after the scores had been released and he had asked me to "stop by" his office for "a chat."

"A hundred points?" I asked hopefully.

"One would think, one would think," he hummed excitedly. "But here at Ivy Prep, our average gain is two hundred points. *Average,* I'd say. And our top-of-the-line tutors, now, I'm not talking people like you, who've just joined, I mean folks who've been perfecting their craft for years . . . they can see upward of three or four hundred points. Rose? Do you see what I'm saying?"

I smiled without showing my teeth.

"So, Rose. Let me be frank. You're a—you consider yourself an educator?"

"Um, I've mostly been writing—"

"*All*"—he held up his finger—"our tutors are educators. Because that's the business we're in. Education. But as I think I mentioned, we only want you to educate in the subjects you're *extremely* good at."

"Right, totally. That makes sense."

"But I don't want you to think of this like you're getting into trouble, because the truth is that we actually have a really wonderful opportunity for you."

Icy sweat slid down my back. It was so *typical* of Ivy, of every elitist institution, that the first hint that you've royally fucked up is the emphatic insistence that you have in fact not fucked up.

"I really do like the SAT. I'm beginning to develop a real soft spot for it," I improvised, but Griffin was squinting and dabbing at his iPad.

When he finally found what he wanted, he swanned his fingers out and announced, "The Wests. Now. It's a very tricky situation."

"Yes," I said ambiguously.

"Rose," and his voice had an *okay, you got me* tone, as if I were driving a particularly devilish bargain, "I'm going to be perfectly frank here. I wouldn't say this to everyone, but I'm saying it to you, because I like you. I trust you. Now. The Wests. They've let a lot of our tutors go. They're picky. *Not* that I blame them. You know how these families work." His voice warmed with indignation. "There's the pretty daughter, and then there's the smart daughter. Isabel's sister is *very* smart. And Isabel is *very* beautiful."

There was nothing I could say to this that wouldn't be offensively sardonic or disgustingly creepy, so I stayed mum.

"They're a good family," he insisted, as if I had spoken. "A very good family. Ivy Prep has known them a long time. The sister goes to Columbia," he gave *Columbia* a breathy hush, as if it were an obscure sexual act, "so, just do what you can do. The family has high expectations. They'll want you to work with Isabel a lot. You know, it's college essay time. So I think this will more than make up for . . . the *adjustments* we're making here."

The elevator down from Griffin's office made me sick, dropping so fast, then bouncing to abrupt stops at random floors. Once outside, I nearly ran, furiously navigating the stalled ballet of shopping carts in front of Fairway, and then heading south on Second, a monologue ramping up in my head. I hated that I hated being bad at tutoring, though it wasn't really being bad at tutoring that I minded; it was the money. I had a money problem.

When I had moved in, Lacie had said she "didn't want to be an asshole" about rent, but introducing financial obligation into the web of debt between us didn't exactly seem like a brilliant idea. But I didn't have another one. The question was how to ask. With a joke? I couldn't believe I was in the position of needing something from her again.

Whenever I passed the plate glass of a store window my footsteps slowed as I glanced at my pale, washed-out reflection. I hated how I looked, yet I kept looking, as if a different glass would give a different answer. But to my question *Who am I?* every store answered: just a pink slab of face.

Of all Lacie's soups, I liked her curry-coconut one best, with its great chunks of butternut squash and leeks, its silken tofu and roasted peanuts, the pale wedges of lime and brilliant green sprays of cilantro served in bright ceramic dishes. This morning I had seen a bulbous squash on the butcher block, and all day—right up until my conversation with Griffin—I had thought longingly of the brown sugar and ginger, garlic and cumin, but by the time I got home Lacie had already eaten, and the soup was cold on the stove.

Lacie at the loom resembled a dedicated queen. For weeks boxes of carmine yarn had been arriving, material for the truly epic blanket she was making. I kept waiting for her to declare it done—by now the tightly stitched bloody shroud nearly covered the daybed—but like Penelope, she kept going.

With a bowl of the cold soup I curled myself into the couch. "What are you making anyway? I'm almost afraid to ask."

She shook it out. Wispy red threads floated up. "A cocoon."

I couldn't tell whether she was joking. "Oh my God, that's what I need. A cocoon. Somewhere I can just hide for the next six months."

"Exactly. That's the plan. I'm going to knit us both cocoons, and we're just going to hibernate this winter. We're going to be baby bears."

"Perfect. You're brilliant. This soup is delicious, by the way." I sliced open a cube of butternut squash.

She held her stitching up to the light, squinting intently. "It's really easy to make," she murmured, lowering her arms and unraveling her last stitch. "How was your day? What's going on?"

"Oh, I don't know. Do you ever feel like the whole city grosses you out? It's just like, I'll *never* have kids here. It's a cruel thing to do to a child."

She smiled in a motherly way, as if touched to hear me figure out such basic facts about New York. "I don't disagree with you."

"It's just—these parents. They're the worst. They're like total Calvinists. They work all the time, and they make their kids work all the time, as if the moral crime of being so ridiculously rich in a city with so many poor people is somehow *negated* by never actually enjoying your wealth."

Her clacking stopped. "Did something happen?"

"No. Just the usual bullshit. It's like, this guy, right? I told you about him. The sex therapist with the freaky dyed eyebrows?"

She nodded vaguely.

"He sat me down in his office the other day, and he just starts going on and on about how *wonderful* his kid is, and then he starts in on how he's *not that kind of parent, he doesn't want to pressure her,* but he also doesn't want her to *miss out on any opportunity,* which is totally code for 'get her into Barnard.' So I'm just supposed to magically pull this high score from her, so she can get into this college where she doesn't even belong, and at the same time not do anything to heighten her anxiety. And when that doesn't happen, I lose my job! After a month! I mean, whatever happened to a learning curve?"

"Wait, what? You lost your job?"

"Not really. They're just taking away my SAT students. Which is totally fine. I suck at it anyway."

"But what are you going to do? Isn't their main business the SAT?" Her concern jolted me. She wanted things right in my life.

"Yeah, they have some new girl for me to work with. Her parents just basically want someone to sit with her while she writes her college essay. It'll be super easy."

"Oh, okay. So it's good. I mean, so it's working out." The lightness in Lacie's voice—how quickly she was assuaged—made me want to smash her calm. I needed her worried ahead of my ask.

"It's kind of good, but what if she gets mono? Or jets off to Vail? These kind of people, they're always *leaving*. And then all my income disappears," I snapped my fingers, "like that."

"Well, I told you. You can give me the rent whenever."

Getting what I wanted so quickly left me breathless. She was so good to me. "Yeah," I sulked. "I feel bad."

"Don't feel bad."

"What pisses me off is that Griffin just sits me down and says they're taking away all my students as if it's no big deal, as if I weren't counting on that money. It's like it would be gauche to say, Hey, actually, that's my income. There's this fiction that we're all doing it out of the goodness of our hearts. It's such bullshit."

"You're freaked out about money."

"No, not really. It's just—maybe I'll get another job."

"Look, Rose. Really don't worry about the rent. I mean, pay me eventually, but don't freak out."

"But don't you need the money?"

The red yarn tangled around her wrist. "I mean, yeah, but not like, immediately."

"I don't understand."

"Well, it's like, I mean, my parents sort of—I mean, I pay *most* of the mortgage."

"Wait, you own this place?" I couldn't keep the shock from my voice.

"I mean, my parents do. My mom. And me, I guess."

"But how did she even—" I was thinking of the small white house where Lacie had grown up, single-story, on the edge of town.

"When Bee died." She shrugged.

Amid the snapshots taped to the fridge there was the program from her grandmother's memorial service. Often when Lacie was out I had taken it down, puzzling over the list of Quaker hymns and Jewish prayers, the Wallace Stevens Lacie had read.

"Oh." I nodded. "I'm sorry."

She laughed. Everything in the room felt pressurized, the objects shuddery and wavering. "Now you're judging me like you judge those rich kids."

"No, I'm not. I mean, I was just thinking about Bee. I wish I could have met her."

"Yeah, well." She held my gaze. I knew we were both thinking that I would have met her all those years ago when I was in Cambridge, if not for what had happened. "She had a good life. That's what everyone says."

As Lacie returned to her weaving I let my gaze roam around the room, seeing anew the clamp and sewing machine, the glass jars of sequins and corked bottles of wine, the homemade sourdough and drizzly twin candle stubs. It wasn't just her grandmother's money in this apartment. It was her whole way of life.

Growing up, Lacie's trips to Boston had been *events,* with hushed discussions of dresses and trips to the symphony and high tea. She always returned with gifts that made me sick with envy: a set of 256 colored pencils, a swirly Venetian drinking glass, a white silk blouse. Bee had practiced immigration law, slept with John Updike, and founded a black-box theater. Once retired, she held a weekly salon. There had been a husband, briefly, but she'd built her life around something other than marriage: she'd had theater and art and old china, friends and wine and conversation instead.

But I couldn't touch these things; I couldn't tell Lacie I had read the program from the memorial service so often I had it memorized, that I had googled Bee more than once, and read her obituaries. I couldn't ask her if she'd given up on love the way her grandmother had, though in that moment I became convinced she had. Leo's betrayal had broken something basic in her. For where was Ian? Why did he never come over? What kind of dating were they doing?

But it was much easier to talk about money, so I said, "Thanks for being chill about the rent. And sorry. It's so hard to talk about money."

"Yeah, totally." She shook her head, relieved. "It's so hard."

But *hard* was not exactly the right word, or *money* was not exactly what we were talking about. We were discussing debt and forgiveness, what I owed Lacie and what would be repaid, but the currency wasn't the dollar.

I hung around the couch, finishing my soup and watching her sort skeins of yarn. There was a sort of itchy neediness in me. "Lace?" I finally said. "Can I ask you a question?"

"Sure." There was exhaustion around her eyes. Talking about her grandmother had upset her.

But I pushed on. I suddenly had to know. "Why did you let me move in?"

She didn't answer right away, and I braced myself for a dodge.

When she finally did speak, it was in a low tone. "I'm not exactly sure, to be honest. I mean"—this a little defensively—"I'd thought about renting out the room before."

"But when I came over, it didn't seem like you had been thinking about it." Something lawyerly had come into my voice. "And you don't need the money."

"I wasn't. I don't," she admitted.

"I feel like in the park you weren't even that happy to see me."

"What, in Bryant Park?" She looked up at me, a quick, searching glance. "Well, it *was* weird."

"Yeah, it was weird. How could it not be? We've never really talked about what happened."

Her whole face quivered, and then a mask dropped over it. "I don't think it matters anymore."

"But—how can it not matter? It happened."

"Yeah," she said softly. "It happened."

Encouraged, I stepped into a fantasy I had had from time to time. "Do you ever think—I mean, if I hadn't crashed, maybe—"

She stepped to me, and then she did the oddest thing. Tenderly, she cupped her hand over my mouth. "Hush, baby. Hush. It's okay. I forgive you."

I squirmed my face away. For the strangest moment I had thought she was about to kiss me. "You do?"

"You were a different person." Gently she tugged the sleeve of my shirt. "We were teenagers. We were all teenagers. I don't know if I even cared about Leo that much. It's just dumb. Can't we forget it?"

I nodded eagerly. "Yeah. Let's just forget it." I thought: I should tell her about the novel. I should just mention it. I should—

But she had her hand by my mouth again. "Shhh, sweetie. I see that little mind of yours whirling away. It's fine. Just stop, okay? Just stop."

Behind Swarthmore College there are woods, and through these woods runs a river, though we called it a creek. Fat and sluggish in places, deep and swift in others, it meanders for a mile before cascading over rocks and disappearing underground.

Spanning this river is a train trestle. Forty feet high, painted a pale, drippy green, the trestle is covered with cocks and hearts. Above the graffiti, out of the vandals' reach, giant screws weep streaky rust. Beneath the train trestle, in the tall grass, there are big granite slabs ringing an ashy pit, and though by day this circle looks absurd, the monumental rocks haphazard in the suburban woods, at night it is grandly suggestive of an ancient rite. In high school, we went there all the time.

There were drugs at Crum Henge, usually a few joints, whiskey in water bottles, occasionally a forty-pack of Miller Lite carried on the shoulders of some Sibley boys, but the hippies and punks of my school were basically good kids, "independent thinkers" who understood the message of *Dead Poets Society* and really, honestly, were trying to carpe diem and question authority and live a little, you know? Feel something.

Or that's what I was trying to do, down in the meadow with the SEPTA trains rattling overhead. But I had a problem. I knew high school was supposed to be *the time of my life,* but I couldn't relax. People were always laughing at jokes I didn't understand. I was scared to smoke pot, and when I did, I became so paranoid I could barely talk. Every flickering light must be the cops. Timidly I toked, convinced I was a criminal.

Lacie came to the fires, too, but she didn't have my problem. Just three chords from some bearded senior, and she'd launch into the opening verse. When had she learned so many songs? I was getting all A's in my classes, but Phish and the Dead were beyond me. Lacie was beyond me, moving toward something I couldn't see.

That night the midges had come out, and we were all swatting. It was the first warm night of the year, the first *real* warm night, and the fire in the woods was bigger than usual, not just the punks and hippies in attendance, but the student council president and half the girls' soccer team and, somehow, miraculously, Leo Kupersky.

The strumming guitars kept breaking off abruptly so that the boys could swipe their legs. Not even the campfire smoke was helping.

"Feckin' bugs," Lacie muttered, slapping her thigh, a bright, piercing sound.

"Goddamn." Grogan whistled. "You've still got that Boston accent."

Lacie never had *that* kind of Boston accent; she was a Jew from Cambridge, not an Irish from Southie, but we all loved *Good Will Hunting,* and so she obliged us; "feckin' right," she said, "pahk the cah in Hahvad Yad." And then, to Leo: "Remember? You used to tease the shit out of me. You were so mean."

"Yeah, that was dumb."

"Hell yeah, it was dumb."

And they both grinned like fools.

Later, I caught him looking at her legs in the firelight. *Whack!* She slapped another midge away. *Whack!* He must have been remembering how he used to smack her, back when we were young.

Collapsing into the black claw of her ergonomic chair, Isabel West, a tiny, perfect pinwheel of a girl, announced: "So this is basically the most important thing I will ever write in my whole entire life. This essay has to be really original, like nothing any college has ever seen before, and the writing has to be really good. The writing has to be"—she lowered her voice—"*perfect.*"

"Perfect is a great goal," I said uneasily. "Why don't you start by getting out the prompts?"

She slid a massive binder over. "In there."

I shivered. Isabel's home was massive, essentially a small suburban house perched atop a boxy wedding cake of a building on Fifth. To reach her "office" we had gone up stairs, a whole flight, carpeted in plush pile so thick and creamy I had curled my toes. (Upon entering I had of course immediately offered to remove my shoes; indifferently Isabel had said, "If you want," but by now I knew that the airing of my stinky, profane feet was a mandatory part of tutoring's ritual humiliations.)

Manhattan no longer seemed like a monolithic block of rich people to me; I could slice and dice each avenue, opine about the East Seventies and the West Eighties, Tribeca and the Meatpacking District. I had been in condos and duplexes and town houses, narrow UWS apartments cut from brownstones and sunny corner units overlooking Gramercy Park, but this—with its handful of circling help, and private elevator, and burnished gold banister—was obviously the mother lode of wealth, just as Isabel was the climactic shudder of our culture's fascination with youth and beauty.

When she told me she modeled, it felt less like new information and more like confirmation of something I'd subliminally known. Undeniably, you wanted to watch her. She had big doe eyes and pouty, puffed lips, the smooth dewy skin of youth. As she poked at her phone, there was something poignant in her profile. Even as I paged through Isabel's binder, hunting for her essay, I couldn't look away.

Between Excel spreadsheets of top-tier schools and professionally typeset résumés, I found a sheet labeled ESSAY PROMPTS: COMMON APPLICATION.

Isabel had circled #5: *Describe a work of literature or art that has been particularly meaningful to you. If you wish, you may explain how this work has informed a particular life experience that you have had.*

"That's the most intellectual one," Isabel explained, but I barely heard her; I was busy having the life experience of seeing, beneath this circled prompt, an "Academic Integrity Form": *Please affirm that you did not receive any outside assistance AT ALL in the writing of your college essay: no tutoring, no help from parents, no help from other students.*

In green gel ink, Isabel's splashy signature.

Isabel puffed out her cheeks. "Don't look at that," she instructed. "That's not important."

"You sure? It looks important."

"It's not. They make everyone sign those. It doesn't mean anything."

"Got it." I turned back the page. "So what do you want to write about?"

"Wait." From her bag she pulled out a glossy Dover Thrift Edition of *The Souls of Black Folk*. "Do you know this guy?" She consulted the cover. "Du Bois?"

I nodded. She seemed dismayed by this news, as if she had hoped her studies were more esoteric. "Well, so, he wrote this book, which was, like, really important, and he invented this phrase in it, *consciousness*."

"You want to write about *The Souls of Black Folk*." Neutral was the word for how I hoped I sounded.

"Well, just that particular phrase." She consulted her notes. "Yeah, *double* consciousness. I like that. It speaks to me. And schools like it when you're diverse."

"Yeah, definitely. So what does double consciousness mean to you?"

A little gray cat nosed aside the door. She was small and light and drawn to high places. All business, she leapt to a perch beside the printer and surveyed us.

Isabel recited, "It's when you see yourself from the inside, like a normal person, but also from the outside."

"Right, great." I bobbed my head. "The only thing I would add is that I think Du Bois was specifically talking about being black. Like, the way that white people see you not as a person, but as a black person. Like, that's all they see. That's all *we* see, I mean. We—us white people."

While I oh-so-cogently explained the African American life experience to Isabel, she tilted the gray matte screen of her MacBook, examining her plucked brows.

"Isabel? Did you get that? Does that make sense?"

"Can you say it again? I missed it."

"Well, I—"

"I'm just really stressed out," she interrupted. "I have a big gala coming up."

"That sucks."

Isabel explained, "Yeah, my whole family is going to this gala for this organization that my sister works for. She goes to Columbia. Oh my God, do you want to see these shoes?"

She scurried off to her room, her little feet pattering along the carpeted hall, and then came hurrying back, clutching a pair of red heels, dagger-sharp, all leather and gloss.

"Aren't they amazing? I love them so much." She cradled them to her breast. "They cost twelve hundred dollars," she announced, and gently slid them onto the desk beside her copy of *The Souls of Black Folk.*

"So what does this group do?" I couldn't stop looking at the heels. Red and gleaming, they were sex weaponized.

"Oh." Isabel straightened importantly. "It's a nonprofit dedicated to—wait. You know that show *Law & Order—SVU*?"

"I do."

"Yeah, well, one of the actresses from there, wait, do you know her?"

She said the name of a woman I knew I should know. I shrugged. "Nope."

Isabel looked at me darkly. "She's, like, really famous."

"Yeah. I don't really know anybody."

Isabel seemed aggrieved. "Yeah, well, my sister was obsessed with this show, so my dad got in touch with the actress, 'cause he, like, had a connection to her through his work, and she agreed to let Aria intern at her nonprofit."

Heartwarming, really. "Right, so what does the nonprofit *do*?"

"Special Victims Unit. Like, *sexual assault*."

"Yeah, right. That's the show." She looked at me blankly. "And in real life," I prompted.

"Oh! And in real life she runs a nonprofit dedicated to ending sexual assault."

"That's such a great idea."

Mistrust blinked across Isabel's face, but her sense of irony was too incipient to catch the mockery, and besides, why would I be mocking her when she owns those heels? Those fuck-me heels she was going to wear to a benefit to end sexual assault?

Later, as I walked down Lexington in the shortened twilight of an October evening—having done little more with Isabel than wrestle an essay topic out of her—I watched the women with their leather jackets, their delicate boots and gold-chained purses, and thought more about Isabel's shoes. Her fuck-me heels. God, but how I longed for the days when the terms of the war had been absolute and unforgiving, when feminism hadn't reclaimed sex and all its accessories: high heels, short skirts, lace. Who cared about femme? It bored me. I couldn't do it.

Pop culture too. Hadn't anyone noticed that pop culture was bad? I was tired of people being proud of their guilty pleasures, tired of these guilty pleasures founding nonprofits and ending up in the news. Everyone should go back to being ashamed. Everyone should go back to sneaking their TV on the sly, so that people like me, basic genetic abnormalities unfit to live in the modern age, people like me, whose preferred form of leisure involved reading a paragraph and then staring into space, people like me, who liked the opera and liked even more zoning out at the opera, could again be part of public discourse. For it was too much, I thought as I walked, to know about Damien Hirst and Honey Boo Boo. We were supposed to be conversant in Honey Boo Boo! The internet! Now, there was a thing that really ticked me off, along with fashion and anti-aging cream and the mainstreaming of BDSM. Just the other day Lacie had told me about a friend whose date had ejaculated on her face. What was with people? I was really whipping myself into a frenzy. I hated the world. I missed the '90s, when everyone was wearing flannel and giant blue jeans. Now, that was a good time.

The thing about the '90s, which had seemed like a drag but in retrospect was quite nice, was depression. Everyone had depression, and the people who didn't, did; they just hadn't realized it yet. We were all very worked up about drugs, and whether depression was normal or something to be fixed, and there were a lot of very earnest surveys going around about whether you couldn't get out of bed some mornings and how often you thought about death and whether you ate too much or not enough or not for the right reasons, or if you slept too much or not enough or not for the right reasons: any of these, we had been told, could be symptoms of depression. It was kind of great.

Not that I'm, like, *into* a crippling illness. But weren't things better when we were a nation of melancholics? In our plaid, with our disheveled hair? Now all we've got is *anxiety.* We're all sped up. Now it's racing hearts, racing minds, ragged breath, nervous sweat. Nobody's depressed anymore. Everybody's anxious. I find it boring.

To be honest, I was never that great at depression, though I did try.

By tenth grade, I had stopped showering regularly or wearing deodorant, the better to advertise my bohemian melancholy. I shopped exclusively at Goodwill, and swam in corduroy pants many sizes too large, belted with gray shoelaces. I wore training bras, little cotton things made for eleven-year-olds, and huge shapeless sweaters. I smelled of BO and mothballs.

There was a phrase, and I don't know where it came from, that Lacie and I loved: *I roll out of bed looking this hot.* We'd sex-growl it, tossing our hair, joking but serious, aspiring to effortless beauty, a sort of sleepy hotness. To me, now, no better phrase epitomizes the '90s, and what it meant back then to be a teenage girl.

But while I shuffled along in shit-colored clothing, my hair a ratty disaster, Lacie found little calico tunics and sweatshirts with wide necks that left her pale clavicles exposed. We were both grunge, but I looked like a golem and she looked like the Little Match Girl, all pale skin, dark locks, and mysterious eyes.

The day she dreadlocked my hair, we had waited in front of the high school after the final bell. "What are these plants anyway?" Lacie kicked the cement planter with her Docs. "I look at them every day."

"Hostas. My mom made me help her plant some last summer."

"They're everywhere. They're, like, the symbol of the suburbs."

Other kids streamed around us, their black violin cases swinging, their sports jerseys silver and slick. A crew of boys from our grade, all scraggy shoulders and loose hair, ambled by, shoving and smoking. Lacie looked, and I looked, too, but Leo was not among them.

Another kick to the planter. "We could just go?" I suggested.

"He said today." Kick. The rubber made a satisfying thunk. She ticked her eyes up to the flag, limply clutching its chrome. "Fucking flag."

"One day Mr. Pawling forgot to put it up."

"Hah."

Then Leo was blocking the sky, backpack swaying from one shoulder; then Leo was leaning over and giving my best friend a kiss. I studied the new scuff marks on my shoe. We turned to go.

I still didn't know the exact moment it had happened. One moment he was watching her slap her legs in the firelight; the next, they were together all the time. Completely, inviolably. I gathered that as the fire was winding down, there had been a walk by the creek, a confession of feeling, some making out, but whenever I brought it up Lacie always got smiley and vague. She did ask me if I minded, though; I'll give her that. I had pretended confusion, then outrage, exclaiming "Seventh grade was a million years ago! And I didn't even *like* him like him!"

Now, down Glovings, Lacie and Leo walked in the dead middle, defiant. They were talking, Leo's voice a soft rumble from barely parted lips, Lacie's head tilted as she gave quiet, serious nods.

Behind us, a car.

"I mean, fuck that shit," Leo said.

The car grew louder as it slowed, drawing close. The engine thrummed inside me, agitating me; I braced for the horn. Nodding vigorously, I drifted sideways, not as if I was *responding* to the car, but as if the left side of the road abruptly intrigued me. Leo kept talking.

A red blast of sound.

I jumped. Lacie jolted. We leapt to the curb. And Leo, Leo of the lazy saunter, broke none of the rhythm of his stroll as idly he made his way to the grass.

In a fresh roar the minivan surged past us. A woman, all mouth, hurled out the single epithet, "Move!"

Leo ran after her and feinted as if throwing a rock. "Fucking bitch!"

"Don't use that word!" Lacie was giggling. My heart was still a furious flutter.

"What?" He swung his arm around her. "Fucking? You don't like that word?"

"No," she said, her grin wider, turning into the crook of his arm. "Not *that* one."

He mouthed something in her ear, and she laughed, scrunching more deeply into him. Casually I kicked a pebble. Shoved my hands in my pocket. Whistled a tune, though I couldn't whistle: what came from my mouth was air.

———

Finally Leo peeled off toward his house, and we made the right and then the left to University Place. In Lacie's kitchen we microwaved dinner plates of Ritz crackers topped with American cheese before heading to her room.

Tacked to Lacie's corkboard were new cutouts, which I studied like a map. A hazy black-and-white photograph of a café in Paris; an elaborate doodle of jointed broken branches; a blueprint. Pages from the Delia*s clothing catalog, laughing girls in chartreuse and violet pants with baby T's snug around their cheery round breasts.

"Do you think we could do it today?"

"Sure, if you want."

She perched on the bed, and I sat on the floor in the crook of her thighs. With a comb she divided my hair into sections. The line of the comb's teeth against my scalp was cool and calming, as were her fingers, humming lightly through my hair, setting my scalp tingling. "Am I hurting you?" she murmured when she tugged the first braid tight. "Do it as hard as you can," I told her, and closed my eyes.

The Saturday before, we had gone in Grogan's car to a Phish show in Camden, and I was still buzzing with all I had seen, the long, lanky girls with ribbons in their hair, the scruffy boys bare-chested in corduroy shorts, the nitrous and burritos and buds for sale. Some of the girls had dreads, clumps as fat as sausages framing their faces, and I had seized on this hairstyle; it seemed the perfect way of announcing my allegiance to all things alternative while I worked on my wardrobe.

"Just don't wash your hair for a month," Lacie coached, giving me a gentle pat on the back. "And keep twisting the braids and running your fingers over them."

I scooted around and looked up at her on the bed. "Awesome, thanks." Gingerly I patted my hair.

"Hey," she said carefully. "Are you coming over to Leo's tonight?"

"Oh, yeah. I think I might stop by." I couldn't admit that I hadn't been invited. People didn't *invite* in those days; you just heard about it, the news was in the air. To not know was worse than not being invited; it meant that people—boys—didn't think to talk to me.

From her dresser I picked up a pair of silver hoops. "Can I borrow these?"

"What?" She craned her neck. "Oh, yeah, sure."

The little victory ran hot through me. Thumbing through her closet, I ticked through her wardrobe: sundresses of burnt yellow and psychedelic green; gray pants with mauve and periwinkle patches; little halter tops printed with leaves and birds, shirts too skimpy to wear to school. I pulled out a turquoise tulle skirt, long and gauzy and flecked with silver sparkles. "And this?"

She shrugged. "For tonight? If you want."

Gladness warmed my heart. In her clothes I would be safe.

In the soft breeze, a layer of tulle brushed my bare knees. It felt lovely. I felt lovely, standing on Leo's porch in Lacie's skirt. For long moments before leaving I had studied myself in the mirror, thinking that in Lacie's dress I was a hippie princess, a girl who belonged at a party at Leo's.

But no one was coming. I tried rapping, ineffectively, on the screen door. Music—a bouncy bubbly twist of Phish—bled from the inside. I knocked again, harder, and rang the bell twice, two quick, frustrated shrills. They should be able to hear me, even over the music. I was beginning to feel stupid, standing there on the cement stoop.

I knocked a fourth time. Nothing. Tentatively, I pushed the front door open. From beyond the hall I could just see a shadowy kitchen, with pools of yellow light. The hair on my scalp—already pulled tight into braids—prickled.

"Hello?" I called.

Why wasn't Lacie waiting for me? Didn't she care?

In the kitchen there was no one—just a pile of dirty dishes in the sink, some smudged glasses, and a sopping sponge on the counter. I picked it up and smacked it, hard, against the floor. *Thwack!* it said, a wet, squishy sound. I descended the stairs.

Suburban basement. Dank blue-gray carpet, a ragged brown couch, a single standing lamp draped in a red T-shirt. A circle of maybe fifteen kids. Glass bubblers going around. Phish noodling from a stereo. When I entered, no one looked up.

Lacie sat leaning with one shoulder against the wall, nodding as Leo talked with rhythmic urgency. Sibley and a few other guys were crowded around her, forming their own little circle within the larger one. Grogan was lying on his back, his hands cupping the crown of his head, as if advertising his total calm.

Uneasily I sat down beside the two Steves. Steve T was saying, "First the government pays them to build the prisons, and then they have to fill them up. That's why they bring the crack in." I nodded emphatically, but neither Steve looked over.

Lacie was laughing. She looked radiant in her starry-blue halter top. Through the opening in the back, the lovely pale ridge of her spine, flecked here and there with dark moles, flexed as she laughed, the shoulder blades moving under her skin like wings.

"They just keep building them and building them," Steve B said, and Steve T echoed, "It's part of their system, part of their plan," and I keyed into the rhythm of the way he kept saying *system* and *plan.* The music circled dizzily, wheeling around the same riff. Everyone but me was stoned. As the two Steves ranted, I zoned out on Leo's face. He had stubble along his jaw, and spiky black hairs above his lip.

"Jesus, Rose," whistled Steve B.

I swung around, blinking. Both Steves were staring at me. Steve T dinged me on the ankle. "Don't you shave your legs?"

Frantically I yanked Lacie's skirt back over my calf. "Shaving is fake," I told them, but they ignored me.

"It's so *hairy,*" Steve B said to Steve T. "She's hairier than a boy."

To prove it, Steve T hiked up his pants. It was undeniable: the skinny toothpick of his leg was lightly dusted with white-blond hairs. Mine was thick like an animal's.

"You smell funny too," Steve B added. "And your hair is weird. Do you actually think it looks good like that?"

The room drained. The air shivered like the shush of a dusty bird wing, thick with pot. The boys started talking about something else, I don't know what; unsteadily, I rose, and pushed toward the stairs, my eyes blurry and burning. I kept waiting for someone—for Lacie—to call my name, but she was lost in conversation with Leo. She was gone.

From then on, she was the kind of girl who always had a boy-friend. Or she *had* been the kind of girl who always had a boyfriend, but I wasn't sure whether she still was. In high school there had been Leo, but I hadn't known her in her twenties. Now there was Ian, but even after eight weeks on Albemarle Road I still hadn't seen him. There were nights Lacie didn't come home, but though I assumed she was with him, I didn't ask.

She had an odd way of talking about him. *Right, Ian,* she would say, as if he were a grocery store item she had forgotten to pick up. Or, in a tone of showy bewilderment, *He says I'm not open enough,* as if, emotionally speaking, she were something like Philip Johnson's Glass House.

A vault would've been a better architectural metaphor for how Lacie handled her feelings, but I joined her in cluck-clucking over Ian's emotional neediness, and mirrored her exasperation over his snuggling and texting.

Her stance of bemused indulgence toward him made it all the more perplexing when she asked, twenty minutes before the guests were due to arrive for Shabbat, whether I thought it was okay that Ian was the only guy coming. "Do you think he'll mind?" she said, which was funny, because she had never, until then, seemed concerned with his feelings, and because—as I tartly replied—he was *her* boyfriend. How should I know? I hadn't even seen him in a year.

She heard my sarcasm, registered my displeasure, and disappeared into the kitchen to stir the tom kha gai. But in truth I was flattered she had asked. Her vulnerability, so flashed, had a tantalizing shine.

———

Soon the guests began to arrive, cooing hellos and tossing jackets onto Lacie's bed. Wine was opened and glasses procured. Some girl, even before introductions, cleared off the table; I envied the familiar way she handled Lacie's things, the way she knew what could be dumped on the floor and what should be carefully tucked into the bookshelves.

The woman clearing turned out to be named Sophie. She was petite and pale-skinned, black-eyed, delicate yet direct. "So you're the one who's known Lacie since forever," she cried. "What *was* she like in high school? You have to tell us." But before I could answer she was distracted by a book on the mantel. "Oh, have you read this yet?" she called to Lacie, and the lightness of her tone convinced me she had no idea what I had done.

Next I was introduced to Dylan, who reminded me of a cloudy day at the beach, sandy brown hair and freckles. While shaking her hand I wondered: did none of Lacie's friends know the story? It would be just like Lacie to be discreet.

I didn't have time to riddle it out. "Dylan gave you the bed," Lacie was prompting.

"Oh God, *thank you*," I obediently cried, and Dylan said it was no problem, they were getting rid of it anyway. *Trash,* I told myself, *you sleep on other people's trash*. But I smiled.

After Sophie and Dylan came Anna, a soft, milky redhead with a twisting mouth. "You're both writers," Lacie exclaimed, and we shook hands warily, but when she heard I was working with Portia Kahn, her green eyes widened. "She's got a *great* list."

There was no Ian yet, but other than the occasional glance at the door, Lacie didn't betray any reaction to his tardiness. We gathered round the dining-room table, now set with silverware and cloth napkins, and Lacie, singing, lit two tall green candles. They all knew the prayers, and slowly scooped their hands before their eyes. I tried to follow. Once I caught Lacie's eye and she smiled apologetically, as if to acknowledge this new part of herself. Later we passed covered bread, and sipped delicate quarter-glasses of wine from jam jars. "Shabbat," Sophie purred happily, leaning back in her chair.

Then the sacred mood, so sudden and fragile, vanished, and we were just five women eating soup. The tom kha gai was oily and fragrant, a warm coconut broth with lemongrass and tender strands of chicken. We all exclaimed over it, but Lacie, laughing, said it was stupidly easy to make. Dylan said that all soups were easy, that was what was so fantastic about them, and we were off, idly sailing the sea of conversation: a mutual friend, Jenny (mutual to all of them, I mean), who used to inflict ghastly lentil soup on her dinner-party guests; Jenny's move to Oakland last summer with her girlfriend; Oakland; San Francisco; rent. Mostly I listened, and tried not to slurp my soup.

The talk drifted from girlfriends to boyfriends. Anna had recently been in Bar Harbor, closing up the summer home of her husband's family, but to all the coos of *I love Maine* she only shook her head. "I spent the whole weekend convinced I had Lyme disease. Is there Lyme disease in Maine? Do you guys know?"

Dylan, laughing: "Did you even see a tick?"

"No, I just . . . got a rash." She turned to me, explaining, "I'm a total hypochondriac, but then I actually get sick. It always turns out that I was right to worry."

"I don't think that's hypochondria. I think that's just being aware." Was I being obsequious? I was having that weird thing where my head felt too big and my teeth grotesque. I couldn't stand the attention, so I rushed to grab more of it. "It's like with me and this toothpick. I *still* think I was right to freak out."

"What's you and the toothpick?" Lacie asked.

"Oh." I rolled my eyes. "Once I thought I had swallowed a toothpick."

The toothpick was a useful story, insofar as it made people laugh, and presented me as a neurotic (read: *intelligent*) mind, but I had never told it in New York before, and the stakes of this particular telling felt oddly high.

I made sure they were all looking at me before I added, "I didn't sleep for days."

Laughter, thank God. Dylan said, "You were worried about it coming out the other end?"

I made a mock solemn face. "Yeah, I mean, it can kill you."

Anna, laughing: "How did you *swallow* a *whole* toothpick?"

But I was distracted by a man in the doorway with big blond curls and scruff on his face: Ian. "Hey," he said, uneasy at interrupting our chatter and yet somehow at ease in his uneasiness. "I brought some bread," he announced, holding up a loaf wrapped in one of our tea towels, and just like that, I knew their relationship was real.

"Ian!" they all cried, and lightly Lacie rose to her feet. Maybe she kissed him on the cheek—I'm not sure. When she reached his side, I found myself averting my eyes.

I had forgotten how big and blond he was, with gold curls of hair and little scabs of dried plaster on his arm. He wore Carhartts and red plaid; he came into the living room still wearing his boots, and Lacie didn't say a word. He kissed all the women on the cheek, and when he got to me he exclaimed, "Rose!" and wrapped me in a big hug. He hugged me so hard my feet left the floor. "You're here!" he kept exclaiming, as if he hadn't known. "You're in New York!"

"It's true." I was back on the ground, grinning like a fool.

"Amazing." Happiness like water trembled behind our smiles.

Then we remembered the others. Lacie slipped off to the kitchen to fix him a bowl of soup, and he poured himself into her chair, graceful despite his bulk. "What are we all talking about?" he asked.

"Hypochondria," Sophie said.

"Toothpicks," Dylan said.

"I was swallowing them," I said, thinking it would be funny, but Ian only nodded. Were we all being girly, too giggly over white wine? I wanted to separate myself from the women I had been so eager to join just a moment before, but how could I when I was the one hold-ing the floor?

"I was eating fish tacos," I explained. "This was in Nebraska. They were held together with toothpicks. I was with"—but I found myself suddenly unable to say *my boyfriend*—"Alex," I finished lamely. Later I would see Lacie, too, refer to people by their first name rather than as *my sister* or *my friend*—it was kind of a trick for engendering intimacy—but at the time I felt like a country rube, assuming every-one knew everyone else in my world.

"And in the middle of eating his second one, there was this *crunch*. And Alex was like, totally matter-of-fact, *Oh, a toothpick.*"

I mimed picking a toothpick out of my mouth.

"And I was like, Oh my God. *That's* what that was."

Barks of laughter. Dylan gasped out, "You didn't *know* it was a toothpick?" Ian smiled.

"Yeah, I had bitten something hard, like a few minutes earlier, and I didn't know what it was, so I swallowed it." Beat. "So of course we went to the ER."

More laughter. Ian's smile deepened, but clearly he was only being polite. I became frantic to wrest a real laugh from him.

"Really, we did. And I said to the nurse, I think I swallowed a toothpick. And you know, they're very polite in Lincoln, but she was like, 'What do you want me to do for you?' She got the doctor, he was like, 'An X-ray? You're asking for an X-ray.' And I was like, 'Yeah, I think that would just help me go to sleep.' So they took an X-ray, and they didn't find anything, and it was such a relief. For me, I mean. I think I was the only one who was worried."

Finally Ian threw back his head and laughed.

Sophie cried, "I am exactly that person. I am exactly the person who thinks she's accidentally swallowed a toothpick."

I had them. I had *him.* I felt it. All wrapped up inside this laughter, I started to believe in a New York life. They *liked* me. I was *funny.*

The soup was done. The candles had pooled waxy eggs. Dylan was pushed back from the table. The pipes began their song, and Lacie rose and stacked the empty bowls, their glazed clay dully chiming. No one joined her. Apparently all those polite, tiresome fights about helping and hosting had played out long ago. Tonight was a ritual, old and familiar.

She wasn't lying, I thought. She does this so often they're used to it. She's a host. But at least I can make them laugh.

When Lacie came back out with a plate of brownies, to much *ooh*ing and *aah*ing, Ian scooped one up in his paw and loped off to wash dishes. From the kitchen soon came the comfortable, easy slosh of suds, the regular clink of silverware, the confident opening of cabinets. He knew this house; it was obvious. But when had he been over? I was almost always home. Had he looked in my room? It creeped me out, and excited me, to think of him seeing my things.

At the table, we were back on boyfriends. "It's weird," Sophie was saying in her hushed, breathy voice. She looked like a blossom, a black-eyed Susan. "I almost feel like something happened to Aaron and his mom during Aaron's childhood, something that neither of them ever got over. Like some boundary got crossed, and you know, it's weird, because Aaron's sister has been in recovery, and so they've all learned these new, non-fucked-up ways of being together, they've learned how to be supportive, and maintain boundaries, but sometimes you can feel this old way of being together haunting them—"

"Yeah," Dylan murmured.

"It's always weird, when you can feel the dysfunctional way of being in the new dynamic." When Lacie spoke, I couldn't look at her. "It's like this shadow. Or a callus. It pushes up against everything else. It shapes it."

"Yeah," I said softly.

"Yeah," Sophie agreed.

Anna began stacking our brownie plates. Dylan rose, stretched, and carried two wine bottles to the kitchen. Sophie followed with the cheese. Lacie and I were left alone. But we weren't looking at each other. Not yet.

Later, I found myself lying in the dark listening for the sounds of Lacie making love. Listening, and pretending I was not. From her bedroom came quiet conversation, a low giggle, and then the croon of Sam Cooke. I pictured Lacie naked, all jutting bone and pale skin, a child's body, though I knew from seeing her step from the shower that her nipples were large and dark, the areoles like brown suns.

The music got turned up.

My skin crackling, I strained to hear. Were they fucking? Talking? Was he touching her? Then came the unmistakable rhythmic squeak of the bed, the light, regular thump of mattress hitting wall.

Slowly, with damp fingers, I drew back my sheets. Eased one leg, then the other, to the ground. Stood. Surgically, I slid my feet across the floorboards to the wall. The feathery gray pinwheels of a head rush spattered my vision, then cleared.

My door beneath my hands opened soundlessly. Blinking, my finger pads against the wall for balance, I crept down the hall.

When I was directly outside her door, I heard above the *shush, shush, shush* of the bed little moans, tiny tender sex noises. My pussy went wet. Thick. There in the dark I pressed my palm against the heat in my crotch.

"No." Lacie's voice, a whispered stab. "No." This second one louder. The bed stopped. The breathing stopped. "I hate that. I told you. No."

Her voice through the music might have been honeyed with flirt—I couldn't quite tell. Then came Ian's low rumble, pleading, cajoling. Apologizing? I stood very still. I listened.

The thunking began again. Lacie's quick, high breathing. Like a tiny scared animal. On socked feet I slid down the hall and dashed to my bed, where I pulled the covers over my head as if I had seen a ghost.

But once there I couldn't fall asleep. I kept lying there, listening.

My ears ached with it, my neck tingled. Finally they got loud again. Finally they forgot me. They got louder, and louder, until Lacie was screaming, high wheels of pleasure, and Ian was barking, bellowing, roaring—and that's when I joined in. Very quietly I moaned. Right in time with them. Matching my exhales to hers, making tiny hurt, delighted noises. Crying out.

In the morning I woke to cups and bowls knocking against one another, the *click, click, hiss* of the gas stove, and a low murmur of voices. A thin gray drizzle fell from the sky. My tiny room was dark and silvery, silent and cold, and even before I was fully awake I wanted to be with them.

When I swooped into the kitchen, Ian smiled from the stove. Lacie said, "Morning, cowgirl. Want Ian to make you some eggs?"

She was perched on the stepladder we kept in the kitchen, wearing a black drapey dress and leggings with a long run. Between her hands she cupped a steaming mug. "Sure," I said, standing in the doorway. "That sounds good."

Ian cracked two eggs into the cast iron. His pale T-shirt showed off his big arms and slight belly. He was so strong, so solid, yet his eyes held a liquid sadness that freighted even a question such as how I liked my eggs with melancholy.

Ian poured me coffee. "Milk?" I nodded. "Let's go to the table."

We shuffled to the dining room, and ate among the stained wine-glasses and spilled black pepper of the previous night.

I was hungover from jealousy and wine, and weirded out by what I had done, but as I drank my coffee and soaked my toast in gold yolk, all the blood vessels in my brain relaxed. Ian and Lacie still murmured quietly, talking about his studio in Red Hook, and though I felt apart from their ease, self-conscious and confused, I didn't feel excluded, exactly; more like I was warming myself by their fire. The memory from the night before dimmed.

Outside the rain picked up. Ian, beside me, smelled like sweat and sleep, a *body,* with a high note of turpentine. It made me edgy. Being with them—I liked it, but it was too much. I began to fiddle with my phone. Two new emails.

"Oh, look, you guys," I interrupted. "Isabel sent me her essay."

They looked over as if they were surprised to find me sitting there.

"Isabel's her student," Lacie explained. "Rose is obsessed with her."

"For good reason. This girl is insane," I told Ian. "She calls herself a feminist but wears twelve-hundred-dollar fuck-me heels."

Ian said, "Huh." God, but it was hard to make him laugh.

The file finished loading. I scanned. "Oh, good Lord, you guys, listen to this. This is actually real." I read:

BE YOU

Ever since I was a little girl I have wanted to be a runway model. The lights, and all those great clothes! To be a runway model, you have to know how you look to people. You have to understand what they see and use it to your advantage. It is almost like being an artist, though people don't think of it that way.

In an essay by WEB Du Bois called "Of Our Spiritual Strivings," he talks about the Veil. "The Veil" is about how you can have double consciousness. This is when you are aware of yourself, but also how you look to everyone else. This is exactly the quality you need to be a supermodel.

"Wait, what?" Lacie was laughing. "You're making this up."

"If only." I kept going:

"Of Our Spiritual Strivings" was very moving to me. I felt that it spoke to my life experience. In my generation, people are always looking at each other. They are posting pictures on Facebook and Instagram. Sometimes when people are out having fun they're just thinking about how it will look on Instagram. Obviously this is not what WEB Du Bois had in mind when he wrote about the

Veil and Double Consciousness but I think it's amazing how he
anticipated modern lifestyles.

Feminism has taught me that it doesn't matter who's watching!
And ironically the models who can look like they don't care who
is looking at them are the ones that the most people want to look
at. Both feminism and WEB Du Bois's essay have shaped my perspective as a young woman working in fashion today.

"Oh my God," Lacie and Ian chorused.

"Yep." I dropped the phone on the table with a dramatic clatter.
"That's Isabel West. She loves the term *life experience.*" Theatrically I
wrinkled my face. This was what I had wanted all morning: their attention. "I mean, I thought I had gotten her to agree that *double
consciousness* referred specifically to the black experience in America,
but I guess it was just too hard to write about something other than
herself."

"Even black thought has to belong to her," Ian said, and we all
shook our heads. How thrilling to catch another white person—a
seventeen-year-old girl—being racist. How superior we felt. "Who is
this girl?" he wanted to know.

"She's the richest. Of all my students, she's the richest. Every time I
go into her house, I have to take off my shoes, and the carpet is so soft
my feet practically have an orgasm," and that did it, thank God: he
finally laughed.

Ian and I had met at an artist residency in a beach town during the crystalline early weeks of September, when a spell of drifty laziness, a sense that the ordinary laws of living had been suspended, had overtaken me. Winning the residency was a significant coup; it meant that I had talent, I thought, not simply potential. But after the hyperactivity of grad school and office life, the million bells of obligation, I simply did not know what to do with the gift of time except squander it. I struggled to stay rooted, like an astronaut on the moon.

The beach town was the last in a string of beach towns, and for many years it had been the lesser of its rivals, a sleepy fishing village mostly housing the help for the more fashionable environs. But in the past five or six years, the town council and the bureau of tourism had begun to aggressively market the town to young people. Nightclubs and bars opened. Motels jacked up their prices. A yoga studio appeared, then two, then a juice bar. But the pose of party town was not struck with complete conviction. The big hair and thick necks that invaded each weekend incensed the locals and at the same time pleased them, for now they had a common enemy and a unifying complaint. At the IGA, down by the docks, at the Shag Wong—the original locals bar—a giddy chorus of outrage echoed, the righteous jubilee of those who have finally been wronged.

Into this tempest we were dropped. After a lucrative Broadway smash, a famous playwright had bought an old stable and converted it to a residency house for artists, both visual and literary; the ramshackle building, bleached bone white and a milky calcium blue, had been welcoming artists during the summer months for nearly four decades, far longer than the royalties had lasted.

The towels were all thin, ragged, and rust-stained; the sheets all had the same dreadful gray, black, and white stripes, as if issued by a youth reformatory. The rooms smelled of mildew and Pine-Sol, and the salt and sand of a thousand beach days were bleached into the fine-grained floors. Everything creaked and popped. The second floor only extended half the footprint, so that the painting studios could rise unimpeded into the hot, dusty air that still carried a hint of manure and hay, the snort and stink of the twenty-five horses that once had been housed there. Great wooden rafters crossed beneath the ceiling, and at night birds and bats, drawn by the electric light, dove and swooped, casting flickering shadows on the rough stone floor thirty feet below. A haunted place, at once particular and anonymous, far removed from the faux-weathered shanties suddenly selling for $2 million, the Barn was layered by time, by the stallions who were now dead and the young artists who were now old, and yet despite its history, the place also seemed strangely out of time, an island on an island, a ruin possessing its own logic.

We had no place in this war between summer folk and locals, and the old groundsman who maintained the Barn left us alone. Not once, during my time there, did anyone ask if my work was going well, or even what I did in the hours I spent in my room with the door shut. They all assumed I was writing, but in truth, flummoxed by Portia's notes, and unable to see my fictionalized Lacie anymore, I slumped all day at my desk, reading a book of theoretical physics.

This was during the bad time, when, trying to follow Portia's suggestions, I had turned what had been alive into something *boring*. Portia thought so; after reading my new draft, I could hear her polite "feedback" avoiding the monstrous judgment she wouldn't allow herself to say. I ran from it, unable to admit that something in my writing had soured. In a daze I turned pages, deducing from the strange diagrams and eager explanations that time was not linear but rather curved like a shining silver bowl. I imagined myself in the bottom of it, spinning.

An hour before sunset I would take one of the beach cruisers donated by the playwright and sail down the long winding road to the beach. I never wore a helmet. In Cambridge and Iowa I had; in fact all my life I had, but although there were blind curves and giant black SUVs and even larger pickup trucks barreling along these blind curves at forty miles an hour, I was convinced nothing bad would happen to me. Like the Barn I was untouched by my surroundings; I flew down straight-backed, my hair flying out behind me, my wire basket filled with towel and book, sure I was safe from tragedy.

Once I reached the beach, I stripped to my underwear and swam in the sea. I never wore a bathing suit; my bikini, the first few days, had kept falling off my narrow chest in the waves. There was no lifeguard this late in the season, but the water was warm and a sparkly deep blue, a color utterly unlike the Atlantic of my childhood, more like a lake than the sea. Even on its crashiest, biggest days it seemed to me benevolent, and so I swam alone, at dusk, with no one on shore to watch me.

Into this weightless immortality, this lulling embrace of risk, came Ian. I had known him for weeks, of course; he was one of the two artists practicing beneath the sweeping rafters, a painter who stood on his artwork as he made it. I knew because I watched him from the high observatory window built into the edge of the second floor. I watched his broad, thick arms, covered with blond hairs, as he flicked house paint around, and I watched his funny yellow shoes, pointed like elves' slippers, which allowed him to walk lightly across his Plexiglas canvas.

We roomed across from each other in the narrow white hall built above the kitchen, and though for the first few days we kept our doors resolutely shut, I soon started leaving mine ajar when I was out—it seemed fussy and distrusting to always keep it closed. Then he started doing the same. After a week or so I stopped making my bed the instant I awoke, preferring to loll about with my coffee for an hour or so; this meant that when I left my room he could see my unmade bed. He soon followed suit, and so I could glimpse beyond the partially shut door the flung-back sheet and the round dent where he had put his head. It was a lovely, finely calibrated game of loosening standards, and it thrilled me to lead it. Meanwhile, we continued to speak politely, if indifferently, to each other.

Then I opened an email, and everything changed. The University of Nebraska had awarded me the Dwight O. McKneight Fellowship; for a single semester's work I would receive $25,000, and all I had to do was teach one fiction-writing class, two hours on Tuesday afternoons.

Wobbly, I walked in a circle around my small wooden room. I sat and read the email a third time, then made another circle. The tidiness of the news left me stunned. I had applied, figuring hundreds, if not thousands, were in the pool; I had dawdled through these weeks, figuring that soon enough I'd be back to early-morning commutes and thirty minutes of scribbling before bed. But no. Summarily, I had been yanked from my life.

I closed my computer, went downstairs, and filled a pot with water. Turned on the electric stove and let the coils darkly glow. While there were still only tiny bubbles on the bottom of the pot my eye sockets began to ache. My nose burned, my temple pulsed, and then there they were: two hot tears trailing down my cheeks, leaving in their wake two lines of cooled air. Then more.

As I was crying and salting the water and shaking the pasta box, Ian walked in—he had swapped his yellow elf shoes for boots, I remember that—and asked me what was the matter.

The story came tumbling out, in between gasps of "I don't know why I'm crying" and "I'm so happy, but it's just so strange" and "I feel crazy—"

"Do you want a hug?" he interrupted. I nodded and folded myself against his belly, the warm, safe swell of it, and his strong painter hands. Beneath them, I steadied.

We stayed up that night talking. After I had said all I could say

about the University of Nebraska, after we had googled Lincoln together and laughed and shrieked at the boxy, bland downtown, we
turned to other things: his upcoming show, my faltering novel draft,
ambition, fate, the literary world, the art world, differences and similarities, rivals and jealousies. Later he put on a Britten opera, and we
simply sat in the warm half-light of a single lamp, sipping red wine as
the contralto unleashed her rich throttle.

We finished the opera, and then the wine. In the flickering yellow
light we sat, saying we would like to take an astronomy class one day;
jokingly, we made plans to do it together. There came a whisper of
wings, a beating, and a bat—a tiny black ball of fury—flapped into
the living room. Shakily it circled, nearly like a baby bird, and then
flapped over the stables.

We raised eyebrows at each other. "That," he said, "means time for
bed. Let the bats take over." I sent him a long despairing glance, all
panic and pleading. For me the air held not bats but the golden thread
of what might happen next. Yet seeing the embarrassed half-smile on
his face, I understood that my expectations were both obvious and
unwelcome.

"Yeah, time for bed," I said briskly, and we parted abruptly, in the
hallway, without even saying good night.

After that night, we tumbled into an easy intimacy built from the
cloudless September days, the butcher block in the center of the
kitchen, and the bottles of wine we biked up the hill from the liquor
store. By unspoken agreement every evening at the golden hour we
would make our way to the beach. Now when I swam he sat on the
shore and watched me. I would bob in the water, and sometimes, if
the ocean was calm, I would turn my back on the waves, and he
would point at the wonders happening in the west—great purple pillars of clouds, yellow rays, darkening pink toward the horizon—and I
would wave and nod, as if he could see my tiny head in the dark sea
nodding. But I didn't care about the sunsets. I liked to see him, his

long thick legs sprawled before him, resting back on his hands, watching me, making sure the sea did not swallow me. I imagined what he saw: my white limbs, my blond hair made dark by seawater, the ocean lifting and dropping me like a paper doll.

We took turns showering in the outdoor shower, and gathered in the kitchen after dark, where we cooked in the messy, careless way I loved, chopping vegetables, scalding them with oil, putting everything we had—pasta sauce, eggs, broccoli florets—in a single bowl, all the while talking.

He told me he had slept with a man. He told me that his ex-girlfriend had screamed like she had been stabbed when he told her, and ran to the shower and turned on the hot water as high as it would go, and shrieked while it scalded her. Wet from the sea and my own shower, I imagined this woman, naked, screaming, slapping her own face. Her pink skin darkening to red.

We talked about monogamy. We talked about desire. We talked the way men and women talk when they've decided that they won't fuck: we talked how men and women talk when they're using each other for research. Slowly there built a kind of tension, but not the usual kind. As the night got later and the kitchen smaller and brighter, the long summer twilight finally blackening, night pushing against the glass, we talked on and on. But never again did we wait for the bats.

Sidewalk glittering with glass. Ocean glittering with sun. It hurt my eyes to be in Red Hook. I walked the cobblestoned streets. The sky was bright, and it was hot, too hot for October. Past the projects I went, past the bars and lobster shacks. In a park I hung my arms over the railing and looked out at the pale green doll on oily waves. Then, feeling stupid, I biked home.

On Sunday I had texted Isabel to arrange the week's lessons. She answered:

Isabel: in la
Me: What?
Isabel: LA
Me: Cool. When are you coming back?
Isabel: for auditions
Me: Nice. When are you coming back?

No reply. I went to bed calculating weekly totals and woke up to a blank phone. In the afternoon I tried her again:

Me: Isabel, do you know when you're coming back to NY?
Isabel: depends

———

On Wednesday I was slow to get out of bed. What did it matter, when there were so many empty hours in the endless day? I did my diligent four at the desk, then ran the Prospect Park loop, my legs lead and the air thick. I couldn't remember October ever being so hot. The leaves weren't turning. I was back to sundresses. Every night a box fan cooled me down.

Obviously the planet was sick. When I really thought about it I felt ill too. I thought about how the PhD students of the future (if they still existed) would read today's novels hungry for any mention of climate change, the same way today there were full-length books on the nineteenth-century novels' "veiled critiques" of colonialism. How desperately we wanted to believe that Austen had comprehended the colossal crime of her motherland, even though for her the sugar trade was probably just a plot device to get the second son out of England. Not that I was better. I was worse. Climate change wasn't even a *plot device* to me. It was just some lousy way to express my mood.

That is to say, I was human. My thoughts always boomeranged back to myself. By the time I had stretched and showered and picked through the kitchen for lunch, I was back on the self-pity truck. It was so hot, and there were so many hours in the day, and though I could hear Church Avenue—horns honking, delivery trucks beeping, a construction crew jackhammering—I had fallen out of the city's daily life. I had nowhere to be. I kept taking Lacie's books off the shelves, touching them, wanting to *have* read them, but unable to sit through a single sentence.

The fridge, too, I kept returning to, looking at all the Christmas cards and gallery announcements, all the engagement photos and save-the-dates. Sophie's wedding invitation, a year old and faded by the sun, particularly bewitched me. Tasteful and discreet, a tiny gray square of paper printed in Garamond, it was, I decided, almost ostentatious in its subdued announcement of impending matrimony, its implicit rebuttal of all the gushing photo-saturated cardstock around it. A dozen times I had taken it down and examined it, but on my third or fourth perusal that restless day, I noticed something new. Rather than some obnoxiously cute joint email account, Sophie had simply included her own personal address for RSVPs.

Sophie. Tiny, forthright, laughing Sophie. Sophie who had wanted to know what Lacie was *like* in high school, Sophie who sensed the dysfunction between her husband and his mother, and called that dysfunction a haunting. Who worked at *The New Yorker.* Who had said she was delighted to meet me.

To write the email I wore one of Lacie's old T-shirts with the neck cut out. Curled on the couch, in her usual spot, with my laptop on my knees, I composed the perfect missive—offhand, casual, charming. I didn't think it was too weird. I was new in town. We had a mutual friend. But I still felt nervous. When Sophie wrote back a few hours later suggesting the following afternoon—adding that it would have to be lunch, it would have to be Midtown, did I mind the schlep, any chance I'd be in that neighborhood anyway?—I did a little dance around the room.

Watery indigo. Cream. Black loops floating in pools of red, a ribbon of emerald green. Silky, fluttery, the dress clung to me, elegant, but vibrating with patterns: oscillating dots on the sleeve, mustard yellow V's edged in cobalt and ore.

Last week, getting ready for dinner with Ian and his gallerist, Lacie had sauntered into the living room wearing this dress. Trailing the clean, bright scent of shampoo, twirling a little and laughing, she had asked, "What do you think? Good enough?"

This was not like her. Usually when I said I liked her outfit, she blinked at me. But now she wanted reassurance. "Gorgeous," I said, putting aside my book, which was really her book: *Excellent Women.* "Wow. That dress is really wild, actually. It's crazy."

She held out the hem. "Yeah, isn't it? This pattern is called Dutch Wax, but it's actually from Southeast Asia."

I considered. "Yeah, it looks kind of batiky."

"*Yes.*" Her eyes shone. "Wait, do you know this story? It's kind of fascinating."

I did not know the story, and I did not particularly care, but I was interested in how her eyes were shining. "Tell me."

"These Dutch traders copied batik patterns from Indonesia, and took them home and started to mass-produce them, thinking they would be a big hit in Europe, but they never really took off. So then they started shipping the clothes to West Africa, and the merchants there *loved* them; they started making their own, with local colors and symbols, and all these allusions to history. So now some people call it African Wax. It's funny because it's totally wrapped up in the story of colonialism, but it's also become this symbol of colonial resistance."

She nodded meaningfully when she said *colonial resistance,* and I thought of her work with Jews for Racial and Economic Justice, and I felt vaguely guilty, because I was basically a political sloth, and then I mirrored her emphatic nodding and hummed, "That is so cool."

"Yeah, and then these high-end designers got into it. I sort of love it because you really can say that it is 'authentically' Asian and European and African. I mean, it *looks* African, whatever that means, but when you trace it back, and back, you end up in Indonesia. It's this endless loop of copying and borrowing."

I thought of the costumes she had made for my play back in high school. That beautiful dress. Leo's suit. Since then her delight in textiles had only grown. She had grown. A sort of fierce, squirmy tenderness shot into my heart.

"That's so cool," I told her, but really I was talking about us, us together, the myth of us, Lacie with her costumes, me with my writing. "That's awesome."

Now, a week later, I knew what I was going to wear to lunch. I had known it ever since I wrote that email, though I did go through the motions of trying my own clothes on first. But it was always going to be the Dutch Wax. When I saw myself in the mirror I grinned, and took from Lacie's dresser a little gold chain to fasten around my neck.

———

Returning later that day, I rounded the corner and saw Ian waiting on our building's front steps.

I froze. Lacie had worn this outfit with him just last week. Could I slip up to Church Avenue? Dash to a coffee shop, wander a grocery store, pace through—

He saw me. He stood, waving. The dress was bold. Even from a distance, recognizable. He squinted, and then a light in his face dimmed.

Lunch with Sophie had been a bust. She had chosen a damp, loud, overbright Indian place on West Forty-Ninth frequented by taxi drivers, and her pose of beleaguered patience told me everything I needed to know. This was a favor. A favor, because she liked Lacie, and because she believed in being nice to strangers. But it was easy to imagine the curl of her lip, the roll of her eye, as she explained to her co-workers her lunch plans. This was a chore.

In a spirit of tentative experimentation we picked our way through a handful of topics—writing, literature, Lacie, Brooklyn, New York—but each was like a rocket flare that shot up energetically before falling inert back to earth. At one point her eyes narrowed. "Isn't that Lacie's dress?"

I flushed, looking down at my chest, as if I'd forgotten exactly what I was wearing. "She let me borrow it." I felt like a toddler clomping around in her mother's heels. And then, gaining confidence: "It's Dutch Wax."

I would have launched into all of it—about Asia and Europe and Africa, about *borrowing,* for God's sake, and global trade—but Sophie only shrugged and said it looked good on me. From her face I knew she didn't mean it at all.

There were other problems too. Her lips were too much. Not in the way Isabel's lips were too much—the warm openness of Sophie's face did something to mitigate the artifice—but her beauty was too direct.

Looking at her was like looking at the sun, not in some clichéd pop-song way, but simply because her beauty was too fully and frankly and unapologetically itself. It made me miss Lacie's beauty, the wavering, inconstant shimmer of it.

From the subway I walked home slowly, full of odd recriminations. Sophie and her performative busyness bored me. She interested me only when I thought of her as Lacie's friend, but even that did not give me a feeling of being inside it. What was *it*, I wondered. New York? A life? Lacie?

No, it was something simpler, stupider: it was just a sense that life was large, that it was exciting, that it *mattered*. I was hooked on this feeling. I could find it after two glasses of wine, or with a new man, or among the clever ones at the Workshop, late at night in the timeless dark of the Foxhead, where everything was silky black or harshly lit, and everyone was hilariously cruel and nothing ever hurt.

It was why people moved to New York, I supposed, to live inside this feeling, to live as if the movie camera was always upon you and even the most banal frustrations of everyday life achieved elevation because they happened "in New York." And though I was not immune to that romanticism, I was also thirty, old enough to be suspicious of it, to dimly suspect that feeling like your life mattered merely because you were living in an economically punishing fantasia of a place was dumb, even dangerous: it might stop you from noticing that you were stuck, your life was stuck, you were just a cog in capitalism's machine—

But then again, I could afford to be suspicious of New York. I didn't need it to make me feel like I mattered. Lacie did that for me. She always had. The wine and the boys and the cynical writers were only attempts to recapture that first blush, the hot excitement of those afternoons when we were ten and the hours stretched out before us, infinite. I was seeking something, I thought, some sense that I mattered, that we mattered, chasing it in my writing, in the apartment, with Lacie, but not, apparently, with Lacie's friends.

So, Ian.

I waved bravely back. "Don't you ever check your phone?" he called, standing and stretching. "Nice dress," he added, and hit me like a big blond wave with a kiss on the cheek.

I swirled around. "What do you think?"

"It looks good on you."

The whole length of the elevator ride I couldn't stop pushing at my hair. My arms felt too long and my cheeks too hot. I rocked back on my heels, I hit him with my shoulder and smiled in what I hoped was a mysterious way. "Lacie usually works until at least six," I explained, and he grinned wolfishly.

That rattled me, that and the dress. Once inside I stupidly invited him to "have a seat," even though he already had sunk onto the day-bed and started removing from his backpack silver cans of beer. "Do you want to put those in the fridge? Those must have been hard to bike with. Where do you live again? Is it far? I feel like it's uphill to here from everywhere."

"I was coming from the studio." He held a beer out to me and took one for himself. "Yeah, that would be great."

When I came back from the kitchen he had put his feet up and balanced his beer on his stomach. He seemed rather proud of his belly. Self-consciously, I sank into an armchair with busted springs and cracked my can. I wanted nothing more than to go change, but what would be my excuse? Going into her room, replacing the dress—it would be an admission of guilt. Fishy. I stayed put.

For a while we didn't talk. Once I tried, "Are you in touch with anyone from the Barn?" and he just shook his head. The air shimmered like oil in a puddle, and Lacie's two fans blew the same stale air around, trembling the chiffon curtains.

"Rose, Rose, what's in a rose?" Ian sang to himself in a high, funny voice, and then lapsed into quiet. I looked desperately at the frozen dancer mid-plié on the mantel.

Finally I broke. "So. You just wanted to stop by? You never come over."

"Yeah, sure." He looked at me. "I wanted to see you."

"You've been, like, MIA since I moved here." A barb of bitterness in my voice.

"This fall is nuts. I'm losing my mind getting ready for this show."

I held his gaze.

"Sorry. I just—" It seemed he was about to say something more. Then, quietly, he added, "I thought it would be good for us to have some space."

What did he mean? Good for *us* to have some space? Was there an *us*? Nothing had ever—but what else could he—"It's fine," I told him. "It's just weird to see you again."

"Is it nice?"

"Of course it's *nice*. It's just weird. We were close, and then you were gone, and then I find out you're dating my childhood best friend. It's weird."

There came over his face a look that made me think it wasn't the desire to "reconnect" that had led him to wait for me on the crumbly brick steps outside. It didn't have anything to do with me. Why was I flattering myself with these thoughts of *us*? It was Lacie, always Lacie.

Cautiously, deliberately, he said, "I heard you guys were out of touch for a long time."

"Yeah. When I saw her in Bryant Park it was the first time in over a decade."

"Wow. But you guys were besties in high school, right? What happened? You just . . . fell out of touch?"

"Yeah." My voice was wood. High school all over again: boys by the water fountain, boys at the lunch table, sweet-talking me, but eyes darting and jittery as they looked for Lacie.

"You didn't even try to stay in touch? Like on Facebook or something?"

"I'm not on Facebook," I reminded him.

Ian put down his can. "But did you have a fight?"

"Why do you ask that? Did Lacie say something?"

"Lacie never says anything. She's not exactly the most forthcoming person in the world."

I laughed, more out of relief than anything.

"I mean"—he was encouraged—"she doesn't relate to her emotions the way most people do."

"Women. You mean most women."

He winced. "Maybe. But do you know what I mean? She's very—"

"She's private."

"Yeah. I mean, she's so charming and nice. Everyone loves her. But she actually doesn't talk about herself so much, not if you really listen."

I smiled at him. "She talks to me."

"But about real stuff? Stuff she's actually dealing with?"

I thought of our long evenings with tea, all the catching up we had done, the delicate way we had discussed all the men in our lives, save the two we shared. For sure, Lacie refused the usual guise of female intimacy. But she cooked for me, she had knit me a hat, she picked up toothpaste when we were out. All our little exchanges were electric pulses; I found them more honest, and more thrilling, than the standard confessional mode. But if Ian hadn't figured this out, I couldn't help him.

"I keep feeling like I can't quite grasp the *critical* things in her life," he was saying now.

I smiled at him again, still feeling smug. "You have to be patient with her. She'll open up."

"Really? She seems *so* elusive." He pulled on his beer. Then, timidly, like a child drawn irresistibly to a forbidden room, he said, "So, really, did you guys have a falling-out, or what?"

I shook my head. "It's not a very interesting story."

"Was it in high school?"

The sound of a key in the door. The dress. I stood. Ian looked at me strangely. I sat. All my nerves danced, like metal filings when a magnet gets too close.

"I can't," I said very quietly, and then there came the clop-clop of Lacie kicking off her shoes in the foyer. "Ian?" I pictured her frowning at his big white Chucks. "You're here?"

It was shocking to see the subject of our conversation walk into the room. She brought with her a swirl of sidewalk and exhaust, tendrils curling out from her loose topknot, several tote bags spilling from her shoulder to the floor.

"What are you guys doing in the dark?" she exclaimed, and there was not an ounce of distrust in her voice.

"Hey, babe." Light like a lion, Ian padded to her and kissed her on the cheek. "We were just waiting for you."

"Why is it so hot?" She went to the window and hoisted up the glass, angry at the heat—I recognized this mood from August. We were all regressing.

"Let's get out of here." She stood in the center of the room, hands on hips, elbows pointed. "Are you guys hungry? I'm starving. Let's go to the Tibetan place."

Then she saw me. Her face went through a thousand explosions of feeling. "You're wearing my clothes."

I stood so hastily I knocked against an old Amazon box. Cat took off, hissing.

"Doesn't she look good in it?" There was eager soothing in Ian's voice.

"I'm sorry. I should have asked." For Ian, I tried to keep my voice light.

Lacie was the mistress of ease, a high priestess of social lubricant, but even so, there stretched between us an electric buzzing. She knows, I thought suddenly. She knows I go through her room every day.

Then, with great effort, and great grace, she shut it down. Her face shut down. "No problem," she said. "Ian's right. It does look good on you."

"Yeah. It totally does. Let's get Tibetan." Ian stretched, faux-casual, his shirt rising a few inches to reveal a pale slice of belly with dark curled hairs. "A spicy curry will help me sweat it out." He ambled toward his shoes. Lacie looked at me expectantly.

"Great," I said. Obediently we all followed Lacie out of the apartment, down the pink-carpeted stairs, and into the dark.

It was cooler outside, and after the stuffy apartment the night air slipped around me like the silk gown. Walking down Rugby, I kept far from Lacie. I didn't want her to say anything more to me.

We ordered extravagantly that night: shrimp and pork dumplings, red and yellow curries, a thick gluey bread from Nepal, and mixed green vegetables in a steamy clump. Drinking cold beers and eating spicy curry, we slid through conversation, chopsticks hovering, eating fast and drinking faster, laughing and interrupting, stabbing the dumplings, desperate to show how much we liked one another, how much *fun* we were having.

"It's going to be great," Lacie announced, pressing her dewy bottle against her neck. Naturally, talk of the weather had turned to talk of the apocalypse, specifically the Zombie Apocalypse. "I'm going to be so good at it."

"Are you?" Ian smiled.

"Oh, totally. I'll get everyone I love in one place and like, ration out the food and *organize* everything." She laughed at herself. "I actually really love thinking about it. It's kind of sick."

"And get guns," Ian advised. "You'll need guns. And a tarp. For water."

"Does that actually work?" Lacie wrinkled her nose. We all laughed—at nothing, just to keep the mood going.

"Yeah. Just lay a tarp out—if you can stake it up a few inches it's really good—and in the morning you collect the condensation."

"So that's like, how much water?"

"Umm," Ian paused for effect, "maybe four ounces."

We both shrieked. "Fabulous," Lacie laughed. "Totally perfect. This is going to be great."

"Or you could just, like, hold up a Duane Reade," I suggested. "With all those guns you'll have." We were all giggling, picturing Lacie in—what? a balaclava?—storming into a drugstore.

"That'll be the *first* thing that everyone does. Storm Duane Reade. Steal all the condoms."

"*Condoms?*" I pretended outrage.

Lacie shrugged. "I hear they're useful in a disaster."

"Oh my God, the sex is going to be great." Ian shook his head. "Disaster sex is going to be *incredible*."

"Maybe everyone will share," I suggested. "Maybe we won't have to *loot*."

Lacie slung her arm around me and twisted me toward Ian. "Isn't she adorable?" she demanded. "Isn't she the cutest?" The crook of her elbow was damp and mean against my neck.

"The cutest," Ian agreed, but he wasn't quite looking at me.

"Anyway"—Lacie unhooked her arm—"it's going to be total *Lord of the Flies*. Though it's sweet that you can even *think* otherwise. But no. We're going to have to rely on my natural charisma."

"Your *overwhelming* charisma," Ian amended, pinching a plump shrimp and holding it out to her. "Your animally *magnetic* charisma."

She ducked her head and made off with the shrimp. "They'll all fall into line like good worker bees."

They locked eyes. A tiny smile tugged at Lacie's lips.

I laughed too loudly. "I don't know," I announced. "Some part of me also thinks there's something deeply unethical about building a bunker. Isn't it just a way of caring less about everyone else?"

Ian had a way of looking at me that was more a looking *into* me. He did it now. He dove in deep. And it was an endless temptation—I remembered this from the Barn—to ask him what he had seen.

"Well," Lacie said. "I don't think there's anything unethical about planning ahead. Or taking care of yourself."

"No, I mean, sure, when the next hurricane comes, I'll be hoarding food like everyone else. But do you know what I mean? Isn't this why we live in cities? Because we believe in this grand, totally imperfect, collective experiment? Because we want to take our chances in being part of an interconnected web, rather than some lone cowboy out in Wyoming with his gun?"

Gravely they both nodded. I felt oddly thrilled. "You're not wrong," Ian said.

"No." Lacie considered. "You're not wrong," and I felt like their child, but in the nicest way, like they would take care of me and approve of everything I did.

Just then an ambulance went by, bleating and beaming its disco lights, so we just sat there, smiling and nodding. Ian said something to Lacie too quietly for me to hear, and by the time the siren had faded she had responded and Ian was saying, "But I could just get a studio somewhere else."

I had ruined Zombie Apocalypse with my prudish ethics.

"But Red Hook is so cheap," Lacie said.

"Red Hook is cheap, but Eli is driving me insane."

I didn't know who Eli was, and I didn't know why he was driving Ian insane. Lacie never told me anything, and I didn't want the thing to start where they forgot about me. I blurted out, "I like to walk in Red Hook."

Lacie's eyes narrowed. "Really? I didn't know you liked it there."

"Where do you walk?" Ian asked.

I didn't know any street names. "Oh, just down by the water, like that little park, you know? Where you can look at the Statue of Liberty?"

"Really? You should let me know when you're around. My studio's right there."

"Oh?" I said innocently. "I don't want to interrupt you."

He waved his hand. "Usually I can use a break. Seriously. Text me."

Lacie took a long draw on her beer, watching us. So, I thought. It's not like we're hiding anything.

On the way home, Lacie pulled me close. "Just ask," she hissed. "With the necklace too. I really don't care, take whatever you want, but just *ask*." And she tugged, hard, on the sleeve of the dress.

On the day I learned that Isabel's father committed, or probably committed, debt fraud, the day I learned that the charges against him were then abruptly and mysteriously dropped, none of his cronies or underlings or the investigating prosecutor willing to explain why the SEC was no longer interested in Ervin West, no longer interested though it acknowledged, and Ervin West acknowledged, and it was generally and widely acknowledged that an "impropriety" had occurred, not an impropriety like sleeping with your best friend's boyfriend, no, nothing like the ordinary, dull, unimaginative sins of small people, but something truly fabulous like remaining the chief shareholder in an entertainment conglomerate whose improper debt swapping you have supervised, and then making, in the four years after said improper debt swap, in excess of $10 million in personal profit, yes, on that day, I chose my clothing carefully. A slouchy sweater dress, pale gray; Oxford loafers; and my leather jacket, soft as creamy lamb.

"Okay." I slid Isabel's paper between her laminated copy of "Be You" and her Cosmic Cranberry Kombucha, whose label promised, as Ivy Prep had promised, to reawaken, repurpose, and redefine Isabel.

I was up for the job: sharply dressed, speaking strongly, and oh so ready to make money again. Ervin West's email to me, which had prompted the googling, and which had had no subject line or salutation, had read in its entirety: *Please confirm five o'clock today*, and though we had not discussed meeting—though I hadn't even known Isabel was back from California—I immediately wrote back, *Confirmed*.

"This is great," I declared. "Really great. But what I find myself wondering is, Do you think you've really gotten to the very heart of it? Do you think—I'm just wondering—do you think *The Souls of Black Folk* is the very best book to help show colleges who you are?"

Isabel blinked. "My teacher says it's not just the job of black people to talk about being black."

"You mean race. It's not just the job of black people to talk about race."

She gave a little moue of impatience. "Yeah, that's what I said."

Sulkily she pushed one bare leg out from the desk. No tennis today, apparently: she was still in her school uniform, plaid skirt and blue polo, dainty gold chain around her neck. Gold her father had bought; skirt her father had bought; skirt to attend private school whose tuition her father had bought. Dirty money. Sometimes being with Isabel was like staring at one of those magical 3-D paintings: one way, she was just a pattern of pretty, psychedelic dots, but dilate your eyes, and from the rich schizoids of red and purple emerged the dinosaur shape of her father's ill-gotten capital.

Briskly she stabbed her paper with her forefinger. "This is the most important thing I'll ever write," she reminded me. "This determines my *future*."

"Absolutely," I agreed. "That's why I want to be sure we get to the heart of who you are." We were both quiet, thinking about her heart. Then I brightened. "You said you were a feminist. That's interesting to me."

"Why?" She sounded suspicious, as if she had no idea what might be remarkable about a wealthy young model/actress with collagen-injected lips and a gluten "allergy" pledging allegiance to absolute gender parity. *Look,* I wanted to say, *I'm fighting for the right to get laid when I'm fifty and single. What are you after? Are we even on the same team?*

"I guess I just mean I want you to write about what you care about. I want you to express yourself. I want you to—" I was emotional, why was I so emotional? I took a deep breath. "Isabel. I think you actually have fascinating things to say about being a woman. A young *white* woman. It's different from how I grew up."

"Because of the internet."

"Because of the internet," I agreed. "And cell phones. We just had pagers. Actually, sometimes we used pay phones. We used to call the pay phone at the train station, just to see who was hanging out there."

"You hung out at the *train station*?"

"Yeah." I wrinkled my mouth. "There wasn't a lot to do."

"But that sounds so *boring*," she exclaimed, delighted. "You would just *sit* there?"

"Yeah. Sometimes the boys would fuck—like, mess up, the trash cans," and honestly, dropping the F bomb was the best thing I could have done for student-tutor relations at that moment. She grinned. I covered my mouth. "Whoops."

Coyly she asked, "Were you guys the bad kids?"

"Not really. We were just, like, bored."

"That's cool." She really did sound impressed. "That's, like, really cool." Thoughtfully, she unscrewed the cap of her Cosmic Cranberry. Took a tiny sip. Winced.

I laughed. "Do you actually like that stuff?"

"Not really. It's kind of gross." She giggled.

"Can I smell it?"

A weird, unprofessional request, but Isabel handed over the drink, warning, "It smells like gym clothes. Seriously, it's foul."

Delicately I took a perfunctory whiff, careful to keep my nose and mouth well clear of the lip. "So foul," I agreed. "It's like something my friend Lacie would like."

As soon as I said her name the air got funny. Wavy and charged.

"Cool. Is she really into juice or something?"

"She's into kombucha. Actually, she makes it."

"*That's* crazy." Isabel flapped her arms, excited. "That's, like, *really* crazy. It's *mold*. Does she know that? How does she know it's not going to *kill* her?"

"She's very careful," I assured her.

Dreamily Isabel rested her head in her hand. *The Souls of Black Folk* was nudged aside. "That's totally something they would do in L.A. Make kombucha. That's, like, totally something they'd be into. Maybe you should go there."

"To L.A.? Yeah, actually, I've been."

"I think you would like it."

"Yeah, no, I *do* like it."

"Yeah," Isabel said. "I think it's your kind of place. 'Cause you're earthy."

The statement was categorical, her conviction absolute. My sweater dress, chosen with such care, shriveled to a shroud. "*Earthy?* What do you mean, *earthy?*"

"It's not bad," she said gently. "I can just tell. You've got that natural hippie look."

"What do you *mean*?" I was mildly hysterical. How could she tell? What gave me away?

But she only fixed me with one of her dead, sexed-out stares. "They're kind of hippies there. They like juice and stuff."

It's odd, the power we give strangers over our lives, how readily we believe they see the truth of us. It's as if the burden of knowing ourselves is so great that we lay it down happily, easily, without complaint; as if we think our friends and family are blind, but strangers, random indifferent strangers, possess judgments as arbitrary and definite as God's.

Isabel wasn't exactly a stranger, but she didn't care about me, and so I trusted her. *Earthy.* Dowdy. Bland. Boring. Refusing to shower, or wear deodorant, or brush hair. Smelling of body odor and thrift-store clothing. Everything I had been, back when I was her age. Everything I thought I had escaped.

L acie in the living room had burrowed deep into the daybed with a book. As I came in she said, "Look at you. You're ador-able."

"Ha. Don't even start." She had on her beautiful face today, the pale gray eyes and pink pallor of a Renaissance maiden. "This tutoring girl is making me feel insane."

She rattled her cubes. "Go get something."

The whiskey was all hers, but she shared readily, carelessly; what was hers was mine, she implied with every action: it should be understood. After two months, I still marveled.

"You do really look cute," she repeated once I had fixed myself a jam jar.

"I don't *feel* cute." My dress hem rode up; I tugged it down. "Isabel just told me I was earthy."

She wrinkled her nose. "What does that even mean?"

I sipped, and whiskey fire lit Isabel's words. "I have no idea. She was like, Oh, you'd like L.A. You're *earthy*. She's such a—she's this total Barbie doll who thinks she's a feminist, and is *totally* unaware of how she's completely complicit in the objectification of women. It drives me absolutely insane."

Lacie was furrowing her brow. "L.A.'s not earthy."

"But how do you think she knew? I mean, is this outfit 'earthy' to you?"

"Well"—Lacie cupped her own jar—"it's definitely more New Agey than here. It's airy. But it's not *earthy*. There's nothing *terrestrial* about it."

"Right." I tried to keep my voice even. "I mean, she's just seventeen. She's not well versed on the difference between earthy and airy."

"Really? I feel like when I was seventeen I knew the difference . . ."

Lacie's voice went all wandery, trying to remember our youth. Annoyance flicked me. Why couldn't she just call the little girl a bitch? All I wanted from friendship was the assurance that I was right, but put-upon, that furthermore all life's troubles were really only hilarious episodes, nothing so dark it couldn't be reframed as a one-liner. But there I was, in that room, still trapped with myself. *Earthy*. Lacie wasn't any help at all.

"Whatever. It doesn't matter. It's just, she's so feminine and girly in this way that kind of mystifies me."

"Well, at least you're working again, right?"

"Yeah, totally." I sipped. Something snagged: the check written out to Lacie tucked in my top drawer. "I still don't—"

"It's cool, it's cool. I told you, whenever is fine."

I sighed. "Thanks. It's so humiliating."

She looked away, though because she wanted to give me privacy or she actually hated this money business, too, I couldn't tell. "What's going on?" I asked. "What's up with you?"

"Nothing. Ian is driving *me* insane."

My mouth was suddenly too wide for my face. "What's he doing?"

"He's just working a lot. He's at the studio all the time."

"Hmm," I said neutrally. "He's got that show coming up."

Lacie scowled over her glass, but the scowl already had some self-mockery in it. "I don't like it," she declared. "Obviously all the attention should be for me all the time."

"Obviously." I grinned. "Me too. All the attention all the time."

It was like any other evening, our little routines and jokes, except that I still had something itchy in me. I still needed out of myself. "Attention is good. But not attention from a dumb teenage girl. *Earthy*. It sounds so musty."

"You're not *musty*." Lacie stretched her arms overhead. "You're fucking hot. You're beautiful. That girl is just jealous."

"Yeah." Something pinchy and mean rose up in me. I wasn't getting what I wanted from this conversation; there was something dismissive in her reassurances. I drained the last of my glass. "Whatever. I'm going to bed."

"And earthy can be a good thing . . ." she called as I drifted down the hall, and I shouted back, "Yeah, totally," and shut the door and got out my phone. Fiddled with it. No new texts, no new emails. The weather was still the weather.

The thing was, I just needed to say to somebody, "This girl thinks I'm a dirty hippie," and have them exclaim back, like a friend, like any normal friend would, "What? Oh my God, that's ridiculous, what a stupid rich girl; her brain has been lobotomized by Instagram. You know how it is. Kids these days."

That's what a friend was for. And Ian was my friend. He had told me to text him. So I did.

Descending the endless escalators at Smith and Ninth, walking past bodegas and skittery paper cups, I imagined in the swirl of sulfur lights an act of violence. A mugging. My body slammed by a city bus. The call to Lacie, her question to me: What were you doing there? To distract her I'd have to get seriously fucked up. Hurt. Hospital.

Beneath the BQE I walked, and around the projects, deep in this bad line of thought. Unlucky. I forced myself from violence to Isabel. What if she were with me tonight? I would point to the trash and the silent, dark-coated men and say, *This is New York too. This is what they're hiding from you.*

At the bar Ian was wearing a T-shirt the color of sky after rain, a depthless bright blue. After my dark thoughts, and amid the steamed windows and piled coats, he shone out, fresh and cool. When he turned I tried to kiss his cheek, but my mouth ended up by his ear.

He smiled distantly. He was so big and blond; his effusions of hair and skin, his broadness, his maleness, delighted me, so rank and hairy and even slightly repellant, so corporeal. So different from my last boyfriend, Alex, who had been petite and pristine.

While I was sinking under his spell we were saying hello, I was ordering a Vinho Verde, Ian was unfolding a twenty, I was saying no, no, and he was saying yes, yes. Let me. In the back room a gypsy band jigged, and beneath their screaming fiddle and nervy tambourine there were glasses clinking, people shouting, a man's rumbling laugh, and yet it felt very quiet to me, very quiet and slow, there in that dark, humid bar with the blue light of his shirt.

Our silence stretched like honey from a spoon.

He had dark eyes, deep and pooling, nearly black. Eyes that talked for him. He wasn't afraid of silence. A minute after my arrival, we had already lapsed into one.

Then the conversation shuddered to life. I asked about his show; he complained about the curator. He asked about my writing; I complained about Portia. We agreed that art was a bitch. I said that I thought Lacie was a frustrated artist: all those craft projects around the house, but stuck in an office all day.

"Maybe. I've thought the same thing a few times." He narrowed his eyes at me. "She can be a little scattered."

"Well, the *house* is very scattered."

He laughed ruefully. "It drives me nuts."

I flashed on his studio at the Barn: pigment plastic-wrapped, brushes soft and clean, yellow babouches lined up by the door.

"I like it," I told him. "Maybe it's a little overwhelming. But it always feels like there's stuff going on. It's so alive."

"Yeah, with Lacie, there's always something happening."

I felt then how we could make a project of Lacie. Pool our observations, fuss over her psyche, and speculate, as we had done the other day. It would make us close again, but I didn't want to do it that way.

As if he had heard my thoughts, he said, "You too."

"What?"

"You too. There's a lot going on with you too."

"Oh, thanks." All I wanted was his praise, but getting it was too much; I squirmed away, and he leaned close.

"No, I mean it. At the Barn? You were the hardest worker. You were up before everyone else. You were in deep. We could all tell."

"I'm a mule." I grinned coquettishly from my wineglass's rim. "Just plowing ahead."

But he didn't take the bait and flirt back. Instead he got serious, *more* serious, which I didn't think was possible. With those brooding eyes and hulking shape Ian's default was serious, so when he actually got serious, the solemnity about knocked you over. "This novel," he said quietly, "it's the one from the Barn?"

"Yep."

"Good." He nodded somberly, as if he had been personally worried about my novel. "I have a feeling it's going to be really good. Don't stop working on it."

He cares about my writing, I thought, but he doesn't even *know* my writing. He hasn't seen it. He cares about my writing, but not about me. Which I recognized, even in the moment, as a stupidly self-pitying thought.

But now we were in *another* silence. His eyes flicked around the bar. He was bored. Misery stamped me. *I* bored him. What did Lacie say to him? What did *they* talk about? I could feel the word *earthy* like soil in my mouth. How I longed to spit it out.

I took another sip of wine—like tasting sky—and said, "Do you think I'm earthy?"

"Earthy? No. What are you talking about?"

"Just this girl." I told my latest Isabel story.

Ian snorted. "Why?"

"I don't know! That's exactly the thing. How could she tell?"

"No, I mean, why did it hurt you? Why do you even care what she thinks?"

Why did I even *care*? Oh boy, could I explain that one. "I thought I had shed my old dirty hippie persona, and it totally freaked me out to think it was still visible on me. Like everyone can see this thing, that I'm *earthy*, that I'm not sexy, like I don't register as sexual, but *I* can't see it, I'm completely oblivious to it."

"I think you're sexy." He was serious.

"Well, that's nice of you."

"No, I mean it. You're sexy. You're totally hot."

Exactly the phrase Lacie had used. *Lacie.* She was sexy. Even back in seventh grade we knew it. "I remember," I said, "being at a school dance in middle school, standing on the edge of the dance floor, and not knowing how it started. How to begin."

"How to become a sexual person."

"Yeah." I dug my eye sockets into my palms. "Like how to announce it. Maybe I still need to announce it."

The rec center. Shellacked pinewood floors, a long, low room, a tiny stage up front. Blue and pink lights. The crooning harmonies of mid-'90s pop. Sitting on a vinyl bench, waiting and waiting for a boy to come over to me. Watching Lacie on the dance floor. Watching Jesse Grogan's hands cup her butt. Her blue-jean butt. How could she stand it? Other girls were asked, girls who were as nerdy as me, who got grades as high as me. Girls with glasses. Girls with braces. But nobody came for me.

Why did that ignored girl still live inside me? Why was I still carrying her around? Men had wanted me since then. Men had chosen me. But still I felt like the girl who hadn't learned the trick, who was marked as a child, gawky-toothed, small-eyed, unsexual.

Ian regarded me carefully. Then: "Watch this," he said, and sauntered over to the bar.

All night I'd been tracking a cluster of young men in polos and fleece, clean-shaven, their elbows on the bar, looking around like *What can you do for me?* They were here—I knew—in this odd jazz club as a kind of adventure. Tourists. Young bucks who lived in Murray Hill, made six figures, and thought Brooklyn a lark.

Now Ian nudged one on the elbow and made some comment. He got a smile, then a nod. I watched, amazed. Ian was good with strangers. It had to do with his beauty; even men responded to it. It was a weight, a force. You just gave in.

Then Ian was motioning, and they were looking over.

Furiously I studied the pale carbonation bubbles of my wine. Was I mad? No, more dazzled. Thrilled he would fish a man for me. Looked back: sure enough, Ian and a fleecy finance bro were trundling my way.

I shot Ian daggers as he slid into our booth. "This is Franklin," he said calmly. "He's never been to Red Hook before."

"Hey, so." Franklin was stocky, with square hipster glasses, a crisp navy fleece embroidered with the words *Credit Suisse* in white. "Does anyone actually live out here?"

"My studio's right over there." Ian didn't point.

"Word," said Franklin, still looking at me. "What about you? Are you an artist too? Everyone here's an artist."

"She's a writer." Ian lifted his glass in a toast.

"Guys. I'm right here. I can talk," I reminded them.

Franklin's buddies at the bar kept glancing over and smirking. "I'm going to buy you a drink," he announced.

"Me too," Ian shouted to his retreating back.

Left alone, we smirked too. Ian hit my thigh under the table. "He thinks you're my sister. You're visiting from Pittsburgh."

"You're such an asshole."

"You go to Carnegie Mellon."

When Franklin returned—with shots for both of us—I nodded at his pec. "Do you like it? Credit Suisse?"

He looked self-consciously down, as if he had forgotten the words over his heart. "It's okay," he said cautiously. "The work I do is actually kind of creative. Not creative like what you do, but I like it."

"Oh, I'm not creative," I assured him.

"You are." He sounded almost petulant. "You're writing a novel."

"How do you know I'm writing a novel?"

"What else would you be doing?"

He looked so confused I genuinely felt bad for him. We had probably grown up in similar kinds of middle-class families, gone to similar kinds of upper-tier schools, and now lived in the same city. But somehow we couldn't comprehend each other. I could see—from his clear plastic glasses, his plaid, even the fact that he was in this bar—that we liked enough of the same things. But we couldn't find each other.

To comfort myself I reached under the table and pinched Ian's thigh. *God,* the texture of his thigh was just so *interesting*—so ropy with muscle. To investigate I crept my hand up.

Then Ian, just as Franklin was explaining his deeply creative work, snaked his arm round my shoulder and kissed me deeply on the mouth.

"*Shit,*" Franklin cried. "That's your sister."

Ian didn't answer. He kept kissing me. I tasted whiskey, burger fat, and the metallic tang of turpentine. When I opened my eyes again Franklin was gone. The blue Christmas lights of the bar spun dizzily.

"Let's go home," Ian said, and we were out the door in a shuffle of jackets and scarves, on the cobblestones of Van Brunt where, crazily enough, a yellow cab was idling.

"Red Hook's really hot," I crowed. "Let's go to Red Hook tonight." One of Franklin's buddies stood in the middle of the street, stunned by our poaching of his cab.

Ian and I, we kept kissing. I kissed him in the taxi and as he paid and in his bathroom after he had taken a piss. By the time we were on his sink I knew we would fuck. His thumb traced the dip of my bra. He smelled of sweat, whiskey, and wood smoke; the bristly blond hairs of his mustache tickled my sternum as his tongue found my nipple.

A shrink would say, *This is envy,* introducing me to a party guest I've already met. *This is desire,* and *this is doubleness,* and *this is fury;* this is you kissing inside the bar, outside the bar, in the taxi, in the hall, against the door, on the bed. This is you kissing Ian, and Ian kissing you, and the way it seems hilariously irrelevant, the distinction between *desire* and *action,* though actualizing does bring Lacie into the room: with every kiss you are confessing that you would hurt her to get close to her. This is the link between you, this is why you are down on the bed, this is why your clothes are coming off, and you both know it and you keep doing it. If you have your mouths on each other you can't speak.

PART TWO

Earthly Delights

As soon as Leo said yes, we began. I sensed it was important to move quickly, before he changed his mind. Mr. Cowan said we could use his room, and that Thursday, after carefully tacking Lacie's red scarf over the door, I turned to my two actors, who were sitting side by side, hands folded, waiting.

Back in February, Mr. Cowan had announced extra credit for anyone who entered a one-act in the Young Playwrights contest. A day later, he added that anyone who performed at Art Night would earn extra credit too—not only the writer but the actors as well. Leo had a C in English; I'd heard him talking to Lacie about how he still hadn't finished his *Beloved* paper. True, it had taken some wrangling, but once I had gotten Lacie hyped about a new project, Leo had fallen in pretty easily.

To say I was glad is an understatement. By junior spring they were nearly mythic in my mind. Their names—*Lacie and Leo*—sounded so good together, like an indie rock band, and they were weirdly, seductively twinned, both long and lanky and sleepily hot. But it wasn't just their beauty; it was also that they were leaving me. Sure, now they were careful to include me—Lacie, especially, made sure I was invited to every party and hang—but I knew it wouldn't last forever. That's why I had concocted my plan, had lured them, with extra credit and the promise that they wouldn't have to do *anything,* to this classroom after school.

But somehow in all my fantasizing about putting on a play, I had imagined only the camaraderie: goofing off during rehearsals, laughing at the costumes, huddling in the hot, bright wings. I had not imagined the first rehearsal, or their blank, expectant gaze. I was used to studying *them* for clues about how to behave.

"Okay, um, so. This play. It's, uh, a retelling of the Adam and Eve story, so basically, like, Eve didn't mess up, she wanted to leave the garden. . . ."

Leo was staring at me so deeply that he was either completely engrossed in what I was saying or entirely spaced out. I trailed off.

Lacie coughed. "Maybe we should just read it."

"Yeah, totally. Good idea." My head bobbed in stupid gratitude. The scripts, which I had carefully photocopied during lunch, were jagged in my hands. Finally I got them onto their desks.

They both immediately began to scan. I was horrified. This, too, was something I hadn't imagined. "It's a work in progress, you know, I mean, this isn't the final script, you'll probably think it's really bad—"

Leo folded back the top page and kept reading. How could I have thought this was a good idea? I might as well have toddled up and pushed a glittery house of Popsicle sticks into his hands.

"Rose? Want us to read?"

"Yeah." I blinked back my attention from Leo. "Let's read. Lacie, you're going to be Eve." Then I blushed furiously. Obviously she would be Eve.

They began, and it was bad. Leo mumbled my words softly into the desk, and Lacie spoke in that childish voice I despised, the one she reserved for teachers and other adults. The lines that had sounded so witty in my head were dead and dull.

Then a kid pushed his face up against the glass and made a farting noise. We all jumped. Word, apparently, had gotten out that Leo Kupersky was in a *play*. "Keep going," I instructed, and repinned the scarf.

But then a funny thing happened. On page twelve, Adam snaps at Eve, "Can't you appreciate all that we have?" and when Leo said those words, something like real emotion came into his voice.

Both Lacie and I straightened. "Don't you have any imagination?"

Lacie cried, and she, too, sounded alive, full of feeling, for the first time all rehearsal.

"But aren't you happy?" Leo said, in a shy, pleading voice, and a little door opened in my mind. I didn't consciously think a thing beyond: Oh. They sound like they mean it.

At the next rehearsal we pushed the desks to the wall, and with masking tape I marked off the boundaries of our imaginary stage. "Blocking," I announced crisply, new authority in my voice.

It was marvelous, like running after lead weights have been released from your legs, to talk to Leo without my usual yoke of self-consciousness. I even touched him lightly on the shoulder to tell him where to go. "Look at her when you say that," I instructed, and: "Throw the apple at her feet, but deliberately miss," using a crumpled brown paper bag to demonstrate.

The best part, though, was getting them to fight. They liked it too: they got into it, yelling themselves hoarse, disgust and scorn in their voices. I kept changing it, making it more dramatic, the insults more personal, and I noticed that they were not as loving to each other afterward. Some of the sourness hung in the air. "Guys," I would say. "That was so good. That was so real."

Yes, in that pale blue classroom, with the long slow late afternoon heaving itself toward night, amid the ancient posters of Impressionist art and cheery reminders about grammar, we made a kind of—it is embarrassing to say—a kind of magic. When Lacie, shivering with outrage, boomed out angry words about paradise, and Leo, playing Adam as a kind of slacker, sulked and whined, I got chills. Maybe it is beyond tacky to say this about your own work; maybe it is even comical to say this about your work from high school. But in accounting for everything, I am trying not to lie.

We spent a lot of time laughing, too, or just hanging out, running to the vending machines for more soda, more M&Ms, more potato chips. Afterward we would all walk back to Swarthmore together, the three of us tromping up the long fishhook of Yale Avenue, and at the top, they went their way and I went mine.

That turning away was always when I first felt the slide back to the ordinary. We weren't really three. Lacie and Leo were dating. Lacie and Leo were a couple. Alone in my room, and alone, later, at a party, my mostly full beer carefully clutched in my hand, I learned again that I was disposable. It was only when we were rehearsing that there was a place for me.

One Saturday, Lacie said we should go pick out material for costumes. I assumed she meant a trip to Joanne's, up Baltimore Pike, but when I offered to drive she looked at me curiously and said, "I was thinking we could go into the city."

On the train out we sat with our feet up, Lacie with her hair in a messy bun held together by a mechanical pencil (alone in my room, I had tried to copy this style, but I could never get the bun to stay). She wore blue jeans, not her usual flowy skirt or dress, as if to say *Today is for work*.

"What did you guys do last night?" I knew she had been with Leo.

"Nothing." Lacie leaned her head against the glass. Behind her profile, the soccer fields strobed past.

Nothing. What did that even mean? Did "nothing" include sex? Was it code for sex? The usual spin cycle began in me: longing to know more, fear of knowing more, annoyance that Lacie wouldn't spill. Agitation that I could be so close and yet so far away.

Yes, she had told me they had done it, but in a handwritten note passed between third and fourth period, and that wasn't the same as *telling*. She had marked off boundaries just as our stage was marked off by masking tape. I wanted to rip it up; I wanted to run ourselves together. I wanted to know all the things she knew.

Normally I never would have asked, but in the warmth and isolation of the train, with bright cheap billboards and loopy graffiti blinking past, I found myself saying, my voice furred with shyness, "This is weird, but what's he like?"

"What do you mean, what's he like?" She looked at me, amused. Then she laughed. "Wait, Rose, do you mean *sex*?"

Not exactly. I wanted to know if he liked to snuggle, if he ever pulled away, if they fought, if they had pet names, if they talked on the phone a lot, if she had discovered his emotional issues. Yes, his emotional issues: I was dying to know.

But *sex* would work. Blushing, I waited. Sometimes, in moments like these, I could almost feel the gears in Lacie winding up.

Slowly, stabbing the seat back with her forefinger, she said, "He always falls asleep right afterward. And I get so lonely I feel like I'm going to scream."

"Yeah?" I quivered with the weight of what she had confided. "That sucks. He shouldn't do that."

"It's okay." Her eyes closed. She seemed so faraway to me in that moment, faraway and yet in need of my protection. I wanted to spread my arms over her like giant wings, I wanted to protect her from all the boys, from Leo, but instead, I stared out the window, buzzing with her, watching the athletic fields of Drexel fly past, and then the winking blue of downtown.

We got off at Market East and Lacie led me past noodle shops to a street that looked perfectly ordinary, gray and commercial, until I noticed that every single store window was cluttered with mannequins dressed in awkward, unmistakably homemade dresses of yellow or purple or green.

"My mom always starts here." We went into a low, crowded shop with fabric stacked three deep. A squat older woman materialized from the back, crooning Yiddish and pressing Lacie to the double rolls of her breasts and belly.

At great length Lacie explained our mission. I blushed when she introduced me as the playwright, though the storekeeper only nodded tolerantly before continuing to pepper Lacie with questions. Like a frugal housewife at the fishmonger, Lacie expertly picked among the cloth, often lingering over two samples that looked identical before, with a sigh or shake of her head, moving on. After she had worked her way around the perimeter, she took the old woman's hands in her own—and I had never seen Lacie make such an adult, confident gesture—and promised solemnly to return soon.

For the next three hours we looked. Up and down that tiny street, in and out of airless shops that smelled of detergent and mold and rattled with giant fans. One by one a series of bent Jewish men and women listened to Lacie describe my play. I blushed when she called it fierce, and studied my feet when she said it was a blend of modern and ancient. I was flattered; I hadn't realized she had spent so much time thinking about the world I had made.

Then together Lacie and the shopkeeper would cluck and sigh over silk or muslin or lace, fingering bright prints, pacing the crowded, narrow aisles, sometimes holding a length up to my chest and sighing thoughtfully before issuing judgment: not quite.

I began to tire. It was just the same thing over and over. "Whatever," I started saying when she asked my opinion. "It looks good," and consternation came over her face. But I was hungry. It was past two, and we hadn't had lunch. Her fingers over the bolts of fabric were invasive, her careful consideration overly mannered, but I tried to bite back my impatience. I had never seen Lacie happy in this particular way before: utterly intent, critical, definite in her opinions and unafraid to share them. And—I had to keep reminding myself of this—she was doing this for me.

Finally she said, "Yes. This is it."

I stared silently. Surely she was joking. "Pink?" I croaked.

"Yes." She nodded happily, and the proprietor beamed. "And black silk for Adam." At my look of disbelief she laughed. "Just wait for it," she said. "You'll see."

For two weeks she didn't show me a scrap. She wouldn't even show me the pattern she had chosen; she had made a separate trip back to the city for that. About her, in class, there was a happy, distracted air.

Other things were changing too. When I passed Leo in the hall now he would give me a wordless high five. For an hour afterward I would glow with the force of the smack. In rehearsals he sometimes stood with his arms crossed, nodding, as I talked. Once, with Grogan and a few other guys, I heard him call me "so fucking smart," and though it wasn't clear he meant me to overhear, he seemed pleased when he caught me smiling. Before, his attention had slid over me, frictionless, but now it snagged.

Sometimes, too, when I stepped into Lacie's place to show her how to say her lines, his hand would linger on my arm. Longer than necessary, his hand would stay, holding me.

We choreographed the killing. We staged it. It was important to get it right; even Leo said so. I think he sensed that his reputation might survive getting onstage if this moment wasn't botched. But if everyone laughed—and I thought it nearly inevitable that they would—his murder would become a joke, and there would be a lifetime of people coming up to Leo in the hall, mocking his bug-eyed disbelief, his stagger backward, his slow crumple to the ground. He didn't want that. I didn't want that. So we practiced it again and again.

The key was the length of the stab. She had to gut him. She had to

drive the retractable knife up to the hilt, and it was essential, absolutely essential, that they lock eyes; it was essential, absolutely essential, that neither of them make a sound. If they groaned theatrically,
either of them, we were sunk; if they cried out, we were done. It must
be quiet.

But Lacie couldn't do it without laughing. Looking so deeply into
Leo's eyes tripped her up. Or the violence did. Or me watching. Yes:
me watching her kill undid her. Closer, I would say. Slower. Not that
slow. Faster. Do it again. And she would giggle, or drop the knife;
"Sorry, sorry," she would say, stepping away and wiping her face.

Finally I said, "Let me do it."

Silently she handed me the knife.

At this point in the play Adam thinks Eve is going to stay. He
thinks he's won. He is hiding the apple behind his back, and there's a
moment—I had explained this to them—when he realizes it's too
late, when his eyes register his mistake, but because he hesitates, she
can get the knife in.

As I drew close, his chipped blue eyes sharpened. In his Chucks he
was half a forehead taller than me, and his skin was an ivory white,
with delicate blue veins underneath. He smelled of clove cigarettes,
and, very faintly, the orange sherbet sold in the cafeteria.

I feinted. I stabbed. Up close his irises had a slow spoil of yellow.
"Like that," I said. "You've got to do it like that."

There was fire in my palm. In that moment I had actually wanted
him dead.

The night of the performance drew close. I kept asking about the costumes and Lacie kept saying "Don't worry" in a way that made me think that I should. It occurred to me that I had never actually seen Lacie sew anything. We were six days away, and then four, and then two, and still nothing.

I was standing on the stage, going over the script with Nathan, a bored and pimply sophomore who had agreed to run the lights, when they emerged. Lacie was in a pale pink slip edged with lace; she looked like a Greek goddess, fierce and frilled. Leo, in black silk trousers, was simply debonair. How had she convinced him to go shirtless? Their feet were bare. They looked like refugees from a champagne lunch.

Staggering back, swooning, I cried, "Oh my God, Lacie, they're beautiful, they're awesome, how did you know? You're a *genius*. When you picked out that fabric, I couldn't see at all how—"

"You hated it." Lacie smiled affectionately.

"Well, I was skeptical. But it's perfect. And Leo—"

"Leo—"

He had wandered to the edge of the stage and now sat with his legs dangling, his dear bony spine curved. We exchanged knowing smirks.

"He's perfect too," I declared, and for once Lacie didn't shrug off the compliment. Her whole face a rush of pleasure as together we looked at her boy.

Of the performance itself I remember very little, only the darkness of the auditorium and the blue-black stage coldly lit, the air smeary with the warm fuzz of listening bodies, and the way, when my play began, my heart dropped like a hanged man.

Never had I felt so violently in love with both of them. Sick with need, I watched, feeling something of what a gambler must feel watching his horse round the track, the soft, urgent moaning of *Oh, please,* the prayer: *Dear God, just get it done.*

And they did. They filled the bare, pockmarked stage with their long grace, and when they fought it was glorious: sneers and cruelties, Leo's pale rib cage flashing as he yelled, and Lacie with her crown of braided hair, circling and circling, trying to find a way out.

When she stuck the knife in him, no one laughed. The woman beside me shook her head. Like the sea the audience flowed away from me. They had been on Eve's side—they had thought her feisty, and laughed at her insults—but they hadn't wanted Adam to *die.*

Afterward, when our principal was introducing me to a school-board member, distaste blinked across the man's face before he blandly, warmly shook my hand. My sickness twisted; my jelly guts were exposed. Was this what it meant to write?

I wanted to see Lacie and Leo. I wanted to give them their flowers; I wanted to be swept up in their hugs. The school-board guy kept talking; then my mom wanted some pictures. By the time I escaped the clutch of grown-ups, I was frantic to find them.

They were at the end of the hall, back by the music classroom. Overjoyed, I hurried over, and even when I heard Leo say, "Why are you trying to cut off my balls, babe?" the sly jokiness in his voice stopped me from realizing what was going on.

"Guys!" I exclaimed. "You were amazing! So good!" I hugged each of them in turn, but their bodies were as stiff as boards. "Here, I brought you flowers."

Their faces were shiny with cold cream, and stoic like masks; I pushed first one, then another bouquet of lilies into their hands, which they accepted without looking away from each other.

"Guys?" I said. "What's going on?"

Darkly Lacie said, "Leo doesn't want to go to the Art Night party."

"Oh, no! Come!" I pleaded, and made a joke of pulling on his arm, but he shook me off without his eyes leaving Lacie's, and that's when I realized they were in deep.

"You always do this." There was iron in his voice.

"I don't 'always' do anything." Something patient, long-suffering, in hers.

"Yes, you do." He gestured angrily, and that's when I really should have left, but I didn't. "You just want me to be your stupid fucking doll!" he snapped.

"Oh, fuck off, Leo. Mr. Cowan wants everyone to come. I'm just trying to help you be polite."

"No, you're not, okay? You're just trying to control me, just like your mother tries to control your dad, okay? And it's fucking pathetic. You think I'm your little plaything."

There was another beat as we all stood in stunned silence. A strange huffing sound filled the air—Lacie was trying not to cry. I put a hand on her back.

"Excuse me," she gasped, shaking me off, and there was something touching in her formality, something poignant in her footsteps as she hurried down the hall. A weird power ticked through my veins. *You think I'm your little plaything* was a line from my play.

"Fuck!" he shouted at her retreating form. "She was my fucking ride!"

I stepped closer. There was no one else around. "I got you."

When we reached Leo's house Stevie Wonder was on the radio. I turned off the engine and together we listened to "Lovin' Cup." Tonight there was something obscene in the swerve of Stevie's voice. Leo bounced his fingers off the car door.

After the song he thanked me for the ride. But he didn't get out. I pictured the tiny huff of Lacie's back as she left us. "Well, so are you happy?" he asked abruptly.

"Happy?" It seemed a strange word.

He flicked his wrist. "Your play. Your big amazing play. Everyone loved it."

"Yeah. Yeah. I am." A big swell of feeling hit. I buried my face in my hands. "I think everyone hated it."

"No, no." He reached out but did not actually touch me. "They loved it," he said softly.

What I said next I can only attribute to the fact that we were alone. Right into his vulnerability I spoke. "Everyone is kind of weirded out by me."

"What do you mean?" His voice was gentle.

"I actually just felt really exposed during the play. Like, really exposed. Even though you guys were the ones onstage, and it was just, like, a bunch of parents, I felt so *exposed*." I reached for another word, but only visions of X-rays came. "It actually just made me feel really emotional."

"Maybe that's a good thing."

"It doesn't *feel* good."

Idly Leo made the automatic window go up and down. In the silence my words came echoing back to me, shaming me. I *was* emotional, but I was also performing my emotion for him.

"Look." He sealed the window tight. "Do you want to come inside?"

I glanced furtively at the dark second floor, the blue shutters like faces. "What about your mom?"

"She's cool."

And so I parked the car and followed Leo Kupersky up the drive. As he unlocked the front door I winced at the jangle of keys. "She's cool, she's cool," he repeated. "Don't worry."

Through the darkened living room we went, and upstairs to his room. While he plugged in his Christmas lights I slowly walked around, taking in the lava lamp, the crooked poster of Phish, the incense holder with its crumbly trail of ash. The tiny white lights twinkled.

We weren't looking at each other. Though everything was completely absurd—Leo and I alone in his bedroom at night—we were acting as if it were normal.

He sat on the bed and began to roll a joint. I crouched down by the bookshelf and pretended to be absorbed in studying his CDs. I was nearly trembling, and yet some other part of me felt calm, intent on memorizing everything, squirreling away each detail to feast on later.

"Rose." He had finished rolling his joint. "What are you doing over there?"

I turned to him and curtsied. "Just looking at your music."

He held up his joint. "You want?"

There really was nowhere else to sit but the bed. As I approached I must have flinched, for he chuckled, a lower sound in his throat; or maybe he was just amused at how far from him I sat. He had to lean over to pass me the joint.

All the time Lacie had been with us, I'd been finding excuses to touch him: letting my hand linger on his arm, or our shoulders bounce when we walked home. He had done the same: with the pressure of

Lacie keeping us apart, we had leaned toward each other. But now she was gone; now we were shy. On the bed, our knees faced out, two sets of headlights shining in different directions.

Carefully I snuck a glance at him. He was staring at the wall. Probably he was thinking about Lacie. We both spent so much time thinking about her; we were both caught on her hook, squirming, trying to win her attention. I knocked my leg against his. "Hey."

He didn't pull away; no, he leaned *into* me. Then he took my hand, and unfolded my fingers, and it was strange, the delicate way he put the roach down on the book; it was strange, the way he said, "Rose." He never called me by my name. He never kissed me; that really was the strangest part of it all.

Soft, delicate lips. He flicked his tongue over my teeth. His hand stroked my hair. For a moment I couldn't breathe, or move; then I threw myself at him, and cupped his head in my hand fiercely, sucking on his lips.

For a while we stalled out at kissing. But eventually, my shirt came off, his shirt came off, and I was on top of him and squirming around. I felt nothing beyond a kind of ruthless mechanical focus. I just wanted it done. There was this *thing* in his pocket, as if he had forgotten to take out his pen, but no matter how frantically I rubbed at it, he wouldn't take off his pants. Finally I said in a weirdly businesslike tone, "I was thinking we could have sex."

"Oh, do you want to have sex?" he asked brightly.

We were both trying not to break the dream of what we were doing, but when we were ready to start, when he had rolled the condom over his dick (I could barely look at it, I couldn't even think the word "dick"), when he had said, "Are you sure this is okay?" and after he had pushed inside me, so that I thought I would split, so that I thought *This can't be right, this can't be what people are so hyped about,* I began to laugh—I mean it was so absurd, so unwieldy, so ridiculous to put *that there,* and when he met my face, his eyes were at first worried, and then he was laughing too, we were both giggling, I mean, it was *ludicrous,* what we were doing, it was obscene. His bare ass moved above me.

Afterward tears welled in me. My eye sockets burned. I wasn't sad, or happy: there was just a tightness in my body, or a tightness in me. It was like he had turned me inside out for sport. Softly he patted the side of my face, and then his breathing—just as Lacie had said it did—got soft and even and regular. Keeping him with me was as futile as pinning a wave to the shore. Out, and out, and out he flowed, while I lay beside him, seething.

While he slept I stared at the ceiling. The tiles had five rows of five holes each: twenty-five. Across the ceiling, there were seven, eight, nine tiles . . . my cheeks were wet and cool with tears. Down there were six, seven . . . I tried to look without moving my neck. Maybe eight tiles. Which made . . . seventy-two times twenty-five . . . I carried the one . . . eighteen *hundred* holes above us.

When he woke something had shifted between us. The room was darker. I could feel him roll out from me, like the tide. He ran his hand along my back, but there was something disinterested in it. His touch was impersonal again.

"God," he muttered. "What time is it?"

I wriggled away. Found my underwear and pulled it up. Sticky damp. "No idea," I told him, and the coldness in my voice surprised us both. I, too, had gone away.

He sat up, put his feet on the floor, and squinted at his pager. "It's weird Lacie hasn't paged me."

The air snagged on her name. Quickly I pulled on my old training bra. Thrashed into my giant Belle & Sebastian T-shirt.

"I should go find her."

"Why? I'm sure she's fine."

He sighed. "I should go."

I crossed my arms. "What, you want to make sure she's not cheating on you?"

He shook his head. Pulled up his boxers. Stabbed by a thousand imaginary knives, I still yearned for his body as it disappeared beneath his clothes. His smooth, round thighs, the softness of his belly, those curling black hairs . . .

"That was my first time," I said loudly. "Did you know that? You didn't even ask. You just took my virginity. I hope you appreciate that."

He puffed out his cheeks. Looked at me beseechingly. Oh. He thought I'd be easy. He thought I'd be chill.

"You're a hypocrite," I announced.

He finished lacing up his shoes. "So are you going to give me a ride, or what?"

So it came to be that an hour after I had lost my virginity to the boy I had loved for over five years we were back in my mom's minivan trawling the empty streets for Lacie.

A fire began in me. Leo, languid in the passenger seat, was slumped and satiated, ready to be returned to Lacie. I had been had. It felt unbearable, this rage; it would consume me unless I gave it some *out*.

The stop sign came out of nowhere. I slammed the brakes, and we both jerked forward, then back. He looked at me, amazed. "This is stupid," I told him.

"What's stupid? Going to find my girlfriend?"

"She's not your *girlfriend*."

He gave me a little scoff of disbelief. "Yeah, she's my girlfriend. When are you going to finally accept that?"

I had made a fatal miscalculation. I had pushed too hard, over-played my hand, and thus the only thing to do was to double down on the strategy proven ineffective. "When you stop having a crush on me."

When he didn't answer right away, I plunged off a thousand-foot cliff into a sea of fangy monsters who tore at my flesh with tiny pointed teeth. "You *like* me," I said. "You're always flirting with me. Always."

"You seduced me." He sounded petulant.

"*What?*" I shrieked, and the car jerked dangerously. "*I* seduced *you*? *You* seduced *me*." It was like learning pronouns in Spanish, hysteri-cally.

"Oh, come on. You've wanted to fuck me since, like, *Peter Pan*. Everyone knows it."

A white sheet of rage dropped over my mind. An incredible tightness came over my skin, and my head burned, and the knives were still stabbing, the sea monsters were still feeding. Blue-hot electricity zapped up my cells. Everything in me radiant with pain. I was screaming but my mouth was closed. I was breathing but no oxygen was getting in. And then we came upon Yale Avenue.

Yale: a wide curve left, a sharp jag right, the long graceful fishhook that connected Swarthmore and Wallingford. Carved from rock, it was a joy to take fast, but tricky, especially if you were a new driver, and angry, and distracted.

"What am I supposed to do? Just because you have a crush on me doesn't mean I *owe* you anything."

The fog coming off the pavement grew thick at the bend, and his laugh distorted horribly in my ears. "You know that everyone knows, right? You're, like, completely obvious. You stare at me *all the time*."

Again and again the cops would ask me: *Are you sure there wasn't another car? A deer? There are deer in the woods right there. Maybe in the corner of your eye?* But the truth is that I turned the wheel. I had to stop the words coming out of his mouth.

There was a moment when I thought, I'm going to crash, and then I was crashing, juddering along the granite face of the rock, *jut, jut, jut,* and the *pop!* of the passenger-side airbag, and the horrible scrape of metal against rock, and then nothing. Silence. Leo lay bloodied up against me, a hot, heavy weight.

"Leo. Leo." He didn't move. He was punishing me. *"Leo."*

When I finally understood that he wouldn't answer, I opened my door and ran.

After dropping my bag on the table in the front hall, beside Lacie's piles of mail—she never seemed to go through it—and last week's paper—why she bothered to subscribe I could not understand—I stood dumbly in the dark, letting Cat spine against my shins. My head was paper-stuffed, my limbs noodly. I was strung-out, half-mad, and exhausted, and when I took off my jacket I could smell the sex and sweat beneath the leather.

Then Lacie came barreling from the bedroom in a flannel and black jeans, barefoot, with a fleck of Crest by her lip. When she saw me she slyly smiled: "*Someone* didn't come home last night."

Her trust enraged me. "Yep." I tugged on yesterday's stupid sweater dress.

"Was it fun?" she called from the kitchen.

There had been a frost that morning, the season's first. Leaving Ian's place, we had walked into a world of silver, every blade of grass etched. The sunshine dazzled, the sky was a fierce blue, and the wind whipped: weather that required an energetic response. At the subway, Ian had pressed my body to his and hugged me hard, his belly pushing into mine.

"Thanks, I guess," I had mumbled. I hadn't felt up to the weather. I might puddle out in a million directions; my insides might come up. I was weak, in danger of dissolving.

He had pressed me to him more gently. I kept waiting for him to issue some kind of verdict on the night before, but all he did was kiss my forehead and squeeze my hand.

"It was okay," I said now. "I'm so hungover, though."

"Oh, boo." Her head appeared around the wall. "That sucks. Want me to make you some toast or something?"

Suddenly I wanted to cry. "Just go," I said. "You'll be late."

When she had finally gone, in a flurry of tote bags and *Please, please promise you'll text if you need anything AT ALL*s, I collapsed on the daybed. Lacie had left her whiskey glass from last night, and a fruit fly hovered by its sticky lip. I knocked it away, and it buzzed back and settled on the sticky mess, rubbing its front legs together. Disgusting how its thorax heaved.

I lay back and let my thoughts swirl, giving myself over to *doing nothing* while my stomach clenched. Okay, I thought. This thing I've done, it's not great. It's not awesome. It might even, in its resemblance to a certain act of long ago, be called perverse. But it's not—it's not—gradually my skin shrank, tighter and tighter, hotter and hotter. When I stood up I found my insides had jellied. Rather than a midsection of muscle, I now had a tumbler of queasy grease sliding around.

Gingerly I moved from the daybed to the floor, from the floor to the chair, trying not to upset my quivery organs quaking over what I had swilled the night before. My insides were holding me hostage, slithering evilly around. *But*, I begged. *It's not about Lacie. It's about* him. *For so long, this thing between us. Last night proves it. He feels it too.*

My organs twisted and jabbed.

But she doesn't even care, I pleaded. Here I waltz in, smelling of sex, and she doesn't even ask his name. Maybe she already knows. Maybe Ian had texted her from the train. Maybe I was a cute toy to them, maybe they thought it was sweet how I got all mealymouthed around him.

My stomach cinched. A cold film of sweat coated my arms.

It's okay, I coached myself. *It's okay. You messed up a little, but it's okay*. I hunched over the toilet, mouth open, waiting. Cat watched with hazel eyes. Eventually I began to feel a bit melodramatic, and slunk back to the couch, totally defeated, unable even to vomit up my mistake.

For days I edged through the world as if a sudden move might slosh out my guts. Nausea burbled in me, dread and sickness, a hangover that didn't end.

It wasn't that I wanted him to get in touch so we could see each other again. No; nothing like that. I just wanted him to give me some clue about how he was feeling so I could know how I should be feeling. Of course we were never going to do it again. I had done it just to touch the darkness inside me. To know again the girl I was trying daily to summon to the desk. But we should just confirm this plan. We should agree on it. He should text me to tell me he wasn't going to text me anymore. God, how I wanted it.

"You still feel sick?" Lacie surveyed me slumped on the couch. "Maybe you have a stomach bug or something."

"Maybe. I honestly feel worse."

"You need tea." Without waiting for an answer she slipped into the kitchen. I heard water rushing into the teapot, and then the click and hiss of a burner. "God, who was this guy?" she called. "I didn't even know you were dating anyone."

She appeared in the doorway, a twist of ginger root in her hand, a quizzical expression on her face. Did she suspect? It was rare for Lacie to reference as conventional a category as "dating."

"I'm not. He was just this guy at the bar. He works at Credit Suisse." Shame thudded in me. On top of everything, I'd betrayed Franklin.

"Jesus. I hope he paid for the drinks, at least." She disappeared into the kitchen, and soon there came the steady whack of ginger dicing, a sound I had heard many times over the past few days. Her kindness was making me ill. I couldn't take much more of it.

That night she went out. Still no word from Ian. I paced around the apartment, looking for the millionth time at all Lacie's things, telling myself I wouldn't finish the tub of caramel gelato in the freezer, and then finishing it. As day became night I began to wonder if they were fucking *right now.* God. I finished off the blackberries, the brie, the sourdough.

Eros has always been structured by waiting. Anne Carson has something to say about this. Roland Barthes too. Such elegant, beautiful things! They almost make you wish you had a little bit of waiting to do. Real waiting's not like that. Real waiting's murder. Waiting! A half dozen times an hour I snatched at my phone, clicked it on, and growled. The very air hummed. Whatever I was doing—staring into space at my desk, staring into space on the daybed, staring into the blue-white space of the fridge—it was blackly bordered by the fact of waiting.

Torture: every minute that Ian did not text me confirmed that he was not thinking about me. Eventually my very actions seemed defined by this implicit indifference from him. It was the opposite of imagining someone is watching you. Someone was *not* watching me. Not wondering about me. Was probably totally absorbed in deeply meaningful art-making, and/or looking deeply into Lacie's eyes as they made passionate love. Regardless. Not thinking about me.

All I could do was think about him.

"Let's go home," he had said.

"Stand on my feet," he had said.

Under the soles of my feet, his cool skin and brittle tendons. "Oh, you're so wet," he had moaned, and bent me over the bed. Slid into me. The bone lust, the revelation. I played that tape again and again. I wore that tape out.

It was hot, my senior spring. The week they announced my play had won, the dogwoods bloomed and wilted, bursting whitely out one Monday and sagging from every branch by Friday. Tulips bloomed and shriveled; the forsythia had just one day of glory. All around me there were brown flowers.

Play rehearsals began, *official* rehearsals, for the staged reading that would happen downtown. I rode the R3 from Swarthmore to the city, back and forth, over and over. My face close to the glass, I watched scenes from my childhood slide by. Always, when we crossed the bridge that spanned the creek, I craned my neck to see the dappled water scattering light.

One pale sunny afternoon on the train I heard my character's voice. I *heard* it. Eve. She was speaking to me; she was telling me why the garden was paradise, and why she had to leave. From my bag I slipped my notebook and began to scribble, desperate not to lose any of the words as they fell into my mind. Eve's monologue. That was what my play needed. I was an idiot—a fool—not to have seen it before.

It was my first taste of that particular intoxication, the hours of drudgery at the desk rewarded with a song you simply wrote down. Eve told me how good it felt to want things. To take, the way a man took. Going for it, going *into* it. Wanting something. Desiring. Desiring and not giving a fuck. Just like a man. I wrote and wrote, and when I brought the pages in the next day, neatly typed, the director read the lines with his mouth agape. "This is incredible," he told me. "You've really got something."

———

Even though I had been literally *running* along Yale Avenue to flag down a car, the EMTs insisted on strapping me to a board. Over and over they shouted, "Your head! Your head! Do you want to be paralyzed?" I kept asking about Leo and they kept telling me my friend was fine.

As they carried me to the ambulance, hot pricks of tears stunned my eyes. The pink Philly sky, light-polluted and crossed by black branches, was like a Japanese woodblock print. It was so beautiful I thought I must be dying.

But at the hospital the young intern said I was fine, maybe a little whiplash, but fine. Lucky, really. No, she couldn't tell us anything about another patient, not even if we had been in the car together. By then my mom had arrived—she had come barreling into the ER, black fleece over a yellow nightie, flip-flops wetly kissing the linoleum— and when she saw my eyes roll back at the doctor's intransigence she slipped out, somehow found Leo's mom, and learned that he had already been released. Head wounds: they bleed a lot even when they don't go deep. Concussion? I asked. Maybe, the nurse shrugged. He was knocked out. But he should be fine.

Well. We drove home in a tentative silence, as if cringing and waiting for another blow. In the front hall my mom hugged me extra-close and I said, "Ah! Ah! My neck!" and she said, "Oh, my sweet baby girl."

Not until the next morning did she ask, "So, what were you and Leo doing driving around at one in the morning?"

I was lifting my cereal spoon high, so that I wouldn't have to bend my neck; I must have looked like a toy soldier. Without turning my head I said, "I was giving him a ride home."

"Where was Lacie?"

"She didn't want to go to the party. She had a headache."

My mom sat down at the table and looked at me a long time. Not like a police inquisitor, but rather in a camera's searching pan. Wondering where her daughter had gone. I didn't mind. I was wondering the same thing. According to our usual script I should be psychologizing *why* Lacie had skipped the cast party, and how that had made Leo feel, and why I had gone, and how I had missed that curve, and why we were so lucky. Between my mother and me there usually existed an abundance of words, but I had scared myself, stepping into this new skin. I was too frightened to speak from it.

At school, reaction was surprisingly mute. A minor car accident that didn't involve drugs or alcohol or serious injury simply did not interest anyone, though Lacie, who had been mostly ignoring me, came up long enough to say, "I'm glad you're okay." As if by agreement, Leo and I ignored each other.

The pain in my neck was exquisite. Any tilt or lean set off shuddering spasms. If I made a sudden turn, I saw stars. I looked fine, though; the pain was private. I kept thinking darkly that the doctor had been wrong, that I had injured my cervical spine in some invisible, permanent way. No one could see the damage I had done. But I knew it was there.

So things might have stayed—simply put, no one seemed that interested in the circumstances of our accident—had *The Swarthmorean* not run a small item in its police blotter the following Friday:

EMTs responding to a 911 call found an immobilized vehicle on the side of Yale Avenue at approximately 1:12 A.M. early last Sunday morning. The driver did not appear to be intoxicated, and a passenger, treated for minor injuries at Crozer-Chester Medical Center, was soon released.

The following day, my mom came back from the Swarthmore Co-op with a funny expression on her face.

As she slung the milk onto the fridge's top shelf and tumbled apples into the crisper, she kept darting glances over to the couch, where I sat ramrod-straight, gingerly turning the pages of *A Delicate Balance*. Finally, folding a canvas bag, she announced, "I saw Janet just now."

"Yeah? What did she say?"

"Actually, she didn't talk to me."

"She didn't see you?" Lacie's mom and my mom were not exactly friends, but they were friendly.

Deliberately, my mom stacked the remaining canvas bags in a lumpy tower. She petted them as if they were alive. "Honey. I don't know how to say this. But if there's anything you want to tell me, I'm here to listen. It can feel so terrible to hold things inside."

"Did she *ignore* you? Like, on *purpose*?"

She faced me. "I'm not saying that. I'm just saying, if there's anything you need to tell me. Or maybe there's something you need to tell Lacie? Is that it? It might make you feel better."

From the couch I pushed off like a rocket and began to pace. While my mom had cooked for me these past seven days, I had just sat there. While my mom had put away the groceries, I had just sat there. I had let her take care of me, and now her insinuations felt like a second violence.

"It's really beautiful, how you've been friends for so long. . . ."

"*Okay.* I get it, Mom. Stop."

She took a deep, shaky breath. "I'm just saying. This is a significant *time* in your life. So you might want to think about what kind of person you want to be."

Knocking on that cornflower-blue door with its tatty wicker wreath of soft cotton flowers, I felt all the years of my knocking run through me. This is *home*, too, I thought, and not even the open dismay on Janet's face erased the feeling.

"Luce!" she called, her eyes fixed on me.

When Lacie appeared, hair damp with grease, sweatpants food-stained, face smushed from sleeping, her arms were crossed. "What?" she said. "I've got nothing to say to you."

We stared deep. It was weird to think of her becoming a stranger. Yet she already looked strange to me. New creases in her face. A new stain on her incisor. "Okay," I whispered.

A silence like the silence of a wave before it breaks. If she had invited me in at that moment, I would have wept; I would have sat on her bed and told her everything, and I know, *I know*, she would have listened, and told me it was all right. I think—I like to think—we could have found each other in that moment.

But instead her gaze hardened. "I heard the party ended early."

"Yeah, we ended up not even going—"

"But wasn't the accident at one in the morning? That's what the paper said."

I didn't move.

"Huh?" She wiped away a tear. "What were you guys *doing* all that time?"

She jerked back into the dark of the house and, real quick and neat, slammed the door. The brass knocker landed a beat behind the door with a dull thud. I stared at the cornflower wreath, gently rocking, then pulled loose a stalk of ersatz straw. All the way home, I mangled it in my pocket.

Our senior year, we didn't talk. We didn't sit together at lunch. We had one class together—Social Studies—and we sat on opposite sides of the room.

Every so often I would forget and smile at her in the halls, or wave or say *What's up,* and the look that she gave me every time was one of utter confusion. As if she couldn't figure out who I was; as if she was wondering if I had mistaken her for someone else. Behind her eyes, none of our history.

I could never forgive her for that.

Sometimes I think this was when the trouble started. Sure, I had idolized her before then, but most of us have a friend we admire when we are young: someone just a little bit cooler, a little bit stronger and more daring. Then we grow up, and see through them; they lose their magic when their faults become clear.

But I never got to diminish Lacie. She became instead a glimmer. A dream I could almost remember. I spent senior year looking for her. Listening for her: she was a refrain, the wisp of a pop song, a hook in my head. There she was, walking with Kathy, safety pins up the sleeve of her sweater. There she was, among Grogan and the two Steves. She was wearing more black. She had joined the literary magazine. A photo of hers was hanging in the art wing. Then, one day, with Leo: they had patched things up. All winter I watched them, stewing. Thinking: they have erased me. What we made together is gone, rubbed out like chalk.

I won the playwriting contest; I got into Harvard; my parents announced we were moving away. My father's firm had given him an option of early semi-retirement, and they'd always wanted to live in the country. After June, I wouldn't be coming back to Swarthmore anymore.

I suppose that is part of why we didn't patch things up. But maybe some summer vacation wouldn't have made a difference. Bad blood between girls tends to stay bad.

ISABEL WEST

College Application Essay

DOUBLE CONSCIOUSNESS AND ME

There is something called double consciousness, where you are aware of yourself as a normal person but also that people see you in a category like black. It's like there's two of you and it's very painful. WEB Du Bois in his bestselling book *The Souls of Black Folk* was the first person to note this phenomenon and give it a name. When I read *The Souls of Black Folk* I really identified with it. This is because even though I am not African American I am a woman and also Jewish. People put me into categories too.

When my boyfriend asks me why I am being so emotional, is it because of my period, when the theater director at school asks for boys to carry the stage sets, when my parents won't let me walk around in Central Park by myself, that's sexism. These are people who see me as a woman. In addition there are things that are not a direct impact on my life but still send me a message about what our society thinks a woman is. Where I live, New York City, there are a lot of billboards with women on them but not that many women in positions of leadership, like the mayor, for instance. What kind of message does that send a young woman like me?

I come from a long line of strong independent women. My mom and dad met at Harvard Business School. My dad says my mom was even smarter than him and got higher grades. They got married and had my sister and me. My mom was not happy in her career so she chose to stay home and raise my sister and me. It was her choice. That's what feminism is: a choice. She raised us to be strong independent women, and it worked. My sister is going to Columbia.

I want to always follow my path. Right now my path is to go to [insert name of school here], be a premed, and then go to medical school while pursuing my dream of being a model. When I'm a breast cancer surgeon I will also design a line of sportswear for active women who want to feel good and strong even if they have had cancer. There will be swimwear for women who still have their real breasts or reconstructive surgery after cancer and also swimwear for women who have had mastectomies, but choose not to have reconstructive surgery because that was their choice and I will respect it. I also want to get my PhD in history.

I'm going to be honest. When we were assigned *The Souls of Black Folk* in Social Studies class at first I didn't want to read it because it seemed boring and like it was written a long time ago (1903). But after reading it I see that there are actually a lot of similarities. Not much has changed. We all want to be free to be seen just as a normal person which is actually a very rare thing when you think about it. To be seen.

Dear Isabel,

Thank you for sending a new draft of your college essay, which I found powerful and moving. I especially like what you wrote about different messages you've received about what it means to be female. Do you think you could be even more clear about how these messages affect your sense of self?

Your writing about your mother is beautiful. Have you ever talked to her about her choice?

I think this represents a big step forward for you with your college essay. You're writing more personally about your individual life experience. Do you know what the word "intersectionality" means? If you want to keep Du Bois in your paper (which I think you should—it's terrific!), you might want to look up this word. Maybe you can write a paragraph about it for me before our next meeting?

Keep up the good work,
Rose

Dear Rose,

Thank you for sending along your new draft, which was an absolute pleasure to read. You've finally found a way to drill down to who Lacie is as a character. I can see her so much more vividly—you've managed to capture so many of her quirks. And the scenes from her point of view give the novel real depth. They burn and sing. She has come brilliantly alive.

Another thing I love: in this draft, adolescence, and all the shifts it brings, is even more minutely rendered. The intensity of the friendship between the two girls is finally caught in all its nuance and complexity. Fantastic work.

I think we're getting very, very close. As a final step, can you elucidate more clearly the narrator's mental map? To sleep with your best friend's boyfriend is such a radical act of betrayal. Help us understand her state of mind. I think that will help complicate this tale of feminine backstabbing, and give your draft the final polish it needs.

Really looking forward to discussing this with you!

All the very best,
Portia

I read the letter once. Twice. And then again and again, as if it might dissolve from my screen. I couldn't believe it. Four years I had been trying this and that, inventing and reinventing, trying to get somewhere, and finally, finally, I had gotten it right. I had scored. She loved this draft. When we talked on the phone, I could hear the energy, the relief in her voice. We were back.

There was only one hitch: *Complicate this tale of feminine backstabbing.* I wasn't sure I liked this note. Why did we all have to stand shoulder to shoulder, anyway, like some Dove commercial or Beyoncé video? Wasn't this injunction to female solidarity just evidence of how generally weak and fucked women were? Only the powerless had to band together.

Besides, the truth was that I liked Ian. What else to say about it? He intoxicated me, just as Leo had, and it's not that my actions had *nothing* to do with Lacie, but I was also in the thrall of lust. Why was that not reason enough? A guy who desires madly, who can't help himself, who commits betrayals and risks everything, is legible to us—why was the same thing either incomprehensible or pathological when it showed up in a woman? Why *couldn't* it just be about sex?

No, I thought. This was a note of Portia's I would reject. No need to clarify my narrator's "mental map." It was already so gloriously clear.

Then, just like that, almost too fast, though I had been waiting and waiting for it, Ian wrote. Picking up my phone to see if Isabel had replied, I saw the text for which I'd yearned:

Dinner tomorrow night?

He chose Song, a Thai restaurant in Park Slope so unhip there was no chance Lacie would ever grace its doorway, a fact I pointed out to him not long after we had ordered our noodles and curry.

Ian looked at me carefully. "The way I feel," he announced, "is that I like Lacie, and I like you. I like both of you."

"Okay. Congratulations. But that's not what I asked."

Steaming plates of greasy noodles arrived. Ian stabbed a big flat fat one and said, "Are you sure?"

"Yeah." I was annoyed, and my annoyance felt good, because it meant we were *in relation,* two semantic steps from *in a relationship.* "I was just pointing out that you chose a place where Lacie would never go and her friends would never go."

"That"—he stabbed another noodle—"sounds like a question to me."

We ate in silence. I was still so awed by his beauty—I mean, it was absurd, him out to dinner with *me*—but something about it made me want to outfox him. "Do you get off on this?" I asked.

"Off on what?"

"Cute," I told him, and that did it: a little smile curled around his lips. I felt as victorious as all the times I'd wrested laughs from him.

"So," I tried again. "You and Lacie have an open relationship."

He looked at me, bemused. "Is that what she said?"

"I'm surmising. I'm an optimist."

"Here is the way I feel." He seemed to be into announcements, as if he had processed everything, *figured everything out*. "It's not like things are open or closed between us, it's not like we've talked or not talked about it. It's like—she doesn't seem to operate by those kinds of categories. So I'm not going to either."

I nodded rapidly. "That makes total sense."

"I just feel like, if I brought it up, she might look at me like, *I don't know what you're talking about*."

I laughed. "Yeah, totally."

He put his hand on my arm. Oh, the heat. *I like Lacie, and I like you*. What bullshit. What a delicious steaming hunk of bullshit; how easy everything would be, though, if it were true. How simple. Maybe, for him, it was. Maybe, for me, it could be.

When the bill came, he said what he had said before: "Want to go home?"

As we were walking down the slope, a light rain began to fall. It misted the cones of orange streetlight and collected along Ian's hair in tiny sparkling droplets. In the windows of duplexes, there were rooms of yellow and blue light, a woman pacing with a phone at her ear, a man setting down a brown paper bag of groceries. Ian was talking, either about Nietzsche or about his childhood superheroes; I couldn't tell which. I liked him draining himself of words, draining himself into me.

He lived at the bottom of the slope, right before it crested upward again. Gowanus: the point of the V, where brownstone Brooklyn sours into industrialization before becoming bourgeois again. Now that I wasn't thick with whiskey I could really look at where he lived:

the stoop's painted red steps and black railing, the building's long carpeted hall, which smelled faintly of vegetable soup, and the cool gray cleanness of his one-bedroom.

Quick as a lynx he slipped off his shoes and plugged in a strand of white Christmas lights. The tangerine kitchen fell into dappled relief. I stood by the door.

"There's bourbon in the hutch." He had his back to me, rinsing out glasses in the sink. "If you want some."

Carefully I shrugged off my coat and hung it on a hook beside his Carhartt. I unlaced my shoes. Everything in the apartment was deliberate, and it made me deliberate, too, as if I were being filmed.

As I was unhooking the pantry's latch he came up behind me and pressed against me, his arm around me, his hand cupping my breast. As his other hand slid down my jeans, he nuzzled my neck. I arched against him. "Come on, get the whiskey," he muttered. "Get it," and when I leaned forward, he plunged his fingers deep into me.

I was pinned. Impaled like a butterfly. *Study me,* I thought. *Push me.* Pink gauze fell over my mind and strange soft pants came from my mouth. He drew my blouse over my head and I lifted up my arms like a child. My breasts, freed from their bra, were one-eyed fish, pink and dumb. He unzipped my jeans. I reached out and undid his belt, and he yanked down my underwear.

Then he had me by the neck, bending me forward. Then he was gliding into me. My head was nearly in the hutch. There was no condom, we were definitely not using a condom, but what the fuck, who did he fuck anyway? Lacie? I'd take that risk.

Fuck me with the same cock, I thought. *Just* try *to knock me up. Just try. If these ancient eggs get whammed off a one-night stand, I'll dress up as the goddess of fertility with corn sheaves next Halloween.*

"We should use," he said, "a condom," and then he scooped me up, carried me to the bed, and poured me out so he could stuff his cock into my mouth. It was that kind of night. He fed his fingers into my mouth. He fed his asshole into my mouth. I tongued it like I was getting a grade. It tasted peppery and dry. Later I sat on his face, and his fingers dug into my hips as he worked me over with his soft, marvelous tongue, his *genius* tongue, and I moaned until I caught sight of myself moaning in the mirror on his closet door, my tiny belly swelling out, my cheeks flushed. I looked beautiful. His fingers dug deep into the flesh of my hips, and his face was lost between my thighs. "Do you see yourself?" he hissed from somewhere deep in my cunt. "Do you see what I'm doing to you?"

Later, when we were fucking again—with a condom—we stared deep into each other, and he looked so old to me. His eyes were deep and sunken, with fine lines around them, and his face kept wavering between human and idol. A stone god. I sensed the evil in him.

When it was over I curled up with my head on his shoulder. I wanted to tell him that I had felt his spirit, that I knew it was not entirely benevolent, but I couldn't find the words. Finally I said, "You're very masculine."

"Yeah." He sounded neither flattered nor surprised. "I've got a lot of dude energy."

I thought of him walking across his canvas or standing in the doorway of the kitchen in the Barn. Watching me. Watching me from the shore.

"I tend to be drawn to really feminine women," he added. "I don't know what it's about exactly." He was talking up to the darkness above his head.

"What does that mean, 'feminine'?" I said. "What's feminine?"

"You know."

But I didn't. Was feminine pliant, was it docile, was it passive? I was sure he meant something good, but everything I remembered from Hinduism and yoga sounded lame. "Do you think I'm feminine?" I asked.

"Yeah." He stroked my eyebrows. "You're very feminine."

So began a period of fucking. Fantastic fucking. We still talked—I'll get to the talking—but conversation was no longer the point. The point was me naked in his bed. The point was him opening my knees like a book. Devoting himself to my cervix, pounding it with three curled fingers, refusing to touch my clit no matter how I begged, until his blunt force spread me into shivery, crumbly coming.

What he liked was to push me just past where I could stand it. Past enjoyment, where my mind went blank and my body limp, and strange words like *no* and *stop* came out of my mouth. "You don't mean them, do you?" he asked, and I said I didn't, though sometimes when we were fucking hard I'd wish desperately for it to end.

Sometimes, too, when his face was between my legs, I would skim below the lip of an orgasm, that elusive short-circuiting so close but sealed away. To reach it, I'd think of Lacie: her breasts, her sprawled out before me, her offering herself up. I'd imagine doing to Lacie what Ian was doing to me.

Later in the night, sitting on the toilet to pee, I'd remember what I'd wanted, and it would rise up before me, garish and obscene. I had never thought of other women this way. I didn't want to *date* her. I just thought of fucking her. And then, only when Ian was fucking me.

"You're like this strange combination," he said one night. "You get very shy, like this little girl who's never seen a cock before, and then you go crazy, you can't get enough. You're actually so sexual. You have these really strong orgasms."

I should have rolled my eyes, but all I said was, "Really?" I liked him telling me what he thought of me. It was like peering into a mirror usually hidden. "You mean stronger than other women?"

"Yeah. I feel your pulse. It's like, *Wham! Wham!* Your whole body shakes. And afterward you're all soft and compliant." Tenderly he touched my face. "It really gets to me."

He did always want to fuck me right after I came. Sometimes I pushed him away—I wanted to be with the waves echoing through my body—but my feeble resistance only brought him on more.

"Good," I told him. "I want to get to you."

Meanwhile, Lacie and I played a round of psychological warfare so excruciatingly subtle it resembled in all essential details normal life. She went to work, I went to work, and in the evenings we cooked large sprawling vegetarian meals with too much oil and cheese. Over kale and squash we offered up precise observations about the subway: the "rapey" vibe of the tunnel between the F and L at Fourteenth Street, the crowded Union Square platform, the smell of wet coats in a humid car.

Sometimes, talking to her, I would remember how I had thought of her, and I would blush or look away. Eating her salad, or some of her fresh-baked sourdough, I'd feel creepy and ashamed. The memory of my fantasies seemed to have nothing to do with our life together. Disconnected from reality, the images floated in the air between us, untethered, extreme.

But it helped that Lacie never stirred when I came home late from Ian's. She never pushed when I said I had been out with friends, though she knew I knew almost no one in the city. She didn't ask whether I had met someone, which made it easier to split off these two parts of myself.

Basically we didn't talk about our dating lives, so the fact that our dating lives involved the same man became irrelevant. We contented ourselves with sly cultural observations and self-conscious rants; we risked nothing; we essentially did stand-up comedy for each other, there on the fourth floor of the only apartment building on Albemarle Road. Did this count as normal? I couldn't decide. The only normal we had ever had was when we were ten years old, infinite and bound to each other. Everything since then had been an attempt to recover our Edenic past.

Ian and I started going to Applewood, a small farm-to-table joint with painted green tables, wide-planked floors, and silvery photographs of Vermont sheep. A fire crackled in the fireplace, and servers in white cotton aprons circled. Applewood was not exactly fashionable, but the meat was humane, the cocktails seasonal, and the mood genteel.

Ian always wanted to meet late. It took me a while to figure out this was because he waited each night to hear from Lacie first. I was his backup. I didn't care. We'd sit at the roughhewn bar and order drinks from a man dressed as a Mennonite. Ian always had whiskey, and I a cocktail. Once the bartender started recognizing us, he gave us pours from the top shelf, mostly scotch that tasted like dirt. Peat, we said knowingly, and kept sipping, until we tasted not dirt but green hills and cold mornings, wool sweaters and wood fires. We sipped and talked of warm places. The yellow slippers he wore came from Morocco. He said, "You'll see, the souks there are insane," and I thought I'd nearly die from the promise inside *you'll see.*

Our Mennonite comped us olives, crostini, and once a liver pâté. Dense flavor bombs, food not to satiate but enthrall. The bill came handwritten, always shockingly large, and sometimes Ian paid and sometimes I did. I sensed it was easier for him, but I never minded slapping down my card. It felt powerful to pay. To spend to the point where it scared me.

We talked about the next day's work, what he hoped to do in the studio, what I hoped would happen at the desk. We talked about art. We talked about philosophy. We talked about Aristotle, and kink, and will to power; we talked about tattoos and vegetarianism and UFOs. We built a little life together, a rhythm. I didn't ask him any more questions about Lacie, and he didn't tell me any more answers. We didn't have to say her name anymore. Simply being together invoked her.

"You've got your dish? Okay. Let me give you one more hug."

The gentle clang of ceramics against coat buttons.

"Okay, good night, lady."

"See you Thursday."

Ding of elevator, slam of door. Sophie, the last guest, gone. Another Shabbat dinner done.

I had come to love these nights, the one stretch where I let what I was doing with Ian drop away. The rest of the week I held myself rigid, ready for a trap, my wrongness a foul skin around me, but when the light on Friday afternoon grew long and mournful, and Lacie began to race around, stirring the soup pot, setting the table, and I trailed after her, helplessly repeating, "Just tell me what to do . . ." the world beyond the windows dissolved. Ian faded to abstraction. There were prayers and candles and eating, the easy, ready laughter of women who plainly adored Lacie and so wrapped me in their affection, thought I was worthy of their attention simply because I knew her. No: because she had chosen me. Assistant mistress of Shabbat.

And as much as I loved the dinners, I loved afterward almost as much, when Lacie would return from escorting the last guest out and collapse onto the couch. I'd get the wine from the table, and we'd sit around, lazily trading tidbits from the night.

Tonight we sat in contemplative silence for a bit, until Lacie chuckled softly to herself. "Well, you've got to hand it to Sophie. First she was bored with her husband, now she's bored with her boyfriend."

"Wait, what are you talking about?"

Lacie leaned forward to scoot her glass onto a paperback. "I know, right? It's crazy. I probably shouldn't talk about it, but yeah, basically Sophie's been having an affair for years."

"An 'affair'?" I hadn't known we were old enough to have affairs. I hadn't known our generation *believed* in affairs. Wasn't the idea that you were supposed to file for nonmonogamy in a procedure that I had always vaguely conflated with filing for bankruptcy? You were supposed to talk about it, at least. We were the talk-about-it generation. "It's been going on for *years*?"

"Well, Aaron's really bad at sex. He's totally hung up on his mother."

"Wait, this has to do with his *mother*?" She sounded so cavalier.

"Don't you remember? How Sophie said there was some thing?"

It took me a moment, but once I did, the memory came back like a chill, Sophie saying, "You can feel this old way of being *haunting them*," and Lacie and I ashamed, avoiding each other's eyes.

"Oh, right," I said now. "But does Sophie think he's like, literally in love with his mother?"

"Something like that. He's just not that into sex. Who knows. Don't repeat this, by the way. I mean, lots of people know, but it's supposedly a secret."

"Oh my God. Oh my God." I was shaking my head like a stunned idiot. "And here I was, thinking that her life was basically perfect. I was *envying* it."

Her life sure looked perfect. She was tiny like a doll. She worked at *The New Yorker*. Regularly she moderated panels and interviewed intellectuals and wrote wry, precise blog posts. Three years ago, she had married the son of a famous Conceptual Minimalist, and together they had bought a two-bedroom and filled it—or so I imagined—with books and limited-edition prints and strange liquors in beautiful bottles from distant lands. To envy her showed no imagination. It was stupid. I tried not to do it, but I couldn't help envying *Lacie* for how much Sophie liked her, how clearly Sophie enjoyed being her friend. Especially given that Sophie had basically rejected me.

Lacie cocked her head at me. "Maybe it is perfect."

"She's having an affair!"

Lacie shrugged. "Well, people do the best with the lives they have. Sophie gets to have her *needs met,*" Lacie used air quotes, "or whatever, and Aaron gets to have this beautiful wife who adores him. It's not ideal, but under the circumstances, I think it's fine. I mean, it sounds like Aaron is just not a very sexual person. For whatever reason."

I tried to imagine what Aaron looked like. I pictured him moist around the mouth, with dark hair that fell into gelled ridges. Finally I said, "I don't know if I believe in someone just not being a sexual person."

"What do you mean? You don't think that's a thing?"

"Not really. Not unless there's been some kind of damage. Which it sounds like maybe there was."

"Like, anyone who's not super into sex must be kind of messed up?"

There was something wrong with Lacie tonight; she was wound up. But I stuck to my guns: "It sounds awful, but yeah. I don't think someone's just born without a sex drive. I don't buy it."

"I don't really like it," she whispered.

"You don't?"

She winced. "Is that horrible to say? It's fine. But it's just—it gets a little boring. I feel like we're all supposed to be these enlightened women who are totally sexually fulfilled, but sometimes I just think, Eh. Couldn't we just read a little? Or go to sleep?"

As someone who had endured several periods of involuntary celibacy, Lacie's attitude was incomprehensible to me. She sighed. "I mean honestly, sometimes I just wish Ian would be more chill."

"You mean about sex?"

"Yeah, kind of. Is that terrible?"

"No. Wait, what's he like?"

Did she suspect? Hesitation played over her face. Primly she said, "I'm sure he wishes we were having sex more often. But sometimes I just don't want to be touched."

A weird triumph snaked through me. Lacie was bad in bed. All my life I'd envied her coolness, the way she never chased men. But—I thought, astonished at the simplicity of it—it's because she doesn't need it. A million bucks said she just lies there, her big gray eyes wandering around the room. No wonder my appetite drove Ian mad. No wonder we couldn't stop.

"I get that," I said slowly. "Sometimes you want your space."

"Yeah, and I mean, maybe eventually he'll go fuck someone else, but whatever. I don't really care. I feel kind of European about it."

"You feel kind of European about it," I repeated slowly.

"Yeah, I mean, it's not like I would want to *know*. But we haven't really talked about exclusivity. It's just obvious that what's happening between us is very intense. It feels big." She looked at me urgently, with that razored stare that she unleashed sometimes, a laser beam shooting out from her usual vagueness.

Probably—I realize now—she only wanted to see if I understood what she meant. But in that moment all her words doubled and stretched. What was she trying to tell me? That she knew? That she didn't mind? Lacie had always worked by implication and discretion, high-stakes negotiations conveyed through metaphor. By her usual standards, this was downright direct.

"It feels big, but you don't care if he's dating someone else." I had to be sure. I held all the muscles in my face absolutely still.

"Well, not *dating*." She frowned. "But sleeping with, sure. It's just, obviously we're significant to each other. It's not like the occasional fuck is going to change that. Whatever's happening between us, it's big." A girlish smile played on her lips.

"You like him." In my voice, accusation. What about all those times she had complained about him? What about the way he never came over? How *big* could it be, especially if she didn't mind "someone else" sleeping with him?

"Yeah." She shook her head, still marveling. "I guess I really like him."

*Y*ou like that, Ian said. *You stupid slut, you like that. You look so good with a cock in your mouth.* That's what my best friend's boyfriend was saying to me. So I bought a bottle of water, and hummus in a tiny tub. I ordered takeout, with plastic silverware, then got some murdered mammal at Applewood. Meanwhile, kids all over this city were taught to the test. Meanwhile, kids all over this city got private tutoring. *You like to be bossed, don't you? You like to be told what to do.* At parties plastic cups with crenulated edges were thrown away, bleached napkins smeared with inky wine were thrown away, books were purchased to be thrown away. Meanwhile, Ervin West was writing generous checks to politicians who would further wreck the earth and his daughter's body, and the feeling he had in the midst of all this wreckage—I would bet money on it—was *I wish I had more control.*

Sometimes, while walking, Ian would slip his hand around the nape of my neck, and squeeze and grip my head there, and I would feel myself completely under his control, as simply as a dog belongs to its master. A great billowing weakness would blow up from my stomach, a wave of sexual feeling so strong I would often stumble and he would catch me by the grip of his five fingers. I was enthralled then, a cat humming, its spine arched against a human hand; I desired him, because I could feel how much he desired me; I was thrown deliciously, girlishly back against myself.

I began to feel—I suppose the word is paranoia, but it felt more like an acceleration of reality, as if my life were a toy top, spinning so fast that even knocking the floor or bumping a wall did not slow it down.

Subtle mistakes proliferated, though it was impossible to say whether they were actually proliferating or whether I was simply paying more attention. For instance, usually when I arrived in the snowy vestibule of the West manse, no one was there to greet me. I would step tentatively into the front hall, calling out "Hello?," my thin voice sounding especially weak and watery in the artificial hush of the house: the silence of the Wests' condo, of every new-construction condo, was the space-signal purr of the computerized home. There might be no one home or a dozen family members secreted away in their own wings or the whole clan lying bloodily murdered behind the kitchen door. In that indifferent hum, who could tell?

But today, when the elevators disgorged me into the lap of that white credenza, Isabel was waiting for me, arms crossed. "It's good you're here," she announced ominously, and turned on her heel.

Rather than athletic apparel, she wore a blue Oxford shirt and dark stonewashed jeans. Her hair was pulled up in a messy bun, and a tiny gold necklace winked from her narrow neck. As she padded along the shadowy hall, past the recessed spotlights that lit up formal portraits of the family—I caught a glimpse of Rachel West's lunar baby bump, cupped by her ringed hand—I decided tonight Isabel looked like an academic or an architect, the lead in a romantic comedy before she lets down her ponytail.

The housekeeper—I still hadn't learned her name, because Isabel called her something like Ooma, which I was 97 percent sure was a pet name, and yet no one had thought to tell me her real name— brought me a dinner plate of three ravioli with a side of grilled asparagus. This had never happened before: the second mistake. When I stammered out a polite protest, Isabel said, "You're always eyeing my food, and it makes me feel weird."

Oh. Isabel was more observant than I thought. Or maybe she was simply being pragmatic. She wanted me fueled up: we were obviously in for a long one. The word from the top—Ervin—was that the current draft had to go. Complete gutting. Apparently Isabel had shown him the same draft she had sent me, and he had announced that he didn't like any of it—not Du Bois, not the line of swimwear, and especially not the "personal stuff."

"He told me family stuff is *private*," Isabel said dolefully, and I flashed on the time I had seen Rachel West, she of the high grades in business school, trailing sadly down the long hall, looking pensively at her portraits.

"And what do you think about that? Do you agree?"

"It'll just be easier to start over." With her fork Isabel sliced a ravioli open and smashed out a puree of pumpkin. "But the thing is, we don't have much time. So I thought you could type"—she nudged her laptop toward me—"and I'll talk."

During training someone had asked "where the line was" between helping and cheating, editing and writing, and rather than address the rich literary tradition of this question, Griffin had nodded sagely. "Personally, I never type anything for them. My hands never touch their keyboard. But you'll have to find what's right for you."

I had vowed, then and there, that I, too, would never type a single word for my students, but when I broke this news to Isabel she argued, "No, I'd still be the one *writing* it, you're just *typing*," and when I said, "I'm not going to be your scribe," she said, "But we have so much to do!" and so I said, "*You* have so much to do. Not me, *you*. I already wrote my college essay, a long time ago," and then she banged her fist so ferociously that I immediately relented, saying, as if I had simply misunderstood her before, "Oh! You want me to type for you? Sure, I'd be happy to type."

It did feel wrong, I'll grant Griffin that. "Umm." Isabel peered expectantly at me, perhaps a mite disappointed that my fingers were not already flying over the keys. "So what do you think I should write about?"

"Do you still want to write about feminism?"

A shy, baffled nod. "It's just like, I know what I want to say, but I just can't, like, *say* it."

"What do you want to say?"

"Just like . . ." She looked at me blankly. "I don't know! Just like, how I'm a feminist, why I'm a feminist. That kind of stuff."

"So why are you a feminist?"

"Because it's not fair!" She screwed up her face in exasperation. "It's not fair! Girls *are* equal to boys!" Then she gave a wolfish grin. "We're actually so much better."

I felt bad for her, I really did. Who could say you were having an experience, a *life experience,* if all that came out of your mouth were the same things showing up on the internet?

"Right, but that's not an essay topic. You need to think about what you want to say about *yourself.*"

"I don't have anything to say about myself," she admitted in a small voice.

We looked at each other then in a kind of mute panic, the same look I caught in my own eyes when, having done absolutely nothing at the desk for an hour, I got up to brush my teeth a third or tenth time.

"God, what is the point of a college essay anyway? Why do they even care? Why can't they just like look at my grades and *know* I'm a good person?"

I didn't laugh. "Well, you know, they want to get a sense of who you are. You just need to tell them something about yourself. It almost doesn't matter what, as long as it's honest. Authentic. Who you *really* are."

But we were past all that. She looked sickened by my platitudes; she knew that her situation was impossible, that the most slick piece of writing she would ever produce would be judged on how *genuine* it was. She had mastered all kinds of gloss, but this was eluding her. Glumly she watched me saw off a piece of asparagus. "Do you actually like that stuff?"

"Asparagus?" I considered the feathery purple-green stalk on my fork. What did asparagus cost in late November? Certainly at my uncle's Thanksgiving feast the week before there had been no asparagus. "Yeah. Even though it makes your pee smell weird."

She shrieked. "Your *pee?*"

"Yeah. You haven't noticed that? Maybe you don't have the gene."

"The pee smelling gene?" She giggled. "That's disgusting." Then suddenly she looked pensive. "Does everyone have a hard time writing their college essay, or is it just me?"

I thought of teenagers in Iowa and California, Seattle and El Paso, squinting at their computer screens, softly moaning. "No, I think everyone hates it."

"But as much as me? I mean, my English teacher is, like, really tough."

"Maybe not as much as you," I granted.

She blew out her fat lips. Her gaze wandered to the corkboard. I watched her look at all the photographs of herself in tight, shimmery dresses, with lushly cascading hair, studying the images as if seeking some key back to herself. In a slow, speculative voice she said, "I mean, real high schools aren't like this, are they?"

"What do you mean, 'real'?"

At the edge in my voice she turned back to me. "Like, normal. Public? The kind you went to. Aren't they really easy?"

Given my obsession with high school, it was strange how little I remembered. Lockers and halls. That's what I remembered: locker-lined halls. The ghostly feeling of never knowing who you might meet. A crush. The clock. I remember the round analog clock on the door, the black digits, the tick marks, the smooth sweep that the second hand made, as soothing as a mother's hand saying *There, there.* Time going by. The sound of the marching band carried on the wind. The old-carpet smell of the auditorium. In Spanish class, in the basement, with the laminated posters conjugating *ser* and *estar,* the clock went *tick-tick,* rude judders like the judders of my heart. I hated Spanish.

"I don't know if it was easy," I finally said. "I did hang out a lot."

"I hang out." She sounded morose.

No, no, I wanted to say: *it was different.* But how to convey the capacious sails of our days, the restlessness and ennui and music, the boredom and what came out of that boredom? "I had this friend named Lacie," I said tentatively. "I think I mentioned her before. We hung out all the time. We did everything together."

"What was she like?"

"I don't know. She was really funny. She was my best friend." The past tense in my mouth horrified me.

"Yeah, but what was she *like?*" Isabel sounded impatient. "Was she popular?"

A memory: walking home from school. So many memories of walking home from school, but in a way they were all one long memory, and that was what I suspected Isabel, with her appointments and tennis lessons and flights to L.A., lacked: the sense of childhood as an unbroken dream.

In this particular memory we were fifteen, and I remember I was upset about something, though I can no longer remember what, only that Lacie was loyally, appropriately sympathetic; as we walked home she let me wear her headphones while *Little Plastic Castle* strobed bluely in her Discman.

Isabel was looking at me expectantly. "What did you like about her?"

I liked singing along to "Gravel" with her. I liked buying every single Ani DiFranco CD with her. I liked making mixtapes; I liked finding live bootlegs with her. I liked singing all the words aloud, knowing that my voice was thin and flat, but trusting her not to care. That was what I wanted to tell Isabel, something about that trust; something about what Lacie gave me.

She gave me Ani. And Ani, with her leather bras, motorcycles, and syringes, made me think that my world of cotton underwear, minivans, and milk was seething with strange forces. Listening, I learned that I must be brilliant and punk and bold. I learned that the best love was demented and doomed. It happened with married men, or nineteen-year-old girls, or heroin addicts from rural Indiana. Really, it was best that Leo didn't love me back. It made our romance more real.

If this doesn't make any sense to you, relax: either you were a suburban white girl in 1998 with all your incipient feminism and loneliness and lust, or you were not. You were some other child, in some other land, with some other piece of vinyl or plastic that set your heart on fire. Think of that album now, the album you endlessly played, whose art is etched into your brain, the lyrics into your DNA. Not the first album you loved, but the one that suggested a pose.

"She was just one of those people," I finally said. "When I was with her, I liked myself so much more."

There was on Isabel's face a sudden intensity, a vulnerability I hadn't seen before. Quietly she said, "I think I know what you mean."

"You do?"

A faint pink blush crept into her cheeks. "Yeah, there's this girl at my high school, and when I'm with her, everything is just more fun. It's hard to explain. But I just always want to be around her."

"Is she your friend?" For some reason I held my breath.

Isabel nodded shyly. "Yeah, I think she's my best friend."

When I got home that night and found the table set for two, gingham napkins folded into soft-eared triangles, the whole apartment pleasantly steamy and smelling of fried garlic and cumin, I was surprised, and obscurely unsettled. More mistakes.

Around the corner came Sophie, cupping two bowls of basmati rice. "Rose!" Her displeasure slipped behind a mask of warmth. "Lacie wasn't sure if you'd be home. Have you eaten?"

"Oh, I don't want to crash your—"

"You're not crashing!" Sophie slipped the bowls onto the table and returned to the kitchen. I watched her go, as amazed as if she'd just pulled a rabbit from her hat. For years she had betrayed her husband. How could she do a thing like casually put rice on the table? Why was she not bent over with guilt, why were her clothes not rent, her feet not bare and bleeding?

And then: Right. Betrayal didn't stop your life. You could do something that rearranged your sense of yourself, and then simply continue on. Life continued on. Long ago God had gotten out of the habit of striking people dead. Even when you wished for it, for volcanoes and brimstone, all you got were crisp fall days, bright sunshine, a disconcertingly robust sense of well-being. You still enjoyed your food. Even liars like dinner.

Lacie, flushed, with tendrils wild, came zooming around the corner with a platter of roasted chicken. "You're back!" she exclaimed. "Perfect!" As if this had been the plan all along.

We sat, and for the first twenty minutes or so everything was fine.

Sure, I had crashed their date, but they were both too polite to say that they minded. We chatted and chewed our food. I didn't mind eating dinner twice; in those days I was always hungry.

At one point Sophie said, "I think the critics put more on Jenny Holzer's work than what's actually there. Her work is really catchy, for sure, but there's not a lot of substance to it," and wild jealousy stabbed me. I didn't even know who this person was, though I knew I should know. Probably even Isabel knew. It had something to do with growing up in New York, I thought. Artists and opera stars were household names; you accumulated from birth the cultural capital you used to slay at cocktail parties until you were ninety.

And the affair, and the sexless husband? Did Sophie privately feel her life was a disaster, even as we all envied the proper nouns—Princeton, *New York Review*, *New Yorker*—she had managed to attract? As she spoke in her precise, careful way, I kept staring.

Then the conversation turned to Ian.

"But I'm not even being controlling. It's not even like I'm angry. I'm just confused. It's like, What is actually going on in your brain? Who *are* you?" From the ferocity in Lacie's voice I could tell he had been the topic of conversation before I had arrived.

"Wait, so, what's he doing?" My voice was twitchy.

"The same old shit." Lacie ripped some meat off the bone.

"He's acting very distant," Sophie explained.

I stared at the roasted and dissected bird, imagining Lacie removing its bloody neck and bagged guts, then washing its pale, slick skin. Tenderly tucking thyme and parsley into its ass.

"It does sound like he's been really busy," I offered tentatively.

Sophie glared at me. "He's perpetually unavailable."

Lacie pinched the bridge of her nose, as if just *remembering* this incident overwhelmed her. "Yeah, it's just like, I get it. He's got this big show, he's totally slammed. I *get* it. But it's just, like . . . *common courtesy*, if you have plans with somebody, to tell them that you can't make it."

"Totally, totally." I bobbed my head.

"I mean, on Wednesday night, we'd said we'd hang out, and I waited and waited for him to call, 'cause I'm, like, trying not to *crowd* him, but then when I finally do text at nine thirty, he says, sorry, still at the studio, think I'm going to work l-l-late tonight." She swallowed a rising sob.

"It's fucked up," Sophie said quietly, rubbing her manicured nails over Lacie's hand, trying to calm her down while her eyes sought mine, as if to say, *Can you believe this? Have you ever seen her this upset?*

I hadn't. A black cloud of truth rose up. He *had* been at the studio that night; he had been at the studio pushing his cock into me. No. I was sucking it into my body with my cunt, feeling like my cunt could consume the world, consume *him* with its hunger, and then his phone dinged. Without taking his eyes from my face he fumbled on the floor and held it up to the light and then looked and muttered *Oh, fuck* and typed some things with his thumb and I didn't ask because I told myself he deserved his privacy, but it didn't feel good to be lying to myself about why I wasn't asking, which was that I already knew.

"Do you think he's having an affair?" I asked.

They both turned to stare at me.

"I mean, is that it? You're worried he's cheating on you?"

They both started to talk at once. "No—" Sophie began, and then Lacie chimed in with, "Cheating is not—I mean, to me *affair* implies marriage."

I couldn't help it, I looked right at Sophie. Then I forced myself to look away. "You know what I mean. Do you think he's seeing someone else?"

There was a real four seconds of silence. Sophie looked in actual physical pain. I had upset her by barging in like this; I could practically see her thinking *Why does she have to make the subtext text?*

"That's not Ian's way," Lacie finally announced. "That's not—I mean, it's like I was saying the other night. That's just not the vibe I'm getting. I think he's actually just really stressed about the show." She brightened. "Are you going to come?"

"When is it?" I pretended to need to know.

"Umm . . . two Wednesdays from now? Something like that. Oh, come! It's going to be really fun. There's going to be a swing band and everything."

I couldn't imagine anything worse than seeing Ian with his arm around Lacie, but I muttered something about trying to make it. So far I had avoided seeing them together. He hadn't been over recently, which I liked to think was a sign of fraying relations between him and Lacie, even though I knew this kind of thinking was a dangerous self-indulgence. Probably he was just avoiding me. But—a tiny part of me protested—maybe he was trying to distance himself from her. Maybe he was working up the nerve to break her heart.

Or maybe it really was this damn show. Maybe when a man—this man—said he had work to do, that's all he meant. For me, the work excuse was never just a work excuse; it was also a way of saying: *I'm busy, I'm important, I care about my work, I care about my work more than you, maybe I don't care about you at all, hey, doesn't my choice make you feel a little insecure and thus intrigued by me?* But I was willing to accept that not everyone operated this way. That sometimes a work night was just a work night.

Although honestly I doubted it.

"I'm going to be there," Sophie offered.

"With Aaron?" I asked.

She startled, surprised, perhaps, that I had remembered her husband's name, which of course I hadn't, not until Lacie had told me she was cheating on him.

"Maybe he'll come," she said slowly.

I smiled at her without teeth. "I was just wondering. How's he doing?"

She looked at me curiously. "He's fine."

The thing about a woman like Sophie is that from the moment of matriculation at Horace Mann, she had been in control. Even her wild youth had probably been a calculated wild youth, designed to give the optimum amount of risk-taking without ever venturing near legitimate danger. But after thirty years of perfect management, she had gotten used to her life being managed. She was a bit slow to recognize a threat.

"I just—I remember you said that thing. About his mother. I just wondered how he was doing with all that."

Beside me I could feel Lacie turn to stone.

"Ohhh, that?" Sophie stuttered out a laugh. "I can't believe you remember all that. Yeah, he's fine. We're doing fine."

"The thing is that I'm not a controlling person!" Lacie practically yelled out of nowhere. "*That's* what pisses me off about this whole situation. He says I'm not giving him space. I always give people space! Everyone thinks I'm the most chill person in the world."

"You are," Sophie reassured.

"You totally are," I added.

"Then what the fuck? I mean really, what the fuck? Why wouldn't he pick up his phone? I know that motherfucker is glued to it."

"I mean, just ask him if he's seeing someone." As a child I could never resist picking my scabs. I always had to see what was underneath. "You said you wouldn't care. You said you felt kind of European about it."

"Somehow the reality is different," Lacie mumbled.

"I don't think this line of thinking is particularly productive—" Sophie began.

"I don't know why we can't just be practical about it. I mean, people have affairs. That's the truth. Even really unlikely people cheat." I turned to Sophie. "You know that."

"I know what?" Sophie's chin jutted up.

"You know that people have affairs. All the time."

Beside me Lacie groaned.

"I don't understand what you're getting at."

"I mean, you're seeing someone else, right? It's not a big deal."

Sophie threw her napkin. Literally dropped her napkin, right onto her plate. "How do you know that?"

Lacie turned to me. "What the fuck is wrong with you?"

"I thought it was just like, a fact. Hasn't it been going on for years?"

Sophie had gone white. She was trembling, and beads of moisture had appeared on her upper lip.

"Jesus," Lacie moaned. "Don't you remember me saying, 'Don't repeat this'?"

"But why did you share it?" Sophie stood. "I told you that in confidence. That wasn't for *gossip*."

"I'm really sorry," I said. I was in fact starting to feel sorry. Somehow in my head it had seemed funny. Or cosmopolitan. Or, I guess, to be precise, I was still pissed about that lame lunch date.

"God, Soph, I'm so sorry." Lacie stretched out her hand, and Sophie recoiled.

"I'm going to go. Not"—she held up her hand—"because I'm mad, but I'm just—I'm going to go. I'm not mad at you." Already she was backing toward the door and patting her hair as if her hair needed preparation for departure.

Lacie and I watched her as if she were an actress in a play. We waited to see what she was going to do next, even as we already knew. She put on her shoes. She put on her coat. Her dark head bobbed in the foyer. She sent us one last desperate glance, and then she was gone.

Lacie and I looked at each other. The meal was not even half done. The wine bottle was still beaded. Sophie's fork remained in her mound of rice.

"I—"

It was lucky that Lacie jumped up at that moment because I had no idea what was coming after that *I*. She yanked the platter of chicken, marched to the kitchen, and slid the whole carcass into the trash. Lacie never wasted food.

I followed her, and began washing dishes. This was our first fight. It was funny how calm I felt.

"You always do this," she said after a moment.

"Do what?" In high school I had been a champ at keeping secrets.

"You just, like . . . you just, like . . . you're like—I can't explain it."

More silence. I ran the water hot and made myself keep my hands under it. Behind me I could hear Lacie slamming down glasses. I could picture them piling up behind me like little soldiers. What we're trying to do, I thought, is really stupid. You're supposed to outgrow your childhood friend. You're not supposed to move in together and try to build a new life on the ash heap of the old.

"I mean, why would you even say that?" Lacie finally said.

I turned from the sink. My hands were chapped and raw pink from the water. "I forgot it was a secret."

"All night, you were like, affairs, affairs, affairs! You couldn't help yourself. You kept bringing it up."

I said nothing.

"Are you trying to sabotage things between Sophie and me? Is that it? You're jealous of our friendship? What's going on?"

"I honestly didn't think she would care so much." But I was mumbling. I didn't believe myself.

"You always do this! It's like you can't see yourself, like you think nobody's paying any attention to you. Take responsibility for yourself!"

She was yelling.

"Okay, okay, I am, I am. I'm sorry. I fucked up. It was really bad. I don't know why I did it. I'm sorry."

We eyed each other. She looked pretty. Her cheeks were flushed, and her T-shirt had slipped off one shoulder, exposing a graceful curve of clavicle.

"Okay," she said. "Thank you. But do you know what I'm saying?"

"Lacie, I really am sorry. I don't know what got into me. Probably I am jealous of how close you are to Sophie, or something." I flapped out my hand, a gesture of honesty. "Probably I'm just jealous of her, period."

"Is that why you asked her to lunch?" She folded her arms.

"What?"

"She told me you asked her to lunch. That you *went* to lunch. You went all the way to Midtown to meet her at some crappy Indian place on her lunch break."

"*She* chose the Indian place."

"*She* thought it was weird."

My heart was shuddering, convulsing in confusion; I couldn't have said if I was scared or angry. "How do you know all this?"

"She texted me. Then I come home, and you're wearing my dress. It's weird, Rose. It's really fucking weird."

Deliberately I turned off the faucet. Made a big production of wringing out the sponge. Wiping my hands on a dirty dishtowel, then rubbing them again on my jeans. "I'm new here," I said, in what I hoped was a tone of great dignity. "I'm trying to make friends. Tell me what is wrong with that."

"Oh, please!" She almost barked a laugh. "Please stop with the outsider thing, okay? You're not an outsider. You *belong*. People like you."

"I am, though," and I hated the whine that crept into my voice. "I just moved here. You guys have known each other for years."

"*We've* known each other for years. Even in high school you were like this. Even in *elementary* school."

"Yeah, but I was an outsider back then too. I was a pretty dorky kid."

"Are you kidding? I was enthralled by you."

"I was enthralled by *you*."

We stopped a minute, panting. "You were so smart," she finally said.

"I was so *smart*?"

"Yeah, you were taking all these AP classes, and you won that playwriting contest. I was a little in awe of you."

"You were in *awe* of me?" I was starting to get furious. "Because I was taking *AP* classes? Come on, Lacie. You guys barely tolerated having me around. All the boys were gaga over you. They would practically follow you around."

"No. Everyone was intimidated by you. We all knew you were this genius."

"That's stupid. That's not true."

She looked directly at me. "It's true."

In the silence that followed there was only the gentle *whap, whap* of the broom hitting the molding. "Relax," I told her, and she grimaced and slowed down.

But there was still this pressure in the room. I made a weird chopping motion with my hands. "Not that it did me any good. I'm all 'youthful promise' that didn't pan out."

"That's the most bullshit thing I've ever heard." She waved the broom. Dust bunnies flew. "Take that back. I'm serious. Take that back right now."

"It's true."

"It's *not*. You're working on your novel. You went to Iowa, and now you're writing your novel, and you're going to sell it for a million dollars. You're brilliant."

"You haven't read anything I've written."

"I read your play. I was *in* your play."

"Come on, Lace. That was a hundred years ago. You have no idea if I'm good."

"I don't need to read anything." She spoke with fierce, trembling dignity. "I know you're good. I just know it."

It unnerved me, this faith of hers. What did I do to deserve it? I was stabbing her in the back, day after day, word after word, stabbing her. I had *just* stabbed her. How could she forgive me so quickly? Why couldn't she see how terrible I was? Her trust in me made me angry. "You don't even know what my book is about."

Just then, if she had asked, I would have told her. Just for the satisfaction of shocking her, I would have divulged. It's strange how you can start to hate the people you're hurting.

"Writers don't like to talk about the books they're writing." She put down the broom and took up a dishtowel, and when she stepped beneath the overhead fluorescent, I saw the hairs growing on her face. "You'll tell me when you're ready."

So invasive to see those pale, transparent hairs. So corporeal. For the briefest and most liberating of moments I saw Lacie as she was, and not as I wanted and feared her to be: not hopelessly hip, not endlessly smart, not carelessly beautiful, and complex, and always angled away from me, but someone tired and full, a little drunk and petulant; a person betrayed and let down and occasionally exhilarated by her body, like everyone else. A girl with a smattering of soft down on her face.

"Right," I said. "I'll tell you when I'm ready."

"I just think it's interesting. That's all." I rotated my glass a quarter inch and the condensation on the bar smeared. "I don't know. Maybe it's not interesting. Maybe it's totally boring."

"People always remember the past differently. Especially that kind of stuff."

We were at Applewood, in our usual spot, at the end of the bar watching back waiters carry steaming plates of locally sourced corpses. It had been a week since we had seen each other, and in that week I realized: we had to stop.

Which was why, after composing long, eloquent texts in my head explaining why we had to stop, which I imagined I would send just as soon as Ian asked me out, and then feeling slightly aggravated that he hadn't asked me out, I decided to ask *him* out so I could tell him it was over. It was best to be clear about these things.

Naturally, the place to tell him was "our spot." It was absolutely essential to ruin "our spot" with a nasty fight, so that it would be haunted by unhappiness and we would never be tempted to go there again. Yes, it was a measure of my commitment to ending things that I had chosen Applewood, for as soon as I told him it was over Applewood would be ruined, yes, in just one minute Applewood would be ruined, as soon as I told him this one fascinating new insight into Lacie's personality . . .

"It was just weird, this talk. I got so angry that she said she idolized me, when I actually spent most of high school feeling completely left out." Over Ian's shoulder the bartender, still with his suspenders and beard, rattled a silver cocktail shaker. "Do you feel like Lacie idolizes you?"

"Me?" Ian pretended to think while I pretended to wait. Really my internal motors were revving in preparation for the brag about to burst from my mouth. "I don't really think so . . ."

"It's just, I feel like Lacie has this idea that I'm some amazing writer, that I'm this genius, but I'm not. All I do is sit at my desk and suffer."

"I think suffering is mainly what writers do. Especially the good ones." He looked down at his highball. Part of Applewood's charm was its solid stemware. It gave your drinking *weight*. "I honestly have no idea what Lacie thinks of my art. I don't really care."

"But do you really not care?"

He said flatly, "I really don't care."

He was obviously about to get all high-minded about making the art you wanted to make, and not giving a shit what other people thought, that stupid argument that I had had a million times before, at Iowa, after Iowa, self-righteous speeches about how the best things came from people who didn't give a fuck (but I gave a fuck, that was the defining thing about me, that was why I was not a Depressed Girl, why I had gone to Harvard, why I was sitting in this bar talking to this man who seemed alternately attracted and indifferent to me: *I gave a fuck*), and so, to head off this pointless philosophical bullshit, I said, "I got so pissed off I almost told her what my novel was about."

"She doesn't know?"

"Nobody knows," and as if those words had flipped a switch, I suddenly felt eager and sensual and like I knew something about art. Maybe we would fuck later. Yes, we would definitely fuck. After I had told him it was over, we'd both be feeling sentimental.

"Really, nobody knows? You haven't shown it to anyone?"

"Just my agent." Ian looked skeptical. "If you talk too much about something while you're writing it, you kill it."

Of course killing it was the point. I wanted Leo ink-dead, dead on the page. I wanted his memory sold, printed, published, and reviewed, our lives no longer our lives but *public property.* Answering the inevitable nosy questions, I would be coy, and gradually the hurt he had caused me would blur.

Ian smiled his inscrutable close-lipped smile. "Maybe you're writing about me."

"Ha. You wish," but my face flushed.

Then *he* blushed. "Oh my God. You are."

"No, come on. Think about it. I've been writing this book for years."

"Then why are you blushing? Are you writing about Lacie?"

"No." But it was pointless to lie. I blushed so hard it hurt.

"Look at you. You are." He sucked at the dregs of his whiskey, and ice cubes clinked his teeth. "That's sick, Rose, that's really sick. Is that why you moved in with her? So you could take notes on her?"

"Oh my God, Ian, no. It's actually so random that we live together. It's just a coincidence."

"Hmm." He sounded like he didn't believe me. Our Mennonite poured out a liquid ribbon of gin. Behind us, a woman laughed loudly, like a hawk. "Does it have to do with that fight?"

"What fight?"

"You told me you guys had a fight. Some kind of falling-out."

At once, that golden Indian summer day came swimming up: the red chiffon curtains billowing with soft breezes, Ian sprawled on the couch and singing my name. It seemed pointless to deny what was so cleanly etched in my memory. "Yeah, we did."

"So what'd you fight about?" Moodily he sipped. "A boy?"

"Jesus! Why do men always think that the only thing women could possibly fight about is a man? It's so sexist."

He looked at me, amused. "So you did."

I laughed. "God, I hate you. You're the worst."

"You should get better at lying. Look at you, you're blushing again." I ducked my head, secretly pleased. "So what was it? You liked the same boy?"

Primly I crossed my legs and folded my hands. "I'm not telling you any of this."

"Who got him?"

"Come on, Ian. You'll just have to read the book."

He sized me up. After a moment, he announced, "Lacie did."

"Yeah. But then I slept with him, so I guess I kind of won."

I meant it as a joke, but he didn't laugh. There was a terrible, splintery silence. "Oh, no." His voice had gone quiet. "You slept with her high school boyfriend? Really, Rose?"

I shrugged. "Really." In that moment I felt deliciously cavalier.

"And that's what your book is about?" His lips bunched as if tasting something sour. "That makes me feel really weird."

"You guys doing all right?" Our bartender clicked away our glasses with two hairy fingers.

"I'll have another," I said, and Ian looked at me, surprised. "Actually, just a whiskey."

"Me too." He sounded resigned.

"Double rye?" the Mennonite asked me.

That was what Ian was drinking. I nodded, then turned back to him. "Look. What's happening between us, it doesn't have anything to do with Lacie. Regardless of what my book is about."

"Right." He rolled a little red straw beneath his palm. "It's just. It's a lot."

Our drinks arrived. Carefully he turned the glass around in his hand as if he were an alien encountering his first drinking vessel. I waited. I *felt* like an alien, incapable of guessing what these earthlings considered solemn and what was glib. Ian had seemed glib back at Song, boldly proclaiming *I like Lacie, and I like you.* Why should something that had happened in high school change any of that?

When he finally looked at me, the light in his eyes had dulled. "Look, Rose. I've actually been thinking this for a while, but this thing about Lacie clarifies it."

He rested his arms on the bar, perfectly parallel to the edge. I got scared. Clearly he was ramping up to a speech, and the only time men make speeches is when they need to smash your heart to smithereens and they think they can do it diplomatically. He sighed. "The thing is. I think we should stop."

My heart dropped to my gut. Everything got real slow and swimmy, and his words stretched like Silly Putty across the bar to me: "There's a way that we're having sex that's not working for me."

"You're not attracted to me."

"That's not what I said."

"That's what you mean."

We both took a deep, shaky breath. My throat ached as I prepared to hear the familiar words about how fantastic, how fucking fantastic I was, how he really, really wanted to stay friends.

"This was the thing I was afraid of. That you would take it this way."

"I'm not taking it any sort of way, I'm just trying to understand what you mean."

"It's my stuff." He spoke sadly. "It really has nothing to do with you. It's my stuff."

If I were playing Breakup Bingo I would've just gotten the center square.

"I thought the sex was really good. I mean, don't you think it's hot?"

I knew he thought it was hot.

"It's just"—he was speaking slowly—"it brings up something I don't like in myself. I know this part of myself. I don't feel the need to explore it anymore."

Okay, so, a few times during sex, I'd cried. Just a bit. It didn't freak me out. It had happened to me before, a hot welling when the wires of sex and emotion got crossed. Not a big deal, but the last time Ian had caught me. He'd been working his fingers into my asshole, working and working them, and I knew he wanted to fuck me there, and I felt trapped, caught, and suddenly there they were: hot shuddery tears shaking from me. He stopped right away. "Oh, honey, honey, what is it?" he had cooed, curling up beside me. "What's going on?"

"You're scared," I suggested now.

"Maybe." He sounded amiable.

"So don't be scared!"

"Look." He chewed the end of his straw. "I think it's clear that we're not good for each other."

"No. I wouldn't say that's clear at all."

"No? You wouldn't say this thing about Lacie makes it clear? We bring out something bad in each other. We should just stop."

"Maybe." I was thinking hard, scrambling. It didn't matter what came out of my mouth, it didn't have to be true, it just had to be convincing enough that he would keep fucking me. "Maybe, maybe we're just like, interested in different kinds of kink. Like, I like the performance of losing control, this sort of overtly playacting, like, *Oh my God, what a big cock you have!,* and I think you actually like this more liminal stuff, where I'm actually ambivalent about the stuff you're doing to me—"

Two pink blooms appeared on his cheeks. He studied the floor as he blew out his cheeks. "Yeah, uh. This conversation is actually really turning me on."

I went hot. Just him saying it: I got hot. But wasn't this game exactly the game he thought we should stop? "It's just like, maybe if I sort out my feelings about us having the kind of sex we're having, I won't be so ambivalent, and then you wouldn't feel so weird about it," I concluded.

He pushed back from the table. He had flushed a darker pink. "I actually can't talk about it. It really turns me on."

Out on the sidewalk we kissed like crazy. Relief made me giddy. He couldn't keep his hands off me. So no one was more surprised than me when Monday came and he did not call. Then Tuesday. Then Wednesday. I sent him one text, and he answered a day later, briefly. That was when I understood. We were done.

There's the thing when you fall in public, and you get up real fast, smiling, thinking it matters more to preserve your dignity than to figure out whether you're hurt. There's the thing where someone says *I still want to be your friend,* and you say yes, as if you even care about the friendship of a guy who no longer wants to fuck you. And then there's the thing when you wake up at five thirty in the morning with your heart thumping *gone, gone, gone* and you think, Actually this is fantastic, when the supermarket opens I'll be first in line. I've been meaning to make some stock, and we could use some more garlic anyway.

But first, because you are an obedient child, you sit at your desk with a cup of coffee trying to write about a thinly fictionalized boy, but quickly you discover that your brain has been colonized by a real boy, and you think, *It's a relief, really* and *But you wanted this too* and *Obviously he cares about you, this doesn't mean he doesn't care about you* but you don't care that he cares about you, you care about him saying, *You're so wet,* saying, *Oh my God, your pussy feels amazing,* and then you're—what? Turned on and sad? Furious and heartbroken and wet? It's a mess. It's time to go to the food store.

Two hours later, Lacie stood in the doorway to the kitchen wearing nothing but her underwear and one of my T-shirts, which naturally looked amazing on her. Clearly baffled to be smelling carrots and onions a half hour before breakfast, she nonetheless tried to play it cool.

"You're making stock," she observed.

"Yeah, I don't know, I woke up early, I can't get any writing done, I figured why not?"

She took in the bubbling pot, the green plastic bag. "You went to the Co-op."

"Yeah, there was no line. I should always go early in the morning."

She cocked her head—that classic Lacie move—trying to decide what all this meant, but in the end all she said was, "That's awesome. Maybe I'll make risotto tonight."

For days it went like this. I woke up, heart pounding, splintery with grief, bright with the knowledge that he was gone. Anything remotely like sitting at my desk was impossible, but the thing is, when you wake up at six A.M. and you can't write and you don't have to tutor until four P.M., there are a lot of hours to slaughter.

So I taught myself to bake bread. I took over feeding the sourdough starter. I scrubbed the woodwork, because God knows the last time that had happened, and replaced the lightbulb that had burnt out in the coat closet. Once the light was fixed I could see how much dust had accumulated down among our winter boots and summer sandals, so I took out all the shoes and the shoe rack, and then I matched up all the fallen gloves with their husbands, and dusted, and then I thought, I might as well mop, and really the closet looked so much brighter than it had before, and I was sure Lacie would be overjoyed with the bright yellow silk scarf that I had discovered crumpled in the back on the floor, especially since I had soaked it in warm water to remove the dirt, but she only took it between her fingers as if it were a letter from a foreign, possibly hostile country and said, "You're not pregnant, are you? It seems like some nesting instinct in you has gone berserk."

I laughed as if this were the funniest thing she had ever said, and she did her head cock as if pretending to consider for the first time whether I was "sexually active," and then she said, "Well, I think you're working too hard, but it is really nice to have all that stuff taken care of," and I saw that Lacie was not as indifferent as I had thought to who was doing which household chores.

So I kept on cleaning. I stepped up my relationship with the toilet-bowl cleaner and started shopping for household goods. The oven door had squeaked since I moved in; with a can of WD-40 I silenced it. The shoe rack had a loose screw; I tightened it. Nothing I did was that complicated or technical—certainly it all seemed worlds easier than the magic Lacie regularly conjured from the kitchen—but I felt a little butch with that blue spray can, or sticking a Phillips head in my back pocket. I was the man of the house, fixing things up, if the man of the house could also be a lovesick little girl.

Would he text? Would he *call*? I daydreamed about his call, I day-dreamed about what he would say, I composed his speech in my head. I told myself to stop it, to get back to work, to finish my draft. I told myself to imagine that the boy in my novel *was* Ian, so I could subli-mate my daydreams into art, but everything I wrote was shit. It was literature. It was a lie.

Then I fell asleep for an hour. When I woke up I thought, in won-der and amazement and hope, Oh my God, it's noon on a Tuesday, and I'm *napping*? Is it finally happening? Am I becoming a Depressed Girl?

If I were a Depressed Girl, Ian would definitely fall in love with me. Later, in my slim autobiographical novel, I'd describe how I'd felt faint when he'd proposed.

After the wedding, I'd become frightened of certain streets. I'd cry often and forget to eat. Naturally, he'd be unspeakably good to me, so I'd have to do something truly unforgivable, like fuck his best friend, leave without warning, or give away his cat. In a foreign country, I'd tell lies to well-meaning strangers. I'd have meaningless, degrading sex. I'd spend a decade drinking too much, sleeping too much, sleep-ing with the wrong people in a studio apartment containing nothing but a mattress and a milk crate, only to emerge from this wasteland with a fully formed literary voice that described this torpid self-destruction in limpid, quasi-spiritual prose which would immediately earn unanimous critical acclaim, and all the disciplined little twats who had actually been writing for all the years that I had been depressed would just about expire from jealousy and frustration.

But who was I kidding? I was a disciplined little twat. Even as I lay on the couch pretending I was too sad to move I was making to-do lists in my head. I would never weep poetry from my fingernails. There was no sense in wallowing. I got up and got back to the desk.

When I got there, I found an email from Isabel. No content, just a single attachment. "College Essay.docx."

WHAT WOMANHOOD MEANS TO ME

By Isabel West

There is a boy in my grade. Actually I should say, there *was* a boy in my grade. Last year he announced that he was actually a woman. He started wearing dresses to school and sitting with girls at lunch. Everyone was very respectful except for some guys on the soccer team who did some disrespectful things, but they were punished and school guidance counselors came to all our classrooms and led a discussion.

I have always been very excepting of Jewel. Her new name is Jewel. But secretly I have a hard time seeing her as a real woman. A bunch of my friends talked about it and we agreed. The thing is that Jewel never got her period. Getting your period the first time is weird. My mom said, "Now you're one of us!" and hugged me, and I felt sort of freaked out inside, like I had turned into a monster.

But now I like getting my period. Not all the time, but sometimes. It makes me feel really powerful and proud, like look, my body made this. Sometimes women who get eating disorders don't get their periods anymore. It's because their body is too weak. I am proud that this never happened to me.

I'm not saying that Jewel isn't a woman. She is. I'm not transphobic. But for me, I realize, my identity as a woman is the feel-

ing that I have about my period, kind of embarrassed, kind of
think it's cool. That is what being a woman means to me. You're
just like a man, except you also get to do all this extra cool stuff,
in your body, without even really meaning to.

I wrote back to Isabel right away: *This is amazing! So great. Maybe
the best thing you've ever written. Just make sure you're always using the
right pronouns, and watch the difference between "except" and "accept."
Otherwise, great! I'm proud of you.*

Yes, she had written it fast. Yes, she would get pilloried for that
opening. But at least she was finally getting weird.

That night, Ian came over. Don't get too excited: with Lacie. From my room I heard them talking in the kitchen. For a while I pretended to read *The Book of Disquiet,* as lonely as I'd been since moving to New York. It would've been better, I thought, if they'd just gone back to his house. I could've been truly alone.

But when I walked past her room after brushing my teeth, Lacie called, "Rose? Come here."

The door was open a crack, and I pushed inside. Lacie and Ian were in bed. Lacie had on some old gray tank that made her boobs look big. Ian was in a white T-shirt. Being so close to them made me flush.

"Come over," she commanded again. "We were just reading."

Ian held up a pink paperback covered in ghoulish cartoons. "Do you know Angela Carter?" I shook my head no. He didn't seem embarrassed. I wondered whether this was some kind of dare.

"Listen for a while," Lacie said. "She's so good."

I inched forward. There was the usual chaos: clothes in mounds and heaps, books and dirty glasses everywhere, unspooled yarn. Her paisley duvet had been pushed off the bed—too hot, the heating in the building was manic. The top sheet was up around their waists. Beneath the sheet, their legs. There was nowhere to sit but the bed, so I perched and listened to Carter's demented fairy tale.

In "The Bloody Chamber," a young bride is whisked away to a remote castle by her new husband, a wealthy older man whose two previous wives died under mysterious circumstances. The castle is huge and dark, with many rooms, one of which is forbidden. Immediately upon arrival, he deflowers her in a tower filled with white lilies and endless mirrors. Then he leaves. Alone, she roams the halls, drawn inexorably to the locked door.

The story was sexy and disturbing, about complicity and depravity, and as I listened I couldn't keep my eyes from Lacie's breasts. Without a bra her boobs were soft and full. I nudged her, and she moved over, so that we could lie next to each other, two little girls sleeping side by side, as we had been at countless sleepovers. On and on Ian read, in a slow, steady voice.

I wanted to drift my fingers up her chest. I imagined: her eyes would close, and she would settle on her back like a good girl, the obedient and passive girl she had always been, and I would peel up her tank top and bury my face in her breasts. Ian would watch. Ian would grow hard . . . These were just thoughts, cloudy dream-forest thoughts; they braided with the bloody chamber, the fairy tale with the cock like a sword. Yes, and Lacie would gently turn me over. She would give me to Ian. It was her way, to share everything. . . .

A heat traveled from my stomach to my toes, a wave of longing so strong I felt ill. Beside me Lacie smelled dusky, of earth and bed, in her thin tank, with her mysterious face, long and plain one moment, incandescent the next. Beside her Ian hulked like a mountain, a dark gravitational force. I wanted them both so badly—the desire was so strong I didn't have to wonder at its strangeness—that my head went thick and my vision blurry, their voices distant through this haze.

A thousand times I've gone back to this moment; a thousand times I've replayed the scene, wondering if my nerves failed me, if another way was unfolding before us and we all lacked the courage to take it. What might we have done? What might have grown from it?

Instead, when the story ended, I stretched and said good night, and they called to me happily, glad for me, and glad for me to go. I thought

Ian might catch my eye, let me know he was grateful to me—how mature I was being, how adult, not fucking up his shit, basically being a good girl, a good and obedient girl, submissive as he tossed me aside—but when I stood in the doorway he reached for the water glass and avoided my eye.

The next night was the gallery opening. First I had to tutor Isabel. When I arrived, however, I was ushered not to Isabel's but to Ervin's office, a lavish leather den as large and dark as Isabel's office was small and white. On the massive cherry desk sat Isabel's new essay. Behind the desk, Ervin West, a squat, bald man dressed entirely in olive khaki, heartily shook my hand. I saw on the essay a big swooping question mark beside the word "period."

Ervin, without comment, positioned the paper so that I could see his incredulous markings (he also, apparently, had hesitations about the line *I'm not saying that Jewel isn't a woman* and the word "monster"), but I was more interested in him: his shortness, his roundness, his pink, fleshy face and bald, shining head. What an unlikely vessel for such a gross quantity of capital. "What do you do, when you're not doing this?"

"What?" It took me a moment to understand. "I'm a writer."

We both silently look at the marked-up paper between us. "Writer," he mused, carefully considering that category of people. "Like that movie. That sick, sick movie. What was it called? With Kathy Bates?"

"*Misery*?" *A book, you fuck. It was a book first.*

"*Misery.*" He clapped his hands with delight. "Yes. What a sick movie. I saw her in a restaurant once, Kathy Bates. I just looked at her and thought, Sick, you're really sick. So. What do you think?"

The transition was so abrupt that it took me a moment to remember my line: "She's such a hard worker. So dedicated."

"Yes, exactly." He seemed stunned by my powers of observation. "She's a very moral being. I don't know if you've noticed this, but she has a really strong sense of right and wrong. I mean, for instance, in this essay. Whatever its, um, shortcomings. She's so accepting. We couldn't be prouder of her."

Behind Ervin, the gray tabby padded silently into the room, then crouched, sprang, and landed, silently, on the polished expanse of the desk. Mindlessly Ervin dribbled his fingers over her face, and she began to lick. Her pink tongue—in and out, in and out, a regular pulsing rhythm—sickened me.

"The thing is," he continued, "Isabel's in a place where she just needs to get on with her life. How long do you think it will take? One hour? Two?"

My laugh was a nervous exploratory trill. "How long will what take?"

"She just needs a model. She just needs to see how it's done. Then, moving forward, she can write her own. But she's spent a lot of time on this paper. Too much, in my opinion."

The tabby, rebuffed by Ervin, prowled to me and, with a delicate corkscrewing motion, a twist both controlled and voluptuous, flopped on her back, offering her belly.

"You mean you want me to write her paper for her?" I tried to keep my voice in another country, far from accusatory; I asked in the spirit of a foot soldier prospecting her mission.

"Well, just provide a teaching aid. Give her a model."

I petted his cat to soften my words. Her nose was dry against my fingers. "I don't write students' papers for them. I just don't. I don't do it."

When he spoke again there was in his voice all the gravitas of true suffering. "When Isabel was two years old, a taxi came up onto the sidewalk and hit her stroller. Right on Madison Avenue. She was in the ICU for four days. The worst"—he leaned forward—"four days of my life. I just—you can't imagine. My little girl. We didn't know what was going to happen."

"That's terrible." I meant it. If it was true, it was terrible.

"Thank God we made it through." Ervin sighed.

The cat, with a languid slow stroke, swung out her paw and snagged the hem of my blouse. Carefully, all the while making eye contact, I unhooked the claw.

"But as a result, sometimes Isabel has trouble getting her thoughts onto the page. Abstract reasoning. You must never"—he held up his hand—"ask her about this. It's been a real struggle. But that's why I knew you'd understand."

"But I don't understand," I said quietly. "If it's difficult, she needs to try harder."

"Absolutely, absolutely. So, you know, we really appreciate *all* the help you can give. We'll see you next week?"

With the same slow underwater motion the cat again swung her claw, and this time she ripped loose from my thumb a crescent of skin.

"Your cat got me." I held up my hand with its bulbing red blood.

He laughed. He laughed for so long I became uneasy. Then, abruptly: "So, let's say it takes you three hours. That's fine. We can cover that. Just show her what real writing looks like. You're a smart girl." He rolled up Isabel's paper and swatted me on the shoulder. "Careful. You've got blood on your hands."

On my way out I saw Isabel in her office and waved. She beckoned me over and announced, "He's completely insane." The blue light of her phone bathed her.

"Who, your dad?"

"He wants me to *completely* rewrite my paper for, like, the *third* time. Wasn't that what he was saying to you? But he can't make me. He's not my teacher."

She was right, so naturally I said the worst possible thing: "He just wants what's best for you."

To my absolute horror she began to cry. Softly at first, just a crinkling at the eyes, and then full-out, shoulders shaking, nose-running sobs.

"It's okay," I cooed. "It's okay. Why do you care about this paper so much? I promise you, it's not even that important." I circled my hand in the vague direction of her back, afraid to touch her.

"But, but," she gasped, "it has to be perfect."

"But why?"

"I can't believe you're even asking me that!" She literally stomped her foot. "Basically this is the most important thing I've ever written in my whole entire life! The whole fate of my *life* is being decided right now." She swung her fists around.

"Isabel, Isabel. It's okay. I hate to tell you this, but where you go to college—it actually doesn't matter that much."

She straightened, and her face hardened.

"It's true. You'll make some friends, you'll take some classes, and then you'll graduate. Wherever you go, you're going to have a good life. That's just"—and who knows why I said this—"that's just *especially* true for you. Your life is going to be fine, no matter where you go to school."

Her face contorted itself into something resembling hate. It was the most reaction I had ever elicited from her. "Where did you go to school? *Harvard?*"

"Yeah, Harvard," I reluctantly admitted.

"So it's easy for you to say!"

"No, yeah, no, that's right, that's true, but, um, you know, the general point still holds true. So"—I tapped her shoulder—"don't drive yourself crazy. Don't let them steal your adolescence from you."

Since learning the name of Ian's gallery—Milk and Honey—it had made me cringe. It seemed too blatant a celebration of gentrification, though it was hard to deny the sentiment: Red Hook did seem like the Promised Land, not least for Milk and Honey's monthly parties, which had become the thing, a free bacchanal where a band played, drinks were served, and all the artists and scientists and philosophers whom Johan Lundberg, the very pale blond Danish founder, had gathered round him opened up their offices and studios.

It all sounded annoyingly hip to me, the kind of New York thing simultaneously overcrowded and over, but I wanted to support Ian, *as a friend,* by going.

It does not exactly take a genius of self-perception to see my true motive.

Lacie, of course, did not know anything about my true motive. Or she pretended not to know, or I was pretending that I didn't know that she knew, or she was pretending that she hadn't guessed that I was pretending not to know that she knew. By the time of Ian's opening, we had reached a hall of mirrors. Her façades, the refractions of knowing, were so convoluted that I couldn't even guess at which level we were operating.

Just this morning she had said, "Do you think it will be weird for you and Ian to see each other?" but when I asked her what she meant, she only shrugged and said, "I don't know. It's so public, and it's his *art,*" as if that made any sense at all.

Regardless. When I told her I'd see her that night at the show, she hugged me—which she didn't often do in those days—and said she'd see me there.

I arrived late. In the stone atrium, a swing band had taken the stage, white guys in goatees with trombones, and I bobbed briefly in the sea of Brooklyn plaid. Behind a card table a woman in a cream-colored dress with sleeve tattoos was pouring wine. I opened my wallet and caught her violet eyes, mouthing *red*.

When she handed me my plastic tumbler, she gave me a shy, pleased smile. As I drank, I thought it must be clear how much I needed it, my tension and anger X-rayed by this priestess of boxed wine. I asked for another. She hummed faintly under the music, a simple lulling tone.

I drank from the second glass of berry-black wine until Ervin had melted from me, and the high vaulted ceilings were a cathedral's, and the party a glittery, shimmery net of meaning. Sobriety, I thought: nothing but a deliberate dodge of beauty.

Walking away from the band and the booze, I found beneath a soaring keystone arch a heap of dirt. Sculpture. In a shadowy corner where once longshoremen had stacked burlap sacks of coffee and crates of alcohol, a flickering film loop showed a hanging; endlessly the hooded body dropped. In the light of a camera obscura I observed a pregnant belly, bare and fuzzed like a peach. Thank God a 3-D printer had been fired up; in four hours we would have a fork. The showstopper, Johan's own contribution, was an upright transparent coffin containing a human collaged from a million tiny cutouts of butterflies. I spent a long time looking.

On the second floor there was a giant cocoon suspended from the ceiling, knit entirely from ruby-red yarn. I climbed inside. The yarn was soft but strong, tightly woven, and the whole hammock swayed when I entered. Instantly the chatter and music softened, and the sterile blue-white gallery lights sank to a warm pinkish glow. A wave of luxuriant warmth swooned over me. Eyes closed, I listened to a fiddle playing down below. Its twang awoke some restlessness in me: I wanted to share. Where was Lacie?

When I wriggled from the red cocoon, I saw a little sign that said LUCINDA SALT. What? My brain assumed an error. Not until I took from a hard, clear folder one of those heinous artist statements did it quite register: Lacie had a piece in the show. *Lacie had a piece in the show.*

I found her down the hall, talking to some skinny Muppet-like hipster, but as soon as she saw me she broke away. In public we were each other's priority.

She was wearing a white dress, like the woman behind the make-shift bar, but Lacie's was vintage shirtwaist with mother-of-pearl buttons, over which she had slung a kind of bolero jacket. It looked absurd, and bold, and she wore it very casually. My black jeans and cardigan, chosen to seem like I didn't care, suddenly seemed shoddy and shapeless. "Do you like it?" she hummed in my ear. She must have seen me climb out of her creation.

"I love it, oh my God, Lacie, I had no idea you had something in the show. Why didn't you *say* something?"

Even as I spoke I was remembering the red yarn at the house, cardboard boxes mail-ordered, full of soft garnet spools, so deep and plush I couldn't resist plunging in my hand, as if plundering a chest of rubies. She had said something. She had told me she was making a cocoon.

"It was just so last-minute, I wasn't even sure it was going to happen," she explained. I could tell she was downplaying it. I felt worse.

"So you're an artist," I said unsteadily.

The truth was that I had never thought of Lacie's crafts as art. True, she was a founding member of the Aftselakhis Spectacle Committee, which every year put on a Purimshpil of impeccable leftist credentials, collaborating with formerly incarcerated women or nannies from Domestic Workers United on bright giant puppets and curtains and papier-mâché masks, but though many jars of sequins were used, and many tambourines played, it had never seemed very serious to me.

She cocked her head. She took my measure. "I make things," she said lightly, and I murmured a bit more about how much I liked the cocoon, how I felt it had held me, and then I said, "Take me to Ian's art."

When we reached his studio there was a pair of teenage girls whispering on Ian's couch, little ghosts of our past selves. When they saw us they hurried out, still giggling and whispering.

"You can stay," Lacie called after them, but they were gone. "They looked like high-schoolers," she added. "What are they doing out so late?"

I was too distracted to answer. For the open house Ian had draped his studio with swaths of velvety pink and Prussian-blue fabric, the better to show off his spindly gold sculpture, great architectural models of dream homes that could never be. "They're beautiful," I breathed.

"Oh, yeah. Haven't you seen his work before?" Lacie got out her phone. "Where is he? He said he'd be a little late."

Until then, I had only seen his work in little glimpses. He was protective of his creations, and usually kept them covered, but now I could look all I wanted. I approached a teepee, maybe a foot high, that swirled upward without a lid, like a cone that never closed; it made me imagine the night sky, navy etched with silver.

This is art, I thought, but that was mean, and I didn't even believe it: what Lacie had made was art too. I knew it, but I was simmering, not exactly with anger but with the growing conviction that I didn't know her at all.

"Come on, let's sit on the couch."

We collapsed onto the sagging plum monstrosity, and Lacie started talking to me, fluidly and rapidly, pulling at my arm to keep my attention, while I darted surreptitious glances, trying to see more of Ian's dream models.

We passed her silver flask between us, giggling at the dark figures that hesitated at the door, safe inside the insular cape of our company.

Soon, drinking, I forgot about Ian and his sculpture, which seemed, the more I drank, annoyingly cerebral anyway. What I wanted was *more:* more Lacie, more intimacy, more *us.* In a conversational lull I took her hand. Uncurling her fist, I said, "You know what I was thinking about today? Remember the letter you wrote me the first time you had sex?"

She laughed. "I never did that."

"You wrote me a letter. It was really sweet. 'Today the grass grew and Leo and I had sex.' Don't you remember?"

"No way." She nestled her head against me. "Were we apart or something?"

"No, I think we were just—young enough that sex felt hard to talk about. That's all." She looked skeptical. "We were really young. Nobody now is ever that young."

"Why were you thinking about all of this?"

"I don't know, just thinking about Isabel." Lacie's eyes flickered dead with boredom, but I couldn't help myself. "She's so sexualized. Before she even knows what it is, she's in it."

"I'm sure she knows what sex is." There it was, the way she cut between warmth and irony. It drove men wild; it drove me wild too.

"I think we had a code," I said loudly. "Didn't we have a code? I think we had a virginity code. *God.* Remember when we used to walk to the Acme and get those vegan moon pies? I thought they were the most delicious things in the world."

"Why are you talking about this?"

"It just seems like we fell out of time." My tongue was not so agile in my mouth.

"Yeah. Did we really eat that stuff? It sounds disgusting now." She smiled, puzzled, but happy to see me happy.

"We've been friends for so long. What is it, like twenty years? It's just so crazy. Am I even twenty years old?"

She bobbed my nose. "Square dance. Gym class."

"You mean so much to me, and we're just so close. That's it. Nothing can break that. I mean, how many people do you know who are actually close to their elementary school friends? Nobody. But here we are. I mean, even when I sleep with Ian, it doesn't change the *basic fact* of the situation."

"Even when you . . ." she said in a dazed, wondering tone.

A flower of frantic love was blooming in my chest; it was imperative that Lacie understand how much she meant to me. "You know?" I said eagerly. "We've just transcended all of that."

Abruptly she scrambled back on the saggy couch cushions. "What are you talking about?" Her voice was dangerous.

"Well, it's not like it's changed anything."

"*What* hasn't changed anything?"

Some of my wine and whiskey buzz dissipated. "Don't you know?" I said more quietly. Over by the night teepee, a couple was circling; I could feel them listening, even as they pretended deep engagement with Ian's art.

"Know what?"

"Know . . ." But I could see by her face that she didn't—and then she did. "Oh my God." She covered her mouth with her hand. "What? Really, Rose? Really?"

Just then the warm, full roll of Ian's laughter came dancing into the studio, noise from another planet. Lacie's face was a crumbling wall, a dam bursting. "Ian's here," she murmured, and reached out, as if to pat my hand. Then she thought better of it, got to her feet, and left.

I snuck a glance at the couple. They immediately averted their eyes. "Fuckers," I muttered, and they scrammed. I sat there like a bug for I don't know how long, thinking—what? At least it's done? Yes. I was strangely elated, in a clean, shocked way, the way a wound is clean before it begins to bleed.

My cell phone rang. I pressed it to my ear and bleated, "Hello!"

"Rose? Ervin West here." He spoke in a sadly automatic tone. Alone in his dark and dustless office, he must be cupping the big flat iPhone to his ear, watching the squares of yellow light in the luxury building across the street. "I want to have a conversation with you about how you've been speaking to Isabel."

"How have I been speaking to Isabel?" I watched Lacie speak to Ian as if that would give me a clue. She had him backed against a wall, and their heads were close. There was something sexy, bright and flaming, in her anger.

"I understand you told her that I'm stealing her adolescence from her. I'm just wondering what you meant by that." He sounded pleasantly inquiring. Was this how he spoke to the feds?

"It's complicated." I swirled my hand to indicate *complicated*.

"What the *fuck*," I heard Lacie moan.

"Well." Ervin cleared his throat. "I don't understand how you can call yourself an educator and then undermine the whole project of education."

"I wasn't—what do you mean?" Ian kept looking my way. Then he said something to Lacie, and the two of them turned and speed-walked out.

Ervin was hesitating. Was he actually thinking? More likely, the noises of Milk and Honey—the new Red Hook—were reaching him. Finally he said, "I can't employ someone who feels so conflicted about her job. Isabel has enough anxiety in her life already."

"Yes, absolutely, I agree—"

Came the flat *spat* of cellular disconnection.

When I took my phone from my ear there was a warm smudge where my cheekbone had been. Silently the numbers climbed on the display, as if our call were continuing. It took time for the network to understand.

Delicately I tapped off. Took a deep, swirly breath.

Strangers were looking at me. Then looking away. The scene had become a scene. The party had gotten smeary, turned up and sloppy, with a wobbly, dark hole where Lacie's emotion had been. I pushed past the spindly, skeletal homes and the textiles of turquoise and green.

Right, I thought to the 3-D printer, still wearily sawing away. *Sure,* I told the pregnant belly, luminous like an egg. The boy with the handlebar mustache, the girl with her tits strangely slung together, the hooded body that dropped and dropped: *Really, guys? This is what you think about violence? This is what you've got?*

No, not the heaps of dirt, not the coffin of butterflies, not the single stream television, *not* most of all the bloody cocoon, the cheap Louise Bourgeois womb: Oh, please! This hadn't been news since 1975. *Come on, Lace.* Say *something.* What the fuck was wrong with our generation? We were all so scared and nice, nice and scared. Even subversion came with a typed white handout. Even tricky art was called "tricky" and dropped in a box. Everyone wanted to be liked. Everyone wanted a write-up in the *Times.* Everyone wanted—

On the street I spotted them. Lacie was still incandescent, Ian shaking his head *no.* So busy was she screaming she didn't see me skulk across the street. He did. He sent me a glance as raw as opened skin, pink and shocked and tender, a universe from the smug satisfaction he had showed me at the bar when he had oh-so-reasonably, oh-so-respectfully suggested we stop, and satisfaction was not the word, then, for what I felt. No, power is the word.

PART THREE

Expulsion

Grand Central at any time is a dream, with the pale gold and pearly green-blue of its celestial signs, but at half-past ten, when there are only cops and panhandlers and drunk suburbanites around, there's a stillness close to church. Slamming through the hall that night, I was aware of destroying something sacrosanct. Furiously I cut a harsh diagonal, my backpack heavy with sweaters and jeans, underwear and socks, running shoes. Basic stuff. I was going home.

The spur from Southeast takes only twenty minutes to reach Harlem Valley–Wingdale, but then it's nearly forty minutes to North Banbury. On the drive back from the station my mom and I didn't talk much. She didn't ask if I was okay, or why I had come home. Over her nightie she'd thrown a North Face fleece, and in the light of the passing headlights her skin was papery and worn.

When we pulled into the driveway Marlo began to bark, and by the time my mom was unlocking the front door he was hysterical. Out he tumbled, all brown wriggly body, his grief over the midnight intrusion magically alchemized to pure canine glee. Reflexively he pushed his long torso against my legs, shaking and snapping his jaw, while I cooed, "Oh, Marlo, Marlo, yes I came home, I'm here, I know, it's so exciting," and then I slapped his side and he trotted off to find me a toy, and my mom kissed me near the lips and said she was happy I was home.

Was it home? When I had brushed my teeth with the extra tube of toothpaste kept in the guest bathroom, and slid between the crisp white sheets of the guest bedroom, wallpapered in cerulean blue, Lacie and Ian and Milk and Honey, at least, seemed a million miles away. Two minutes later I was dreaming.

When the city people had discovered North Banbury, the town had stripped away its hardware stores and food marts, its gas stations and drugstores, to make room for "shoppes" selling penny candy and Shaker furniture. Then the money abruptly veered east, to the hamlet of White Hart, leaving North Banbury with a Main Street of shuttered ceramic stores and out-of-business cafés. It was a funny summer town, mostly deserted, with a strangely prominent post office, and a hot-dog vendor selling his wares exclusively on Wednesdays from eleven to one.

Not that any of this bothered my parents. After I graduated from high school, they had bought a narrow three-story Victorian with rattly windows, wide soft floorboards, and peeling lead paint. To my surprise they'd decorated impeccably: in the airy top room, with its banked four-pointed ceiling, they'd placed giant clay pots filled with sprays of red Japanese maple, a comfortably saggy mauve couch, and a mounted sculptural twist of weathered gray driftwood. It turned out my parents had taste. They were only waiting for me to leave to display it.

I awoke the next morning to crunching gravel. From the window I watched my dad walk down the driveway with his gym bag over his shoulder. Downstairs, a burner clicked and caught.

While I was washing my face my phone trilled.

"Rose? It's Griffin," Griffin shouted when I picked up, and with my finger I plugged the ear that was not pressed to the phone, as if I were having trouble hearing, though my parents' house was silent. "I just got off the phone with Erv. Ervin West? He's very upset."

"Oh, no." I squinted at the tiny analog clock on the dresser. Seven thirty in the morning. "I'm really sorry to hear that."

"Do you remember what you said to Isabel last night?"

So I came to learn that after I left, Isabel cried so hard her mother thought she might need to be sedated. Said that she *hated* me. Said that she *never wanted to see me again.* Said that *I didn't believe in her,* that I had *told her she was a failure.*

"So, needless to say, you won't be working with Isabel anymore." He sounded grimly satisfied.

"Did he tell you he asked me to write her college essay for her? Because he did. He asked me to do it." Panic made my voice mean.

"Be that as it may." Griffin did not sound surprised. "Be that as it may. The thing is, Rose. I know that you're very smart. But at Ivy Prep, we don't hire for book smarts. There are lots of geniuses in the world. That's actually very common. What we need are people who can *read people*. Who are *emotionally* intelligent."

Of course he had it exactly backward. Any modern female who'd gone through the whole *please others* indoctrination—who had been socialized, in other words—was *emotionally intelligent.* Emotional intelligence was as common as dirt.

"Look, Rose," and now he sounded genuinely grieved. "If I were your friend, I'd tell you to get another job. Not that I'm *not* your friend," he quickly added.

"You're firing me?"

He chuckled. "I'd like to think that being your friend and being your boss, they're not mutually incompatible. And I like you a lot. That's why it's difficult for me to have this conversation. But as your friend, I'd tell you to start looking for a different job."

"So you're firing me."

"No, no, no. At Ivy Prep we don't *fire* people. We just, well. It's an algorithm."

"An algorithm," I repeated.

"The tutors at the top of our ranking system, they get the most referrals. Those at the bottom get the least."

"And I'm at the bottom."

"Well, actually you're off our list."

"But you're not firing me."

"I like you a lot," he repeated helplessly.

I looked in the mirror. I'd slept in my sweats, and my hoodie had left a red crease across my cheek. "I like you too," I told Griffin Chin, and then I hung up the phone.

They say that people who lose everything—in a fire, or a flood—often feel an odd exultation. I had never understood that until now. Lightness swam up in me. The shoddy apartment, and roaring subway; the endless coaxing of Isabel to more sentences, clearer sentences. Why did I need any of it? Over months I'd erected a life I had imagined was as solid as stone pillars, only to discover I'd built a paper tent. Down it came in a single yank.

If I told my parents I'd lost my job they'd want to have a sober conversation about how, and why, and what I felt, and because my mom knew how to listen, because she was a very, very good shrink, she'd pull the loose threads in my conversation until I was talking about Isabel's adolescence and my adolescence and then, inevitably, *Lacie's* adolescence, and then Lacie today, and my mom would see it all, my cloak would unravel and I would be psychically naked before her, which was how I always ended up in front of my mother: bare. Unable to keep anything from her.

No. Not today. I vowed not to blab my mistakes. I would not—under no circumstances—bring up Isabel. I definitely wouldn't say the name *Lacie*. I would keep myself locked away.

Once I had decided to hide my distress from my parents, I joined my mom in the breakfast nook, where we sat drinking coffee with milk fresh from the local dairy. Chunks of fat floated in our cups, slowly dissolving into yellow greasy circles. Steel-cut oats bubbled on the cast-iron stove.

"How's Lacie?" my mom asked.

"Fine," I said carefully. "She's just sort of the same."

When I'd moved in with her my parents had naturally been surprised, and rehashed many old memories of our sleepovers from years ago. But there was something probing in my mom's voice now. "Is she still talking in that babyish voice?"

Actually, my dad had been the one who did most of the reminiscing about our old friendship. My mom had never liked Lacie. Or rather, she had liked her when she was a fearless ten-year-old girl, but when she had become giggly and coy, popular with the boys, my mom, unlike the rest of us, was not charmed. My mom was a practical woman.

"Um, not really. She's not really so girly anymore." I hesitated, annoyed that my mom was caricaturing Lacie in this way, but also glad. Maybe I could allow myself to say this one thing about Lacie. Just one thing. "It's more like, she pretends she's this brilliant absentminded artist, but really she's totally savvy and careerist and smart about things like that."

My mom waited. I wanted to tell her more. I wanted to describe the red cocoon. I wanted to explain how I thought it was bad, but that I also secretly loved it, and how much it terrified me to love it, because I thought it must mean Lacie was more talented than me, in addition to more everything else, but I knew my mom, the therapist, would say something vaguely chiding about jealousy and remind me that brilliance was not a zero-sum game; she would straighten me out, and nudge me an inch closer to psychological health. So annoying.

"How are you guys doing?" I said instead, playfully poking her. "Tell me about *you.*"

Overnight my parents had donned the garb of old people. My dad had new stiffness in his joints, instructions to replace his daily run with a swim, plus pills to take each morning. If my mom sat for too long it took her forever to stand. She'd bend over and massage her knee, muttering, *I'm fine, I'm fine.* It worried me. Also I wanted to poke at her vulnerability, since she had so quickly sensed mine.

But all she said was, "Oh, honey, we're good, we're good. It's a very sweet time of life, really."

"Yeah?" I tried to make my face open.

"Yeah, it is. Your father and I are in a really good place, we're financially secure, there's not"—she looked at me hesitantly—"you know, when you're young there's all this rushing around and scrambling, you're trying to get ahead in your career, you're building a family . . ." She hesitated again, knowing my prickly spots, but unable to resist them, as I could never resist hers, "or you're trying to *meet someone,* but when you're older, that stuff is resolved, you can just enjoy life." She looked at me squarely, and I was surprised to see tears in her eyes. "There's so much of life to be enjoyed."

Up in North Banbury, life did seem to consist of simple pleasures. Every morning the sky was a deep saturated blue, and on my runs the sun warmed me. Writing in the kitchen, I listened to the humming creek, and on breaks watched the quicksilver water. Marlo dug holes. One night I let him up on the bed, where he curled nose to tail like a fox. The warmth of his body soothed me.

Evenings we had long meals. My mom cooked. Gradually I forgave my parents for wearing the masks of old people. I saw that beneath their tentative questions there was a real desire to know me. Somewhere in their cool, polite interest was love. It was just love that stayed in its lane.

And yet, it bothered me: no matter how often I checked my phone, there were no messages from Ian or Lacie. My background photo, of the beach where Ian had watched me swim in the waves, was never overlaid with a message. It got so just the sight of that curling Atlantic made my heart pound.

My plan had been to stay indefinitely, but the following Wednesday my mom announced that the Duffields were coming for the weekend. Not that this meant that I had to vacate the guest bedroom—no, not at all. She was just interested in knowing my plans; she just wanted to get a "sense" of what I was "thinking."

When she brought this up, we were sitting at the kitchen table again looking at the gold-torched forest, so different from the dusty suburban woods of my childhood. Fog was burning off the hillside, and even through the shut window we could hear the creek.

"What's your tutoring schedule like?" she asked, false enthusiasm in her voice. "Is it like a Monday to Thursday thing, do you take weekends off, how does it work?" Needlessly she added, "We're so happy you're here."

I looked at her face, her gently exfoliated face, plumped and smoothed by expensive creams. "I don't have a job." I hurled the words. "I got fired."

She recoiled. "Fired?"

"Fired." God, what a word. Suggestive of the kiln.

"Oh, Rose. What on earth happened? How did you get *fired*?"

Haltingly, I told the story. She kept nodding, taking big gulps, and when I had finished, my dad, who had wandered in halfway through, and now stood at the stove eating his oatmeal, offered, "Well, she's not wrong. You did go to Harvard. It *is* easy for you to say."

"Right." I held my face in my hands. "It's just, maybe I'm not cut out for this kind of work. I kind of hate the kids."

"Well, you hate *the way they've been raised*. Such a culture of *materialism* in that city . . ." My mom shook her head sadly. "And now of course there's the *internet* . . ."

"No." For some reason I had to make this clear. It wasn't the internet. "Not *the way they've been raised*. Not the culture. The kids. I hate the kids." God, it felt good to say. Even as I recognized how deeply untrue it was—even as I was thinking that I had some real affection for Isabel—I relished claiming harsh land. Always, with my parents, I ended up saying things I didn't mean, just to shock them, just because I was tired of how infinitely reasonable and adult they were. But what really shocked them was when I began to weep.

"Oh, honey." My mom covered my hand with hers. "It's over-whelming, isn't it?"

Mutely I nodded, squashing flat with my thumb the tears on my face.

"Are you worried about money?"

Mind you, this question didn't portend an offer of money. Unlike every other middle-class Baby Boomer parent, mine thought it was character building to *figure it out*. "You're educated," they would say, as if a liberal-arts degree were the equivalent of a fishing rod and the world a stocked pond. "Debt-free," they'd remind me, and I agreed, I *agreed*, but it was hard, when you lived in New York, when you sat with teenagers "just back" from Japan or starting their unpaid intern-ship at a small prestigious literary magazine, not to echo with *not enough, not enough*. That was the disease of the city, the beat it drummed into you, the crazy rhythm throbbing inside every single person you passed on the street.

At my silence, my dad pushed. "Are you worried about rent?" And oh boy, that's what really did it. Waterworks. I wanted to say I was weeping for all the pain I had caused but really I was weeping for myself, me and my infinite capacity to fuck things up. In between sobs I huffed out, "I don't want to live with Lacie. It's too hard. There's too much hist-hist-history."

"You don't want to go back?" my mom asked. She spoke gently, but I could hear her satisfaction, like a ripple of peanut-butter fudge. Fi-nally she had figured out what my last-minute arrival was all about.

"I can't," I said, biting back my tears and using the same flat tone in which I had announced my firing. Then like a good daughter I closed my eyes, so my parents could confer with worried glances about my fate.

"What about Julia?" said my dad. "If you don't want to live with Lacie, maybe you could crash with her again?"

Julia was his brother's daughter, the surgical resident who had shot daggers at me every time she had found me lounging on her couch. Mutely I shook my head. Impossible.

Over my head my parents exchanged more glances. "Alyssa and Marcus are . . ." my mom started to say.

"Were you going to . . . ?" my dad asked.

My mom made a moue of *Maybe?* and my dad indicated *What about the?* and my mom made a face that meant *It doesn't matter,* and my dad with a one-handed shrug said *Then it's okay with me,* and while I thought dear God let me one day marry someone with whom I can carry out full conversations without even opening my mouth, my mom said, "Our good friends just left for Oaxaca for a few weeks. Do you want me to see if they would let you stay in their place? It's Washington Heights, but . . ."

Before I left I did all my laundry. My mom gave me a sandwich. My dad said, "Take care, sweetie," and kissed me on the cheek.

On the train, I told myself it was good I was going back. I had to get my stuff. I'd go midday, when Lacie would be at work. It'd be easy and quick, and then my New York chapter would be done.

Self-satisfied, I took out my paperback and began to read. Almost immediately, my phone buzzed. I had squirreled it deep in my bag, hoping to resist its siren call, but at the chirp I fished it out.

Ian.

I stared a long time. Not even opening the message, just reading the alert, savoring the shape of his name on my screen. He was still in there as *Ian The Barn.* I hadn't changed it; I liked the reminder that we had met in a beach town and lived together in that rambly old converted stable. I studied the pretty shape of the capital letters. *Ian The Barn.* Then hit the message: *Can we talk?* he wanted to know. He had made me wait for a week and a day, but I couldn't resist. Within minutes I replied: *How about this afternoon? Prospect Park?*

Yes, he wrote back immediately. *Great.*

I f a man describes his girlfriend as "totally psycho," he cheated on her, but he still loves her. Listen for the admiration in his voice, the awe that means *I didn't think she'd print out every email I had ever sent her, collate all the text messages, and leave them in a shredded heap on my front stoop, but when I saw the pages burning, that's when I knew this was real.* Do not think, even for a moment, that this man might love you instead. Do not be fooled by *I need to talk to you* or *I thought I could trust you.* A man who is involved with a woman who burns is not interested in *nice* or *trust*, no matter what he says, no matter if he writes *I don't understand. Usually you're so good.*

I was not good. But I didn't believe in good anymore. I believed in beauty. Ian was a beautiful man, but—even though I had been waiting and waiting for his text—when the time came I didn't want to go. Ian said please. He was freaking out: *please its like I dont understand* he wrote, and that's when I took pity, which is the problem with people like me, the whole reason we don't become queen: we take pity.

Really, it was the lack of apostrophes that did it for me. Ian was a fastidious texter, in the way of our generation: no abbreviations or emojis, no punctuation omissions, and certainly no typos. He must be upset.

If sunshine in September is always of the piercing, pristine kind, then December clouds are always dull, wrapping the world in dirty cotton. "You're making that up," I told him after he had described the Gmail flambé. "I don't believe you."

He bit his thumb. "I'm terrified of her. Do you know how much time that must have taken? God!" He swung his arm out toward the duck pond.

Cyclists in Spandex buzzed past like neon centaurs.

"I just—what the fuck? Why the fuck would you tell her? Why would you do something like that?"

"I didn't do something *like* that," I observed. "I did exactly that."

Two Orthodox families went by, the men talking with their heads close, the women behind, pushing baby strollers and leading children by the hand. A parade of dark human shapes against the pale shimmering lake, the women in wigs, impossibly young, the men ahead, talking Talmud. Women with children, men with ideas. I had wanted to live a life of ideas. I had never wanted to worship a man, hoist his flag, join his parade. Years ago, women had helped Ian make a giant flag and carry it through the park. An "art project." I had seen the pictures, and thought: At least I'm not one of them. But maybe I was worse.

"I just don't get why you did that," he spat out, and I realized he had been seething during my silence. "I thought we were friends."

He had lines on his face, soft etchings by his eyes, deeper curves by his mouth. When I had first noticed them, we had been fucking, and they had seemed evil, but now they just made me tender. "I was drunk," I told him gently.

"Drunk is not an answer."

I tried again: "I was trying to be honest."

"That's bullshit."

"Okay, yeah. It's bullshit. But isn't it better to have told her? Shouldn't she know?"

"We could have told her together. We should have told her together. If we were going to tell her, it should have been together."

"*That* sounds like a nightmare."

"It can't be worse than this. I woke up to the fire department on my front stoop."

I laughed. Lacie's gesture seemed funny to me, something her devilish ten-year-old self might have done. Where Ian saw an inferno, a blaze of desperation, I sensed something more mocking. An imitation of heartbreak.

"It's not funny," Ian snapped. I had never heard him snap before. "It's scary. She's not like that. She's not the kind of person to do something like that."

I tried to keep a straight face. "Is she going to get in trouble?"

"No," he said simply, and something in the sobriety of his tone made me not ask more questions.

"Do you think I should call her?"

"No," he said, and now it was his lips curling with irony. "I don't think you should call her. I don't think she wants to talk to you right now."

Once I had watched the sea lions sunbathe on the Monterey pier. From a distance they seemed cute, those piles of squeaking mammals waddling on flipper feet, but when I got closer I saw they had jagged wounds ribboned with blood and yellow pus. "Sometimes they fight," the man I was with had said, and I knew he meant "over mates." The heaps of sunbathing sea lions didn't look so sweet anymore: they paid for their terrible desire to live close with chunks of flesh.

My friendship with Lacie was like the body of these sea lions, infected and weak. It occurred to me, strangely for the first time, that this could be the end. It would not be remarkable for Lacie and me never to speak again. It was in fact the expected thing.

The grass where we were walking was frostbitten, the color of chalk. On the horse trail there were mounds of shit, but in the cold, dry air I couldn't smell them. I couldn't hide anything from him. He looked directly into my brain as he said, "Lacie told me about the accident."

I cut a quick glance over but kept walking.

"Why didn't you tell me?" he asked.

I thought how I had been smirking, cavalier with whiskey as I'd said, *But then I slept with him, so I guess I kind of won.* I had been lying, even if everything I had said was literally true.

"She said you crashed into the side of the road. There was no one else around." He looked at me. "I don't get it. You just—crashed?"

"I was a new driver," I finally said.

"Had you been drinking?"

"No. It just happened. No one was hurt. It wasn't a big deal."

He shook his head. "I can't believe you guys never talked about this. Didn't you ever talk about high school?"

We were by the boarded-up bandshell, shut tight with plywood. "What was the point? It was a long time ago. We were children."

I flinched as he studied me. "Rose. You scare people, you know that?"

I didn't answer him.

"Nobody knows what to make of you. Rose? You scare *me*."

orning. Sunlight drifting in pale, watery squares along powder-blue walls. Beyond a black-boxed window, the looping grandeur of the GW, tiny silver cars winking as they slid cityward.

Alyssa and Marcus had an apartment of clean lines. Glossy floors. An Eames chair, a modern sofa of blue-gray, punishingly hard. A sheepskin rug. A brass circle serving as a coffee table. One of those vertical bookshelves, like a scraggly tree, blooming here and there with big art books, some still shrink-wrapped.

When I had gotten in the night before, I had wandered aimlessly through the place, and now I did so again, opening drawers, studying the bookshelves, perusing the refrigerator, Ian's verdict (*You scare me*) ringing like a bell in my head.

In the library I learned that Marcus was the author of several serious tomes on diet; it was his measured opinion, I gathered from the jacket copy, that three bloody steaks a day were ideal for human flourishing. Alyssa was an artist: she posed little baby chickens doing New Yorky things in elaborate dioramas, photographs of which decorated the walls. Here yellow chicks in downward dog; there yellow chicks swilling Cosmos; and, in a rather heartbreaking series, at the fertility clinic, draped in blue-and-white checked gowns, and then beneath the sheets with their chickie husbands, clucking about ovulation.

The chicks made me mad. They were so *dumb*. They were little more than an elaborate diary, apparently: fertility books lay around the apartment, too, and printouts from trips to a Dr. Kaplan-Finke, and a calendar with circled and starred days.

Why did every stupid successful New York woman brood and squawk with the need for a baby, as if *that* would fulfill her? Why was a *baby* the final accessory, the thing you needed to go with the big apartment and big career and shiny gift books of your chicks, which apparently sold at Urban Outfitters for $17.99? *I* didn't want a baby. Not even an inch of me. I wanted Ian. I wanted a handsome artistic man to be hopelessly devoted to me and listen to me narrate every moment of my every day before making sweet and hot and mildly kinky love to me. For this, I was willing to skip the big ego trip of a mini me.

Now I rifled through Alyssa's dresses before flopping down on the sofa to eat some of her yogurt. It was thick, tangy, delightfully sour; I let it dissolve on my tongue while I lay propped up on the midcentury couch, then got up and paced the room once more. The chicks! I couldn't stop looking at the chicks.

Suddenly I thought I'd go to the Met. See some real art. In the past months I'd spent hours and hours on the Upper East Side without ever gracing its doorway, trudging up and down Park and Lex, always thinking I'd fit in a trip soon, but never quite making it. But now I was free. True, I had to get to Albemarle Road before Lacie got home from work, but I had hours and hours before that.

From the wide gray benches surrounding the Temple of Dendur, I watched school kids in uniforms of pressed slacks and navy sweaters spread like liquid through the temple, squealing at the hieroglyphics. They bunched at the entrance, thrilling at its etched codes, but trepidatious of the depths. They had crayons and worksheets to fill out; eventually, their teacher, a mild-looking man in his own navy sweater, got them to sit cross-legged before the ancient rock and draw. A woman in a long calico skirt hovered off to the left, talking to herself, as if reading the flat gesticulating figures.

Most of us were sitting here, in this luminous gray room, lit by glass windows that curved into the ceiling and overlooked the park.

Listening to echoing footsteps, and the shouts of kids bouncing off glass and old rock, I waited for magic, for my soul to re-form around beauty. I wanted art to be a private well of meaning, something so incredible that my soul would ignite—for what else are these public institutions for?—but I just kept talking to Lacie in my head.

I composed missives, I explained myself, I saw her slowly nodding and saying she understood. I promised her that what had happened would never happen again. Some fierce knot in me protested: I wanted it to happen again.

A few people walked the length of the hall, studying the grainy black-and-white reproductions of the temple in Egypt, and I joined them. The photographs told the story of how in Egypt there was a canal planned, a valley to be flooded, a holy site in its path. How a Rockefeller stepped in, paid for the temple to be dismantled and shipped, block by block, to this northern island.

Funny how stealing and salvaging can look the same, I thought. How you can call one by the other's name.

When I looked at my phone again, it was already five thirty. I had spaced, and now Lacie would be home in an hour.

It was still in those halcyon early days of my time in New York, when I was actually surprised that the 4/5/6 was delayed, surprised and then annoyed—yes, in those days I still managed indignation at the MTA. The time clocks predicted trains in 17, 21, 27 minutes, but minutes passed and the numbers did not drop.

When a train finally did arrive it was as if a giant malicious alien had packed a silver tube with a hive of buzzing humans. The windows were steamed. Limbs, suit jackets, babies were pressed up against the glass. The door slid open, and the hostile riders looked out at the pack on the platform with murder eyes. One younger woman wielding a yoga mat stumbled out. Several nannies barreled on. The rest of us were left with our hair fluttering softly in the tailwind of a tardy, unrepentant 4 train.

All this is to say that by the time I transferred at Union Square— the transfer not an indescribable horror like a genocide but an indescribable horror nonetheless—and another cheery silver can had chugged over the Manhattan Bridge and stalled in the tunnel right before DeKalb, I was very late. Saving some train disaster on Lacie's part, she had definitely beat me home.

They must have heard me turning the lock, for when I came into the living room Lacie was already standing, and Anna and Dylan were furiously studying their plates. On the table, amid goblets of wine and platters of root vegetables, tiny tea lights flickered.

"Oh my God." I stopped mid-room. "It's Shabbat. I forgot."

"Shoes," said Lacie.

Mechanically I returned to the foyer. Of course these nights would go on without me. Lacie had already moved on, apparently excised Sophie, and cooked up a storm without my help. God, it was hard to untie my shoes. The laces kept knotting up.

When I returned, Dylan was thoughtfully sawing at a hunk of rutabaga, and Anna was breaking off a piece of bread with the kind of concentration usually reserved for heart surgery. Lacie had her arms crossed.

"I'm not, like, here," I explained. "I'm just going to get some things real quick."

Spine prickling, I swiveled and strode away, imagining their glances meeting over the lamb, Anna mouthing *cunt*, Dylan patting Lacie's hand.

In my room, I sensed it right away. Nothing was out of place, but there was some subtle rearrangement, the smoke trail of her presence. She had snooped.

From the back of my closet I pulled the old green duffel that had been my home, a long floppy, shapeless tube in which I would yet again stuff the small props of my thin life. When I opened my drawers, my clothing looked obscene, like the discarded skin of corpses. Cast-offs from a dead girl, disgustingly suggestive of armpits, breasts, and legs.

I sat back on my heels and looked around the room. What had she moved? What had she taken? Weariness washed over me. Did it matter? This was my old life. My one poster I would leave. The succulent I had bought in a burst of optimism, the copy of *As a Friend* I had found in a used bookshop, the few other paperbacks bought these past months. My old novel drafts. Let her read them. Recycle them. We were done.

The women were murmuring, but when I darkened the doorway—never has the phrase felt more apt; I was practically a killer with a knife—they fell silent.

"Um, okay." I lifted up a wobbly hand. "I think that's it. Have a good dinner."

For about five seconds I really thought it was going to be that easy. I dropped my duffel to pull on my shoes. There was silence from the table, but not *super* hostile silence. Maybe they'd just lapse into conversation when I left. Hurl a few insults, then move on to discussing holiday plans.

Then, just as I was pulling on my coat, Lacie slipped across the room, quick and quiet as her cat. "One thing." Her breath was hot with garlic. "I need the rent."

I straightened. She wasn't a very good angry person. Her fluttery hands and high, agitated voice belonged to a bad actor from a community theater troupe. "Oh, yeah. Okay, sure." I kept my voice casual.

"*All* of it. From September too."

September had sort of floated from my mind. Lacie had been so cavalier this fall, so quick to forgive my debt when I had lost my SAT students. Though I had never paid her back, I had forgotten to think about it as a gift; it just seemed like we were both enjoying the pile of gold her grandmother had left behind.

Also, my credit cards were maxed out. I didn't have eighteen hundred dollars lying around; I didn't even have a job. "Okay, yeah, for sure." I bobbed my head. "I can totally get that to you. It just might take me a minute, but I totally can. It's just that, um, I lost my job."

"What?"

"I lost my job. I got fired, actually."

"You got *fired*?" Lacie began to laugh hysterically.

"Yeah, I got fired." Every time I said it aloud it hurt more.

Still laughing, Lacie staggered back to the couch and collapsed. Head on hands, shoulders shaking, she moaned, "Oh my God, oh my

God." From the table, Anna and Dylan swiveled their legs to me, their eyes lasering *Now what did you do?*

"Lace?" I stood over her. "Are you laughing or crying? I can't tell." She continued to convulse. "Oh God. I'm really sorry."

Anna coughed.

"How could you," Lacie sobbed. "How could you."

Dylan stood. "We can go. We can totally go."

"You're fine," I told her. "I'm about to go."

"Yeah, but"—Dylan cast a glance back at Anna—"maybe we shouldn't be here."

"You're fine," I snapped, and they stepped back. "Lace?" Again I reached out my hand, but she was projecting a force field I couldn't penetrate. "I'm really sorry. It was really stupid." Now I sounded like the bad actor, tinny and hysterical. I fought a terrible urge to smile. The women were watching. My almost-friends, my near New York life: even now they were receding. It was okay. I'd move back home. Home was nice. "I think, ever since moving here, I've just been—I mean. All our history. I haven't been dealing with—"

"You were *living* in my *house,*" she exploded, and the women rose and drifted toward the door.

"We're going out for a walk," Anna said.

"We'll be nearby," Dylan said.

"We love you, Lacie," Anna added, and as one, they slid on their coats and slipped out the door.

With her friends gone, the apartment seemed darker. Smaller. Lacie straightened up. "I never want to see you again."

"Okay."

"If you come by the house again, for any reason, I will take out a restraining order."

"Totally," I agreed.

"I read your stupid fucking novel. I feel bad for you, I really do. You're actually just a pathetic, small person."

So it had been an old draft. Somewhere deep inside me, a small nub of confidence budded. To read my stuff, to talk like that, she must still want to wound me. We weren't done yet. And the inferno she had built on Ian's stoop, what was that but a way, too, of keeping the story going?

She wiped her eyes. "By the way. It's really fucked up you never told me what it was about."

"Well, I wasn't telling anyone."

"But you were writing about me while living in this house. You were like a spy. It's so creepy."

"I wasn't spying *on* you," I started, but my words sounded empty, even to me. Who was a writer, anyway, but a voyeur? "And I wasn't telling anyone what the novel was about. Ian just happened to guess. He's so curious about you." And then, a nasty flash of inspiration: "Maybe if you were a more open person, he wouldn't have come to me begging for dirt."

"Oh, so it's *my* fault you guys fucked?"

"That's not what I said."

"How long was it going on?"

I crossed my arms. I was still standing over her, but I couldn't bring myself to sit. She was like a wild animal. "Not long," I mumbled.

"How *long* was it going on? I'm such an idiot. You were always out late, but I never asked, I just figured, She's a private person. . . ."

"*You're* the private person. Ian is mystified by you."

Her elbows slid around her thighs as the heels of her hands worked her face. With slow, tentative movements, I lowered myself onto the far corner of the daybed, keeping an embroidered tangerine pillow between us.

When she looked up, the pressure of her palms had left red clouds around her eyes. "It's just like . . . who are you? You move into my apartment, wear my clothes—yeah, I noticed that my stuff kept moving around—write about me, write as if you *are* me, steal my boyfriend . . . what is it, Rose? You take and take."

It hadn't felt like taking. It had felt like a way to be close to her.

"I don't get it. I literally don't get it. You've got this, like, *vampiric* relationship to my life, but when I offer you something genuine, like friendship, you don't take it, you can't even see it."

The heat turned on. That old familiar gurgle of pipes, followed by clanking, as if a little man in our radiator were banging away with his hammer, banging away at my heart. "You're right." I found myself whispering. "I'm sorry."

She straightened. "I think you should go."

What could I do? By saying *sorry* I had ended our game. All that remained was a reversal: the retrieval of my coat, the slow, careful winding of scarf around neck. Lacie wouldn't look at me; she wouldn't speak to me, except to remind me, again, that she needed the rent.

With a heave I shouldered the green duffel and stepped over the threshold. I turned back, to say one last thing, one final whatever, and found that her face had screwed even further into damage and rage. "So, what?" She gestured at my bag. "Back to his place now? Just, you got all your stuff, go running back to Ian?"

I dropped the duffel, and my gut dropped with it. "*What?* No." Then my heart began to swell. She had just told me everything I needed to know.

When I got home that night I wrote an email:

Dear Ervin,

First of all, I want to apologize for upsetting Isabel so badly. Obviously, that was not my intention, and I feel horrible about it.

Over the past week I've been thinking about our conversation, and I've come to believe you're right in your assessment. Isabel does need to move on with her life. I'd be more than happy to send along a sample essay for "inspiration," if you think that might help Izzy with her process.

As you may have heard, I've parted ways with Ivy Prep. However, I've consulted with their pay structure, and the fee for this kind of sample essay is $1,800, paid directly to me.

Please let me know as soon as you can if this appeals.

All best,
Rose

Ervin never replied. But an hour later, a bright notice on my phone told me I had received a PayPal payment in the amount of $900. The accompanying note promised the balance "upon receipt of the deliverables."

The next morning I wrote the ending to my novel.

I had written it many times before, in Iowa City, delusionally triumphant, and then chastised, again, upon my return to Oakland, and three times at the Barn, once in Nebraska, a tinkering on Albemarle Road, each time with the faith that it would be the last, each time pumped up on epiphany and insight, but now was different: Now I had fresh the shining example of Lacie's rage, so much of which I had forgotten: the way she couldn't quite do it; the way you had to scrutinize her words, hold them to the light, to really understand she meant it; the way her emotions swung about, somewhere beyond you, so that even fighting with her you still felt you were missing her, that she was lost in a private sea. Yes, that morning I sailed our fight like a ship back to high school, to senior year, to the island where she had stranded me.

All that day I wrote and revised, declaiming my paragraphs from the hard gray sofa before returning to the study to smooth them out. The words came cleanly, falling into my mind, the right rhythm and shape, the right inflection of noun and verb; *as music* they were perfect, and yet somehow they also made sense. Hours passed. I ate more of Alyssa's yogurt and fruit. Some of Marcus's chorizo. I found myself re-adding a sentence I had deleted, and then cutting it an hour later: the loop. The loop was always a sign I was done. So—trying not to overthink it—I pasted the new ending into the final draft, hit Save, and sent it to Portia Kahn.

With the novel I included a note saying that I thought this was it. If she liked what I had done, she could submit it to editors.

―――――――

Only then did I allow myself to unwrap the present Lacie had given me. Only then did I take her final question in that final moment and unfurl its glorious implications. If she thought I was with Ian, they were not talking. No amends had been made. Maybe he was even waiting for me. Maybe. But I had to be careful. I had to fish him with just the right words.

Dusk was falling, the purple-black December night close. Ian and I had talked so much about dusk. Often we had commented *The darkness feels especially dark this year;* showing off our poetic chops, we had discussed how the winter light both drained and saturated, the yellow deepening into gold until the pooling shadows swam out and swallowed the land. Then, we agreed, the darkness came fast and total, a black scrim yanked down upon the world, changing the city, making strangers wary of one another, turning quiet side streets menacing and squeezing the stomach of every pedestrian with dread.

Now, with the light stabbing through the high, uncurtained windows of this stylish apartment, I could practically feel him thinking these thoughts. I got out my phone and wrote: *Every time the light gets like this I think of you.* No. Too saccharine. I tried: *God, dark so early.* And then: *Don't know how you're feeling, but I'm leaving town & would love to see you before I go.* The word love. With a tap I sent it out.

For twenty minutes I furiously ate Marcus's salted almonds and waited for my phone to chime. Finally, frustrated, I shut the phone in a desk drawer and went out into the gathering night.

Up by 179th Street the neighborhood gets a little funny. Not only the usual funny of uneasy gentrification, though there's that, too, but the crazy funny of the nation's busiest bridge belching thousands of cars through twin cloverleafs directly above a quiet residential neighborhood. The scale is all wrong: there are eighteen-wheelers and commuter buses pounding concrete and families heartbreaking in their helmeted vulnerability wobbling up the pedestrian ramp on their bikes, and meanwhile quaint brownstones and Dominican bakeries and bodegas with dyed roses all seeming to slide down the impossibly San Franciscan hill that announces the bald fact that we are on an island, and this is the shore.

As I sloped in the chilly twilight down to the water, I came upon a screaming boy. Wailing, he clutched his shin, his dark eyes bright with tears, the front wheel of his overturned bicycle still slowly spinning.

A man brushed past. He was tall and slender as a wisp, so that when he knelt by the boy he was like a string dropping. "Aw, kiddo," he said, and kissed the crown of the boy's head. "That hurt, didn't it?" Soon he had his son standing, and together they were reciting the names of the body, the boy dutifully squeezing his arms and legs, cheerfully reporting back that each part of himself was okay.

This tender parenting so moved me that I found myself a step or two later nearly blinded by sentimental tears. The dad had been neither overly fussy nor indifferent to the boy's pain; I decided he must be a doctor, an ER doctor who had had to regularly assess for life-threatening bleeds; that he had turned this dire task into a playful game to distract a hurt child charmed me, and when, a minute later, I saw the boy and dad wheeling the trike up the hill, I almost looped back and asked the man for his number. Though of course that kind of nice man usually comes with a wife.

By the time I had wandered down to the water the darkness was a gauzy gray, the sky blushing. Three men were sitting on overturned milk crates drinking beers. They regarded me steadily as I wobbled across the rocks, my shoes grinding on the pebbles, scraping and sighing in complaint. The Hudson was a dull overturned skyscraper.

For long minutes I stood with my back to them, regarding the last band of pink above New Jersey. Their eyes bore into me. If one of them came toward me, I would never hear it: the water was slapping violently at the shore, and humming bridge traffic zinged the air. Studying the dying light, acutely aware of my ass, my calves, I thought:

either they are nice men or they are not. I felt I was offering myself, as I had offered my novel to Portia and my guilt to Lacie, submitting to the world's scalding, letting it do what it would with me, and if these men—

But when I turned to go they were deep in conversation, having apparently forgotten all about me. As I crunched past on the sliding rocks, one man touched his hat. His eyes under the brim were tiny and red.

When I got back to the apartment the electric light seemed an abomination. Still buzzing from the imagined danger, I blipped on my phone: no Ian. An email from Portia: she was "excited!" to read my draft. An email from Ervin, reminding me that he had already paid me nine hundred dollars, a "substantial sum." To maximize the effectiveness of my contribution to Isabel's college application process, it was essential to receive the sample essay "as soon as possible, preferably before 7 P.M. tonight." I tapped to the home screen. Half-past four.

Quickly, confidently, I folded open my laptop and clicked a new Word document. Then I stood at the window a long time, watching the cars on the bridge. The GW from a distance was majestic and calm, but mostly what happened there were traffic jams and suicides. People fuming, people jumping. I pictured again the men under the bridge. Suddenly I knew what I wanted to say. I returned to the laptop and wrote:

In my mind it always happens slowly, almost gracefully, the front wheels of the taxi rolling over the curb, the body of the cab swinging like the arm of a prizefighting boxer. Yes, in my mind it is graceful, and slow; there's an aria playing, the unfurling of a soprano, an epic feel—though of course it all actually happened very fast.

The cab came onto the curb, bent a No Parking sign, and

knocked the stroller right out of my nanny's hands. That's what she later said, what she couldn't stop saying: just knocked it away. I was rushed to the hospital, given less than half a chance of making it. I was two years old.

The driver lost his medallion. He lost his green card. He lost his family, for a little while; he lost his freedom. I don't know all the things he lost. Sometimes I think I'd like to learn them; sometimes I think it might help me make an accounting of all the things that I lost.

But the truth is that I can't remember. At the start of my life there is an act of violence that is lost to me. I live every day with the consequences; it has marked my body and brain, this story that has been told to me, repeated endlessly: it's as elemental and slippery as myth.

But I don't tell you this to make you sorry for me. This is not the place where I tell you about an obstacle that I've overcome. No, I want to use this myth as a metaphor, which is exactly what a myth always already is.

I have tried and tried this autumn, with the help of my teachers, my parents, and my tutor, to write about womanhood, or feminism, to make some statement about life on this planet as a girl. But when I think about life on this planet as a girl it seems remarkably fine, at least for me, at least until I was about twelve. But then puberty came like that taxi and changed my life. It was impersonal. It didn't have any particular interest in me. I was just in its path.

Now when I try to write a sentence and it comes out strange, when I try to read a book and my mind slides all over the place, when I know what I think but I can't get it onto the page, I wish I could go back to that moment before the cab jumped the curb. Or back even further, to five, six minutes before. I would make my nanny linger at the shop window, or miss the light, somehow move us fifteen or twenty feet back, out of harm's way.

And sometimes when I see a ten-year-old walking along Park Avenue with a soccer ball under her arm, plucky and upright, ponytail swinging, I wish I could go back. For a long time, that's all feminism meant to me: the desire to go back. But you can't. You shouldn't. It's good to be an adult. When I think about college, I think about learning to live in my adult body. To be an adult woman, with everything that that means.

Eesh, that ending! But maybe the whole thing was crap. I couldn't tell. I uploaded the file to an email, addressed it to Ervin West, and wrote, *Here is Isabel's college essay. Thank you for sending the balance of the fee by this evening.*

Then I curled up on the tasteful couch and slept.

That night I dreamt I was looking for Leo in a hospital. The emergency room was nothing but a long corridor of doors, all locked. A father, cradling his blood-soaked son, told me to find Room 18.

When at last I found Leo he was soft and vulnerable, bare under his hospital gown. I crawled onto the big mechanical bed with him and held him; he put his face against my chest and told me that he loved me.

Then he said he had to go. He was late for his opening. He had to fix one of his sculptures. Hadn't he told me before that he was a sculptor? The dream ended on a beach somewhere, me in tears, stupidly begging him to stay.

When I woke again it was past ten A.M. I went to the kitchen and stood in front of the sink, drinking a glass of water and staring dumbly at the announcement for Alyssa's gallery show. My unconscious was really annoying. It was so *literal,* so unimaginative. For shit's sake, I thought. I get it. I get the message.

To prove that I got it, I retrieved my checkbook and wrote *Lucinda Salt* where it said *Pay to the Order of.* Eighteen hundred dollars. Everything I owed her. Then I found an envelope, stole one of Alyssa's stamps from the immaculate desk drawer where she kept her office supplies, and wrote for the very last time the words *Albemarle Road.*

Strangely, I didn't feel bad about writing Isabel's admissions essay. In the grand scheme of the world's injustices, it was a pittance. Really, the only twinge I felt was the umbrage of my ego. In the end, I had decided I was proud of my taxi essay, amused by the metaphor of puberty-as-car-crash, and sad to think of my words floating around in the world unattached—that is, if they made it off Ervin's computer. I could imagine him trashing the thing; in fact, I kept waiting for him to demand his money back, though the fact that he hadn't didn't mean anything. Eighteen hundred dollars to them was like twenty dollars to me.

My mother hadn't said how long the DeSalvanos were going to be in Mexico, but now that I had no more business in New York, I thought it best to be on my way. I called my mom. Her voice knit with concern, but not surprise, as she told me she could pick me up at the station anytime, I could stay for as long as I wanted, I shouldn't worry about it, she hoped I was okay, was there anything she could do for me?

I had been sending so many letters, but I thought I'd send one last one. Well, a text. I drafted it with my heart pounding, then stood there running my thumb over the screen. *This is our last chance to see each other.* Before I could whirlpool into deliberation, I hit Send.

Not two minutes later, the response came. *Rose! I'd love to see you. I was thinking about going to the Brooklyn Banya tomorrow. Want to come?*

It's like church, isn't it, standing inside a man's doorway moments after he's buzzed you in? Everything hushed and still, the quiet before the service, with just his voice wafting from the bedroom, and starry silver lights bathing the kitchen in a soft glow.

"Rose!" Ian came swinging into the kitchen, shoving his phone into his back pocket, twirling swim trunks from his finger, a gliding, swaying ballet that paused only for the instant it took to kiss my cheek. "Ready to shvitz?"

I shyly nodded. Even thinking of him constantly, I'd still managed to forget how big and crazy his curls were, how thick and muscular his forearms were, how deep the notch ran between his eyes. There was the tang of his smell, and the way he looked at me. It was all new, always.

"This place is a trip." He unplugged the string of Christmas lights and grabbed his keys from a hook by the door. "Let's go."

We took the F, and from the F walked to Coney Island Avenue. The Brooklyn Banya sat sandwiched between an auto repair shop and a Pakistani patisserie, a squat gray box with multi-hued floodlights that bathed the word "banya" red, then indigo, then green. I turned to Ian, my eyes a question, and not a nice one.

"What?" he said, and then more defensively, "What?"

I overturned my hands in supplication. Was he really going to make me say it? If I squinted, I could see the street sign for Albemarle Road.

"Oh, come on. It's fine. She never goes here."

Were they teasing me, testing me, was I supposed to act oblivious, was this an offer, or a joke? I thought again of that night reading Angela Carter's fairy tale, the three of us in bed, the heave of my smoky desire and the ammonia of my panic.

"Shall we?" Ian pushed open the gunmetal door.

I bowed, fake courteous, and decided to let it go. Some people inhabit New York as if it were a series of sealed bubbles: you could stroll a few blocks from your ex-girlfriend's apartment, and as long as you didn't have plans to see her, you wouldn't. People like this believe in the city's anonymity, its density; they trust it the way a rock climber trusts the rope.

Ian paid my admission fee, and we separated to change. I stripped amid beatifically obese older women and teenage girls furious with curling irons. I'd had to buy a bathing suit, and the one I'd found, amid December's paltry offerings, was nautical and stupidly skimpy, the blue and white striped triangles held to my chest by a complex system of strings disguised as thick sailors' ropes.

We met again in the dim, echoey main hall, redolent of chlorine and fried pierogies. Nearly naked couples sat at white plastic tables, men and women alike draped with gold chains and felt hats, eating and drinking beers, sucking on orange slices, calling to their children who ran between the hot tub and the cold pool and pressed their little faces against the glass doors of the sauna, leaving ghostly imprints.

Along the back wall there was a mural in faded acrylics of a Grecian garden, with squarish Greek gods reclining beside turquoise pools, as if to reflect back to us in amateur hands the Platonic ideal of what we were doing. To counterbalance this, a twelve-inch TV bolted to the wall blared a Russian Christmas music spectacular, with a leggy blonde in a sparkly gown and a chorus of children singing through falling snow.

"It's very . . . Russian," I said, tucking my thin towel more tightly around my waist. In his orange trunks Ian seemed somehow even more massive.

He grinned, delighted. "Isn't it amazing? Let's do the wet sauna first."

In the bright tiled room, thick with condensation, there were a few middle-aged men with their heads bowed over their tremendous bellies as if in great sorrow. We took our seats closest to the door, and Ian sighed deeply. Soon buds of sweat bloomed on his thighs, pearls that grew large and luminous before trickling away. My skin, pasty white, welled up tears.

A man dumped a wooden bucket of water over the vent and a wall of steam enveloped us. Ian sat back, shiny sweat slicking him. His curls were slack and damp against his skull. Glistening rivulets ran over his stomach and puddled down to his shorts.

I kept thinking we were going to talk but talking was impossible with all the sweating and sighing. The great Russian men sat like totems around us. The truth was that I hated saunas but I was determined not to flee before Ian did.

"God." The sigh came from the back of his throat. "I like you so much." He opened his eyes and patted my thigh briskly, and then stood and pushed open the steamed glass door.

I followed, my heart yammering. Out in the atrium, the chlorinated air now felt brisk. We eased into the cold pool, gasping. I crossed my arms over my chest. Ian did soft, slow breaststrokes in circles.

Not until we had moved to the hot tub did he say, "So. You're skipping town."

"Yeah."

"When?"

"Tonight, actually."

He laughed, as if at an old familiar joke. "So you're just, like, leaving. You're going to move away."

I nodded. "Pretty much. I got fired. Did I tell you that?" He curled his lips *no*. "Yeah, I got fired. So. There's not really anything for me here."

With an indifference that broke my heart, he skimmed his arm along the water's surface, watching the chlorinated bubbles cling to his puckered skin. "This city is too expensive anyway. You're smart to get out."

The jets rumbled to life, kicking up a white frothy stew of bubbles. Ian slid over to one and let it throb against his neck, vacantly staring up at the ceiling. Somewhere, someone turned on a shower.

He reached out and touched the sailors' rope slung over my shoulder. "Cute suit."

The noise of the banya, the wet thwack of flip-flops and echoing voices, receded. I dropped my gaze. "Thanks," I muttered. Underwater, our legs touched. He slid his foot over mine. His old tricks. He leaned close and gently kissed my temple.

Then he pushed himself up to the lip of the pool, swung his legs around, and walked away. "Be right back," he called.

I stared after him. How could he give himself so completely, then withdraw so easily? There was a lightness, an emotional agility to him, that I lacked. On the TV, more fake snow was falling.

A girl and her boyfriend lowered themselves into the pool. "Aah, aah," the girl said, flinching as the hot water lapped her thighs. "It feels nice," the boy insisted, and they circled briefly before perching opposite me.

When Ian returned he said there was a man who wanted to beat me.

"What are you talking about?" Intrigue curled my gut.

He pointed with his chin, and a man sitting at one of the plastic tables, whom I recognized from the steam room, nodded shyly. He was round and bald, with a white wool hat that gave him a courtly dignity.

Around him—and everywhere—lay the limp green leaves of the birch branches.

"Should I do it?" I whispered.

"I would."

"Come with me?"

"Obviously."

We approached the man in his pink chair. He nodded formally at Ian, and the three of us went off to the dry sauna. While the wet sauna had been bright and tiled, with silver vents, the dry sauna was darkly lined with cedar, reminiscent of hell, if hell were a cabin on the shores of Lake Michigan with the thermostat cranked to a hundred and twelve degrees.

"Is your first time?" the man asked. Up close, the pink rolls of his belly were damp and gleaming.

"Yeah." Ian settled himself on the top riser—he seemed immune to the heat—and cupped his chin in his palm. Mischief gleamed in his eyes.

"I will be gentle," the man promised. "Not too hard. Is too hard, you tell me. Okay?"

I said I would, and lay down on the middle bench, belly-down. As the man picked up the branch, I heard its feathery flutter. "You tell me, is too hard," he repeated. I closed my eyes.

Now, the sauna is hot. I know you know, but let me tell you: this heat cooks you. It has nothing to do with August, or the tropics. This is the kitchen's heat. Either you fight it, or you go limp. I went limp.

Crack, the branch came down and lingered on my scapula. "Is okay?" the man murmured above me, lost in steamy clouds. The leaves held the heat, making a glowing bloom on my back. Then, with a gentle suction, as if it yearned to linger, the branch—and the heat— lifted up. The patch of coolness left behind was divine. *Smack!* The leaves came down on my other shoulder blade, and again that warmth, again that cooling spot.

Carefully the man worked his way down my back and over my legs, asking if I liked it. He gave a delighted laugh when I said yes, and pressed the birch branch firmly against my ass. "Is okay?" he whispered. I nodded, my eyes closed.

My insides were baking. I was gloriously relaxed, as soft as a puddle of mush, and yet, when I thought about Ian watching me laid out, nearly naked, flogged by a fat Russian man, a delicious golden lead flooded my cunt.

"Turn over," the man said, and I did, offering him new territory: my breasts, my stomach, my thighs. Not rushed, but methodical and thorough, he covered me with his wet, hot smacks. To finish he pressed the branch between my legs, like a seal. Stamping me. I couldn't help it, I moaned.

"Is okay," he told me. We were done.

I sat up. He disappeared, then returned carrying a wooden bucket brimming with dark water. "For the heart," he declared, and, with much ceremony, dumped it over my head. Icy cold. I gasped, stifling a shriek. Both men chuckled.

"Thank you." Speaking felt strange, like becoming a person again.

"You are very welcome. Very good for the heart," he repeated. Then, with another courteous nod at Ian, almost a genuflection, he was gone.

We stood there smiling. "What was that?" I whispered.

"It was fucking hot, was what it was."

Playfully I swatted him. He caught my arm and twisted it behind my back. From behind me he whispered, "You liked that, didn't you?"

I nodded, my head hitting his chest. He pressed against me, his dick nestling my ass crack. "You like being beaten," he said into my ear, and then he was bending me over, and tugging aside my swimsuit; then he was squishing himself inside. I thought I might faint. Deeper into me, and faster, he fucked: I shivered with pleasure, and a black poppy bloomed in the center of my vision. His cock slammed my brain, scrambled my cells, while he incanted, "You like that, you like that," and blackness swam before my eyes. I was glad to do this for him. Do this to him. Take away his speech: now only moans were coming from his mouth, sharp noises, and then he was coming, gurgling, so deep inside me that my elbows buckled and my forehead hit wood.

In the sudden stillness there was only the sound of panting. Slowly I waddled forward until he slid out. Coyly I turned around. His face was a mottled red.

"God, it's hot," he exclaimed, and half-rolled, half-collapsed onto the bench.

"We should get out of here." I giggled a little as I pulled my swimsuit back into place. "It's a miracle no one came in. At least as far as *I* know."

He didn't respond. I sat beside him and stroked his hair, rocking back and forth, feeling his cum pool in my bikini; everything was sweat, everything was cum, everything was water here in this room. The black poppies were constant now, dark flowers unfurling and exploding. It was so *hot*. "Let's go. Let's get out of here."

"Where do you want to go?" he mumbled, his eyes still closed.

A vision: his clean apartment, a shower, those big towels, his white Christmas lights. "Your house."

"What?" He shuddered a little and pinched his temple.

"Come on. Let's go back to your place."

He sat up, shaking the sweat from his hair. Beneath the pink flush of his skin there was now a grayish hue. "I can't tonight." He wiped his eyes. "I'm busy."

My heart jigged. "You're busy? You've got plans?"

"Yeah," he said shortly, using the tone he always used with me when I asked for too much. "I've got plans."

And then, all at once, I understood. It was obvious. "You're going to her place, aren't you?"

He put his head in his hands. He was so wet and soggy and magnificent, a rumpled lion. "Look, Rose. I'm really happy to see you. It's really nice."

"It's *nice*? What we just did was *nice*?"

He looked at me warily. "Yeah, it was nice. It's a good thing." He was turning the color of cardboard.

"Do you feel okay?" My heart seemed to be pounding all over my body—my head, my chest, my hands.

"Yeah, I'm fine." He squeezed his temple again. "My head hurts, though. I should get going. I'm already late."

He stood, and there it was, hot tears sliding down my eyes, tears and sweat and cum in this room. "I just thought," I pulled him back down to the bench, "I just thought that, when I heard you hadn't gotten back together with her, I mean, since that always was the main obstacle with us, I mean the main reason we weren't—" I couldn't tell the difference on my face, what was sweat, what was tears.

"Oh, honey," he tightened a wet grip on my thigh, "that's not the reason." His voice was faint and airy.

"It's not?" He had only called me "honey" once before.

"It's not. And besides, Rose," and he looked deep in my eyes, "I want you to know, I think Lacie and I are finding our way back to each other."

All I did, really the smallest thing, was shove him. Sure, hard, like his chest was a fire door and the building was in flames. Like I had to find my way out, hard, yes, both hands on his chest, and his legs swung out on the slick floor and he toppled over backward. *Thunk* went his head: very dramatic. Very dramatic of him to stay like that, to pretend he couldn't move. His eyes rolled back in his head. He had already been sitting, I thought wildly. How dare he pretend I had hurt him?

What an unbelievable joke, an unbelievably cowardly move, especially after he had taken me, fucked me in this room. It was so *dumb*. I stood over his prone body, shouting and shaking him, my pulse bellowing in my brain, and slowly it occurred to me that I should probably get some help. Act as if this dumb joke *might* be real.

But when I stepped outside the sauna my legs buckled, and darkness swam over me. I sank down, my back against the tiled wall. Better to cool down first, I decided. Just calm my heart for a minute. In the cold plunge pool I doggy paddled around, feeling sore and used between the legs. With curiosity I watched the pale hairs on my arm stand up.

With curiosity, too, I watched the hot-tub boy and girl go into the sauna. I waited. I skimmed my hand along the surface of the water. Finally it came, and it was almost funny, her shriek. Even from outside the room I heard it.

Three months after Ian's death, Portia sold my book, and a year later it came out: a modest commercial success, but with mixed reviews. Some called it *beautifully honest;* others, *troubling.* Many decried the narrator's morals, calling her self-delusional, a narcissist, emotionally blind. *We're all blind,* I wanted to protest. *We're all masters of denial.* But I kept my peace. I didn't write any huffy letters to the editor, didn't publish a personal essay snidely suggesting *misogyny* had played a role in the reception of my book. I accepted the debut prize nomination, and was then gracious when I lost; I celebrated when the film rights sold, and agreed that yes, someone else should write the screenplay. I was obedient and cooperative in all respects.

For publishing a novel had indeed changed my life: it had cured me of the desire to write. At great cost, I had gotten down on paper the shame of my childhood; I had killed it dead, and now it seemed nothing would ever be so interesting again. Somewhere deep inside me, I felt it: I was done.

Lacie, as you've probably guessed, is the gallerist Lucinda Salt. She got her start when she inherited Ian's art—or rather, his parents gifted it to her, all the sculptures and paintings, all the textiles and paper works. Apparently they had always wanted him to go to law school. Or maybe they just didn't know how lucrative death can be for an artist.

A few years after the accident, I found a press release online, announcing a retrospective of Ian's work. Instantly, I knew I would go. I was living in Boston at the time, making minimum wage at a bookstore, but BoltBus was cheap and my curiosity was too much.

The gallery, I was given to understand, was known as smart, tough, boundary-pushing, though it was so small—tucked away on a side street, down a half-flight of stairs—that I almost missed it. A sheet at the front desk informed me that the model homes in the show were not homes at all but depictions of the artist's brain, that in these sculptures the artist had been wrestling with the fate that had waited, suspended, in his blood vessels, the mortality under which we all live.

Funny, to catch the moment the story changed. To see the lie as it clicked into place. I was sure Ian knew nothing of the aneurysm that had, ultimately, killed him. He was a creature of pleasure, fundamentally; his art was about speculation and fantasy. He wasn't morbid. He just hadn't left the sauna in time. But in the hands of a curator, his death had become poetic. His art, his entire life, now led up to it.

And I had been excised from it. No one had ever connected me to the sauna, no one had ever realized that Ian had been pushed. But still, it astonished me how much it hurt to see myself excluded from the myth.

Across the thin-planked pinewood floor, perhaps two dozen people were scattered. Ian's sculptures hung suspended from the ceiling, slowly turning. I barely glanced at them, so astonished was I by the oil paintings. Big and gloppy, maybe six of them, in loud, electric blues and greens, and even though all the color dazzled, I narrowed in on her portrait right away.

He had done her in pink and gray, with a nasty neon yellow at the edge. He had painted her on her back; he had painted her—I knew, because I recognized her duvet, even as an abstracted smear—on her bed. Her expression was guarded, her beauty ambiguous: her face wavering, her nose too long, her cheeks flushed. He had painted her exactly as I had seen her. He had captured the flickering inconstant quality to her beauty that I loved.

God, I missed him.

So struck was I by her painted gaze that it took me a moment to see the second Lacie. But then the sea of expensive eyeglasses shifted, and she came into view.

She had on kitten heels and a full pleated skirt. Intently she talked to an older man, her hand motions vigorous. I stood to one side, watching. There was something different about her, something beyond the heels and tidy chignon. She was sharper. Cleaner. As if loss had brought her into focus.

For a long time she didn't see me, though the older man kept looking over. I think my gaze unsettled him. Finally she turned. Our eyes met. She got very upright and pale.

Something inside me said: *Good.*

She cut across the room, stopping just before her portrait, so I saw her doubled: Lacie on her back with terse lips, and Lacie flushed, and dazzling, and very real. "Rose. You're here."

I was an idiot: I didn't read her tone. It was neutral, and I guess I hoped it was tipping toward excitement. "Yeah," I exclaimed warmly. "I just happened to be back, and . . ."

I trailed off. The side of her face had dented, like fruit collapsed in the sun.

"You're unbelievable."

I dropped my head.

"You're just . . ." She wiped her forehead.

"How have you been?" I said weakly. "It's so wonderful about the show. It's amazing."

She shook her head, as if this was the most revolting thing I could have said. "I knew you wouldn't be able to stay away. I knew it."

The last time I had seen her, her anger had been nothing but a bad costume; she had shed it easily enough. Now, though, grief had made her carbon-hard. Looking around, as if she expected someone to overhear, she said, "Will you come with me? There's something I need to ask you."

Dread settled in my stomach. As she led me back into the gallery—

it seemed to be made of smaller and smaller rooms—I felt as if I were going down and down, back and back, to that tile-lined hall, the smell of chlorine, the way children's voices bounced around. . . . It must have been a short distance, but it felt like forever, this trip past little empty rooms of blond desks piled with silky catalogs. "Wait, is this yours?" I asked when we reached the final office, large and impressively bare.

She looked at me as if I were an idiot. "Were you with him?"

"What?" Though of course I knew what she meant.

"That day. You were with him, weren't you? What did you do, just skulk away?"

I turned to stone. I turned to pasteboard. I felt as though all the book buyers in Boston were screaming my name. As though my menstrual blood were on the floor, as though my forehead had burst into flames.

"I keep wondering about it." She sounded dead inside. "I just can't shake this feeling that you were there."

She folded her arms, waiting, but when I folded my arms too—when she saw that I wasn't going to tell her anything—she sighed heavily and said, "I don't even want to know. That's what I keep coming back to. I don't even want to know."

From the shallow top drawer of the desk that was not hers, she withdrew a key labeled *12.* "There's something for you in the basement." She smiled wryly. "His parents gave it to me, but I think you should have it."

In the basement? It seemed impossible to go down. We were already down, set below the level of the street, dug a half foot into the earth, in this sterile gallery that tried with artful lighting to disguise the fact that it was submerged.

She pressed the key into my hand. "Take the elevator down. There are storage lockers for the studio spaces next door. His is the last one on the left."

I tried to find her eyes. I yearned, suddenly, for the clarity of her hissing accusation. I even muttered, "Why are you giving me something"—but all she said was: "Move it soon. I told the gallery we'd have it out by Tuesday."

She smiled once, no teeth. Then she spun on her heel and clattered off. She did not say goodbye, or that it had been nice to see me, or that I should take care of myself. Apparently our friendship was to have a smooth, bureaucratic death.

The sub-basement was unfinished, with a floor of poured concrete. A bare bulb flickered on when I descended the stairs. Unlike the other storage units, Ian's did not have raw lumber or canvas or paint. There was no chainsaw or laser printer or speckled work boots. All of the making had been made; all of the doing had been done.

There had been a stretch when Ian had thought he needed to work big, and during that time he had constructed several shells, like the hulls of boats, massive pod-shaped husks made from bamboo. These were the pieces waiting for me. The smallest one came up to my chest.

I unlocked the chain-link door and stepped inside his cage, which smelled dankly of the sea. Was he here? Pressing the palm of my hand against the cheap wood, I tried to feel something. Anything. After all, this wood had been shaped by his hands. But it wasn't something he had chosen for me.

And then I was deep in the place where I never let my mind go. Swimming slowly in circles in that pool, utterly unable to do the thing I needed to do. Split off from myself. Bruised and sore. Pale, transparent hairs.

I brushed again, and the wood—cheap, unvarnished—bent a splinter into my hands. Where was he? Where did he go? I had left part of myself in that pool forever, some essential part of me that believed I could be good.

Then I knew what she was trying to do. She was trying to chain me to him so I'd never be free. For these boats were horrible, dumb. Undergraduate work, at best. Mediocre undergraduate work. And heavy, and bulky, and big. If Ian had known he was going to die he would have destroyed them himself. I was sure of it.

But Lacie was counting on me not to be able to destroy them. She wanted me to carry around these shells like a penance, she wanted their weight on me, she wanted them to take up space in my house. She was counting on me to be too nostalgic to give them away.

But Lacie didn't know me now. She didn't know that I had already done the worst. I didn't need to salvage. I wasn't in search of the past, I didn't need to cling to artifacts to remind me of who I was. I wasn't sentimental. I wasn't a writer anymore.

I turned to go, and found that the door was latched. Dumb. Dully I remembered its click. When I tried the handle, my fingers slid on the brass. Taking a deep, shaky breath, I tried again. Nope. I twisted the key and heard the dead bolt swing around, failing to catch.

Then with an automated tick the bare bulb blinked out: blackness. Stopping up a scream, I rattled the chain link of the cage, yanking the door so hard I stumbled back and hit a boat, which clattered to the floor, clobbering my shin. I yelped and collapsed in the dark, knocking another boat, and with a tremendous crash it, too, fell to the floor.

For a long time I lay still, panting. Gradually my eyes adjusted to the dim, murky light. Gradually I got used to the smell of rot. Maybe because I was afraid of hitting another boat, maybe because I missed him, I climbed inside the small canoe that lay beside me and curled up, pulsing, vibrating, my muscles clenched tight.

When I rose from the boat—I do not know after how long—my motion turned the light back on. All was lit. All was plain. It wasn't difficult to unlock the door and step outside the cage. It wasn't hard to pull the door snug behind me, to drop the little key down the drain in the floor, to say goodbye. All this I could leave behind.

Acknowledgments

Hearty thanks to Sara Weiss, my editor, whose many wise suggestions helped shape this book, and to my agent, PJ Mark, champion par excellence. I feel so lucky to work with both of you. Thanks also to Elana Seplow-Jolley of Ballantine Books and Ian Bonaparte of Janklow & Nesbit, who provided helpful reads and key assistance, and to Rachelle Mandik for a meticulous copyedit.

To the Edward F. Albee Foundation and Lighthouse Works for generous gifts of time and space at the start, and to the Elizabeth George Foundation for a much-needed financial boost at the finish, I am deeply indebted.

A big thank-you to Rebecca Markovits, who published the short story that became the germ of this novel, and to everyone else at American Short Fiction, especially Nate Brown, for cheerleading.

I have been blessed with many incredible teachers, most especially Ethan Canin, Lan Samantha Chang, Allan Gurganus, Paul Harding, the late James Alan McPherson, and Marilynne Robinson. An especial note of gratitude to Lan Samantha Chang, who patiently and brilliantly read endless drafts of my early work.

My good friends Emma Borges-Scott and Michelle Huneven, along with the stalwart members of the novel-writing group, Joe Fassler, Thom Parry, and Chris Leslie-Hynan, all provided wise editorial counsel. A special thank-you to my first reader, last reader, and true-blue friend, Leslie Jamison.

Conversations, short- and long-lived book clubs, epic phone calls, and long walks with David Bukszpan, Will Frank, Jessica Gross, Evan James, Jessica Marglin, Amanda Martin, Dan Poppick, Ilana Sichel, Bridget Talone, and Han Yu all fed my soul and kept me steady. Last but hardly least, thanks to my running buddy, travel buddy, and co-founder of Boundary Club, David Mahfouda.

Deep gratitude to the Council of Siblings: Emily, Chris, and Lauren. And to my parents, Cate and Patrick, who have cheered every victory and salved every setback, who have always believed, even when I doubted: thank you, thank you, thank you. You have taught me how to live, you have taught me how to love, you have given me everything worthwhile in this world. I love you to the moon and back.

ABOUT THE AUTHOR

KYLE MCCARTHY's short stories have appeared in *Best American Short Stories, American Short Fiction,* and the *Harvard Review,* and on *Selected Shorts.* She is a graduate of the Iowa Writers' Workshop and lives in Brooklyn, New York.

kylemccarthy.com

ABOUT THE TYPE

This book was set in Garamond, a typeface originally designed by the Parisian type cutter Claude Garamond (c. 1500–61). This version of Garamond was modeled on a 1592 specimen sheet from the Egenolff-Berner foundry, which was produced from types assumed to have been brought to Frankfurt by the punch cutter Jacques Sabon (c. 1520–80).

Claude Garamond's distinguished romans and italics first appeared in *Opera Ciceronis* in 1543–44. The Garamond types are clear, open, and elegant.